GLOCKS ON SATIN SHEETS

Adrian Dulan

**Lock Down Publications and Ca$h
Presents**

Glocks on Satin Sheets

A Novel by *Adrian Dulan*

Adrian Dulan

Lock Down Publications
P.O. Box 870494
Mesquite, Tx 75187

Visit our website @
www.lockdownpublications.com

Lock Down Publications
Like our page on Facebook: Lock Down Publications @
www.facebook.com/lockdownpublications.ldp
Cover design and layout by: **Dynasty Cover Me**
Book interior design by: **Shawn Walker**
Edited by: **Lashonda Johnson**

Stay Connected with Us!

Text **LOCKDOWN** to 22828 to stay up-to-date with new releases, sneak peaks, contests and more...

Thank you.

Submission Guideline.

Submit the first three chapters of your completed manuscript to ldpsubmissions@gmail.com, subject line: Your book's title. The manuscript must be in a .doc file and sent as an attachment. Document should be in Times New Roman, double spaced and in size 12 font. Also, provide your synopsis and full contact information. If sending multiple submissions, they must each be in a separate email.

Have a story but no way to send it electronically? You can still submit to LDP/Ca$h Presents. Send in the first three chapters, written or typed, of your completed manuscript to:

LDP: Submissions Dept
Po Box 870494
Mesquite, Tx 75187

DO NOT send original manuscript. Must be a duplicate.

Provide your synopsis and a cover letter containing your full contact information.

Thanks for considering LDP and Ca$h Presents.

ACKNOWLEDGEMENTS

First off, I would like to thank God for blessing me with my talents and being the Great Loving Heavenly Father that he's been to me. Without Him, I am nothing. To my mother Sandra Lewis and my stepfather, Ronald Lewis. I love you two dearly. I couldn't imagine how hard this journey would have been without you two in my life. To my little sis, Sparkle and her husband Donnavan- thanks for coming to see your big, bruh. Our conversations give me something to look forward to. Know that in the near future we'll be doing big things. God has blessed me with the vision, so those that have been by my side through this struggle, I'll share it with you.

To my beautiful daughter, Ceairra. Babe, you've done a great job. I'm so proud of you. Keep up the good work and know that I love you dearly. To my youngest daughter, Adrianna Dena Dulan let's get this money, babe. You be sure and keep up the good work, and I'll make sure that I finish our book like I promised. To my daughter, Adrian Hinton. I love you, babe. I'm glad to see that you graduated now it's on to the next step, you're moving up in the world. To my oldest daughter, Tangala. Don't let anyone tell you otherwise—your Daddy loves you. I look forward to the day when we can sit down and talk. To all my other daughters and Granddaughters, I love each and every one of you. Hi, Shelby, I love you!

I-10 what up, bruh? Author of I-10 2 The Pen. Eric Reedus— what it do, fam? My guy Bud from Detroit—checkmate! I couldn't end these acknowledgments without a special shout out to those that didn't stay down. It's because of you that sparked my motivation to grind harder, so I owe each of you a special thanks. Anyone I didn't mention, know that it's not because I forgot you, I just ran out of Tru-Links. Peace!

Adrian Dulan

PROLOGUE

IN THE BEGINNING

"Do you like that?" Derrick asked Erica as he dove deeper and deeper inside of her.

"Ughhhh!!!" she cried out, pulling her face away from the pillow, basking in a zone.

"Oh, you're not going to tell me how much you like the way daddy is giving you this dick?" He whispered softly into her ear. Unbeknownst to him, she hadn't heard a single word he said. She was completely submerged in a whole other world filled with ecstasy. He had her flat on her stomach with her ass slightly raised by a pillow that lay under her waist. He looked down at his rod, each time he pulled out, and saw the undeniable evidence of just how much he pleased her.

"I want you to suck it," he growled while nibbling on her earlobe, holding his dick deep inside of her.

She loved the feeling of him deep inside of her. She ground her ass back up into him. The mixture of her juices and their sweaty bodies created a slight suction sound. She was cumming.

"I'll do whatever you want me to do," she moaned, pushing on the headboard to allow Derrick to get as far inside of her as possible. "This pussy is yours...and I will do whatever it takes to make sure that my man is satisfied."

Derrick eased his dick out of her and slid to the edge of the bed. He stood to his feet and slowly jacked his hand up and down on his throbbing penis. With all the work he'd just put in, he wanted to keep that feeling of sexual ecstasy right there in his groin.

"Uhmmmm look at you," Erica purred, crawling seductively to the edge of the bed. "Allow me to see if I can help you relieve all that pressure you've built up."

She took hold of his dick and immediately ran her tongue across the helmet. The first swipe from the small of her tongue removed pre-cum that had built up on the tip of the head. Lifting

9

his dick straight up to his navel, she then used the tip of her tongue a second time to remove all of her cum from around his testicles.

"Stop teasing me," he insisted, recognizing the little game she was trying to play. "You know exactly how I like it, so why are you trying to play me?"

She stopped licking and peered up at him with a devilish smile. She loved teasing him. She wanted him to beg her to release inside of her mouth. She knew her head game was off the chain, and Derrick loved it. She opened her mouth wide and took in as much of Derrick's long thick dick as she could.

The warm feeling of her tongue sliding back and forth on the soft spot underneath his dick caused Derrick to throw his head back as he released a loud moan. "Sss-hell yeah," he exclaimed. "That's what the fuck I'm talking about."

Derrick glanced down at her. She was a strikingly gorgeous woman. He massaged her shoulders with one hand while gently palming and pulling on her curly hair with the other. She loved his soft touch.

Erica was a stone-cold freak and knew exactly what she was doing. She stood at 5'9 with a beautiful, well-proportioned body. She had soft, welcoming bedroom eyes, with a stylish short hairdo that she almost always kept dyed white. Her stylish hairstyles, and the fact that she always kept it hot and spicy in the bedroom, was exactly what kept Derrick coming back. He also loved the fact that once their lovemaking session began, he never knew what to expect.

He braced himself, feeling his climax rapidly coming on. He stared down at his long thick dick as it violently slammed into the back of Erica's throat. "I'm about to cum," he growled as she slurped, sucked, and pulled at the semen that gradually built in his shaft.

He closed his eyes and began to grind harder. She locked onto his thighs and pulled him deeper into her mouth. "Errgghhh," he cried out, shooting his creamy white load into Erica's mouth.

"Uhmmmm," she moaned, savoring the taste and loving every drop of it. She in no way, shape, or form backed off for one second. She eagerly sat on the edge of the bed, sucking and pulling, slurping and sucking, until every last drop came and went.

Forty-Five minutes later, Erica lay sound asleep, snoring with Derrick awake at her side. In an attempt to avoid waking her up, Derrick slowly peeled the comforter off himself and quietly made his way towards the bathroom. He spotted his clothing carelessly tossed on the floor and quickly scooped them up before heading into the bathroom and quietly locking the door behind him.

He hastily dug through his pockets in search of his cell phone and immediately took notice of the message he'd been dreading to see.

"Three missed calls. Fuck," he quietly cursed, peering at his reflection in the bathroom mirror.

His wife Martina had called three times, and once again he had failed to answer the phone as they had agreed upon. Derrick and Martina had been married for the past four years, but there was something inside of him over the last year that had him intrigued, stirring a desire to cheat. Sadly, he had been sneaking around and cheating on his wife for some time now.

Before getting dressed, he carefully inspected his perfectly chiseled chest, which he worked on religiously. He needed to be sure there were no scratches or passion marks left behind. Making love to Erica could be a very brutal experience at times. Sometimes she could get so caught up that she might accidentally bite or scratch Derrick, leaving marks.

After a brief inspection of his body, he quickly showered, got dressed, and prepared to leave. He then cautiously turned the bathroom knob so as not to make a sound and crept out the bathroom before making his way towards the bedroom door. Just as his foot crossed into the hallway, Erica's groggy voice cut through the darkness of the bedroom, slightly startling him.

"Just where the hell do you think you're going?" She questioned.

He fumbled around in the darkness in search of the light switch and flipped it on. "Damn, I gotta go pick Jonathan up from the bar," he lied. "He's had way too much to drink, and he called me to come get him."

She stared up at him, processing his statement. "It's 2 o'clock in the morning. He can call a cab to make sure he gets home alright. Why you gotta be the one that gets up this early in the morning, just to make sure he gets home?"

Derrick sighed, knowing he was stumped. He knew he needed to come up with an explanation quickly because once Erica made up her mind about something it was Hell on earth to get her to change it.

"Babe, this is my best friend we're talking about here. There is no way in the world I'm just going to lay up and leave him stranded when he obviously needs my help," he explained.

Erica sat bobbing her head as if she agreed with him.

"Well I'm going with you," she replied, flinging the covers off herself and trying to get out of the bed.

"Nah, hold up," he protested, darting back across the room to stop her from getting up. "You have to be at work at six in the morning. There is no need for you to be trying to get up and go on this run. I got this. All you need to focus on is trying to go back to sleep. Jonathan called me. It won't take but a second for me to shoot over there, pick him up, and get back here to you."

She searched his eyes hoping to find the truth, but her gut told her she was probably contending with some gold-digging, thirsty ass bitch. She fought day and night to hold those ill thoughts at bay.

"You better come back," she demanded, eyeing him suspiciously. "Don't I always?" He leaned down and gently kissed her on the forehead. "I'll be right back." He quickly made his way out of Erica's bedroom, out of her apartment, and down to his car. As soon as he was safely out of sight, he pulled out his cell phone and called Martina.

"Hello," Martina answered on the second ring.

"Do you need me to stop by the store to grab something for you before I get to the house?" he offered, hoping to catch some sort of vibe as to what kind of situation he was going home to.

"Really Derrick? It's after 2 o'clock in the morning, and here you are waking me up to some lame-ass questions?"

"Martina, come on, Babe. I was just trying to check and see if you needed anything before, I made it home. Now, what could be so lame about that?"

"Pssttt, anyway," Martina snarled. "Don't come trying to check on me now. You weren't trying to check on me when I was blowing your phone up, and you ain't answer."

He couldn't do anything but shake his head to that. She was right. He had already suspected that she would be furious with him. All he could have hoped for was that the argument wouldn't last all night.

"A'ight, Martina," he conceded. "I'll be pulling up in just a second." He immediately disconnected the call, not giving Martina another moments grace to throw her little temper tantrum. He already knew by the time he made it home, there would be plenty of that waiting for him.

He pulled into his driveway fifteen minutes later. He hit the remote to open the garage door and was shocked to see Martina standing in the middle of the garage, barefoot, in one of his long white t-shirts. He tapped his horn twice in an attempt to get her to move.

"Come on, Babe," he whined. "Don't be like that." After a brief staredown between the two, Martina reluctantly stepped aside, allowing him access into the garage. "Martina, stop acting like that towards me, Babe," he insisted as he finally parked and stepped out of the car.

"No, you don't act like that towards me," she fired back. "How long are we going to have to keep going through this shit, Derrick? I'm sick of being home alone, wondering if you're going to come back or not."

He sighed in regret, fully understanding why she felt the way she did. He knew the way he'd been neglecting his relationship with his wife was bound to catch up with him, but his selfish desires had allowed the seed of adultery to be planted firmly in their relationship.

"Come on, let's just go inside. We can talk about it in there," he said. "You're going to catch a cold standing out here barefoot on this cold concrete."

Derrick tried to walk up to Martina and calmly grab her by the hand, but she quickly snatched away from him.

"I don't want to go in the house and talk about it, Derrick. I want you to tell me how long we have to keep going through this same bullshit!"

Derrick shook his head and stared up at the ceiling. If he didn't tell Martina exactly what she wanted to hear, the whole scenario could go on for hours.

"Babe, I swear to you that this will never happen again. Now can we please just go inside? We can talk about this in there." Derrick reached out again, except this time he was allowed to embrace her hand inside of his. Not wanting her to change her mind, he quickly led her into the house and guided her to the living room. He then sat on the ottoman while she sat on the couch in front of him.

"I just want all of these negative thoughts and feelings that I keep having to just go away," she admitted. "It's like our marriage has gotten so far off track that I almost feel as if I'm starting to lose you."

He reached for Martina's hand again, quickly bringing her fingertips to his lips and kissing them. "I don't ever want to hear you say something as silly as that again. Do you understand me? I ain't going anywhere. And to prove it, tell me what I have to do to make this thing right between us."

Martina sighed as she pondered Derrick's comment. His words were truly heartfelt, causing her to doubt what she already knew to be the truth. The fact of the matter was Martina would go through hell and damnation if that's what it took to get her relationship back on track with her husband. She loved everything about Derrick, from his beautiful cocoa skin tone to his long dreadlocks that hung down to the middle of his back. His olive-green eyes gave him that exotic look that drove her wild. What made him even sexier to Martina was his business sense and the way his mind worked. That in itself drove her hormones through the roof.

"If you'll do whatever it takes to make this thing right between us, then start by telling me the truth. Just where exactly have you been hiding these last few nights, I've been trying to reach you?"

He lowered his chin to his chest and rested his forehead in the palms of his hands. His plan to try and deter Martina from continuing to question his whereabouts had backfired. He needed to figure out a new approach, a way to switch things around and get her mind in another place.

"You already know if I'm not at work, then I'm most likely out with the guys having a drink, or just chilling somewhere," he said, getting down on his knees to slowly ease between her legs. "Where is all of this doubt coming from anyways? You are my wife. You act like you've heard I put another woman above you." He planted small kisses on her thick thighs, trying to work his way up to her love box.

"No, stop Derrick, we need to talk about this."

He continued what he was doing, showing total disregard to her demands for them to talk. Martina looked on in horror as Derrick made his way up her thighs to her soaking wet thong. She squirmed around beneath him, struggling to break free from his bear tight grip, but it was to no avail. Derrick was far stronger than her, and she knew he could have his way with her if he chose to. He moved her thong to the side and ran his tongue across her clit.

"Babe—no—stop, we need to—" she gasped when she felt his tongue plunged inside of her.

He licked, kissed, and slurped at her juicy pussy as she grew wetter and wetter. Guilt, fear, and pleasure all flooded Martina's mind at the same time. As much as she wanted him to stop, she wanted him to continue doing what he was doing. She loved the way his tongue kissed her pussy. She wanted to cry out for more, but out of fear of what he might find if he continued to plunge deeper, she said nothing. Derrick had his secrets, but she had hers, too.

CHAPTER ONE

WE BOTH SHARE SECRETS

Buzz! Buzz! Buzz! The alarm clock blared on the side of the bed, waking the couple up. Derrick knew it was time to get ready for work.

So, he peered over at the clock. Stretching, he then wiped the crust from the corners of his eyes. Daylight had rapidly come upon him, bringing him to face yet another day.

"Damn, it feels like we just went to sleep," he said, looking over at his wife, who was digging through the clothes in the closet trying to find something to wear for work. "I wish I could just lay here and take the whole day off. I really need to get some rest."

Martina smirked, peering back over at Derrick with envy in her eyes. "Well, you're Mr. Big Shot that owns his own business. It's up to you when you get to work and when everyone else has to be there. I know if I were you, I would have someone else doing all the crap that goes along with opening and closing. You're the boss. You should have it made."

"Well, I love what I do," he replied, tossing the covers off him. "Even though it's totally up to me when I or anyone else arrives at work, it's also up to me how successful my company is going to be." He got up and out of bed as if his words gave him a little motivation to get ready for the day.

The couple showered, got dressed, and ate, then Martina headed towards the front door to exit for work. She held a corporate position. Her work hours were slightly different than Derrick's. She had to leave for work at least an hour before he had to.

"Will you be coming straight home after work?" she inquired as she picked up her keys off the dining room table and slung her Gucci bag over her shoulder.

"Now, what kind of question is that?" he said, softly chuckling. "Don't I still live here and pay bills here?"

She rolled her eyes and opened the front door prepared to

leave without replying but was unable to. "Hey, it ain't like you come home every night after work," she quipped. "Just wanted to know so I would know if I should cook or not."

Derrick knew to just let her little sassy remarks slide. She could very well still be caught up in her feelings about last night, so there was no way in hell he would say anything that could fuel that negative energy.

"I love you," he said, flipping the conversation around.

"I'll see you when you get home, Okay!" Martina blew him a kiss and eagerly stepped out of the house in a rush to get to her car.

Her conscience was eating her alive. She felt like a stone-cold hypocrite, and when she hopped in the car and caught a glimpse of her reflection in the rearview mirror, that's exactly what she saw. She quickly pulled out her cell phone to call her friend and tell him exactly what was going on. Last night's experience had come so close to them getting caught that she was almost reluctant to meet at her house again.

"Hello," a man's groggy voice answered. "Hey, it's me," Martina replied.

"Well, good morning sexy. Glad to know I'm the first person on your mind when you wake up."

"You almost got us busted," Martina exclaimed, giggling. Her side piece made her feel so special. She was always glad to hear his voice and was also excited to tell him about what happened. "We can't ever cut things that close again. I thought I was good as dead after you left."

"You thought you were as good as dead?" the man repeated quizzically, trying to get a better understanding as to what Martina was talking about.

"You heard me, dead! Do you know as soon as you pulled out the garage, I let the door back down and Derrick pulled right up, hitting the button and letting the damn thing right back up."

"You're kidding," he said in shock.

"The hell if I am," Martina responded. "I could have sworn he saw you pull out, and that's not to mention I didn't even have a chance to freshen up."

He chuckled. "So, what did he say? What was his excuse? Did he say where he was, or what's been taking him so long to get home?"

"You don't even wanna know," Martina said. She was trying to remember the words Derrick said in his attempt to convince her of his whereabouts. "I will tell you this much, he claims to be spending his time chilling with you."

The man on the other end of the line burst into loud laughter. "That is hilarious. That dude has way too much game. I told you, he didn't respect you. I don't even know how the hell you two ended up getting married in the first place."

"Wow, if it isn't the pot calling the kettle black. What about you?" Martina asked sarcastically. "You're supposed to be his so-called best friend. Maybe you can tell me how you two got to become so close."

"First of all, the best friend comment is a huge overstatement. Me and your man just share some of the same taste." Jonathan fell silent for a moment, allowing his thoughts to travel back to the night before. "Speaking of taste, you tasted quite amazing. I told you I was nice with it, didn't I?"

Now it was Martina's turn to fall silent. She drove in silence immediately replaying every detail of last night's experience. She had a double dose of some good dick, fire lip service, and her fair share of orgasms. The mere thought of the night before made her pussy moist, causing her not to utter another word.

"Speechless," Jonathan exclaimed arrogantly.

"Boy, boo," Martina snapped, realizing the assumption he made by her not responding. "I ain't even about to go there with you right now," she said still softly laughing. "What do you have planned for this evening, once I get off work?"

"Nothing that I know of. Why? Should I be expecting a round two?"

"See there you go again. You need to bring it down just a notch," Martina said, seeing how his ego quickly shot past ten. "I was just going to let you know we could hook up again tonight if

Derrick doesn't come straight in."

"A'ight, a'ight," Jonathan said, agreeing with Martina. "I'll stop being so big-headed. Just give me a call when and if you see that Derrick is not coming home."

"Umm, I'm like 99.999 percent sure he won't be bringing his ass home like he said he would," she quipped. "Just call me later. I'll be there waiting on you."

***

"Ladies, ladies," Derrick said to his employees as he walked through the front doors of his women's clothing store. "Good morning to you all. I hope everyone had a good night's rest and is up and ready for a productive day." He spotted his store manager folding a few shirts and headed over in her direction.

"Well, if no one else was able to get a good night's rest, it sure looks like you were able to," April jokingly said as Derrick drew closer.

April was one of the main reasons why Derrick's store had been so successful. April brought a certain touch of class to Derrick's selection of clothing that most women's clothing stores seemed to be lacking. While most of his competitors' stores had slowly fizzled out, Derricks had continued to burn strong. April brought a touch of class to his selection that was out of this world.

"I sure did," Derrick replied, now standing next to April as she continued working. "But if you were to say you've completed that fall selection, I've been waiting on for two weeks, all my nights would be filled with good rest."

April smirked, looking up at Derrick with confidence in her eyes. "As a matter of fact, I did. If you have some time this evening after we close the store, I'll gladly show you the changes I've made."

"*Changes*," Derrick repeated.

"Yes, I made a few changes. I went with a different outlet, and I'm sure you'll be very pleased with the new merchandise."

Derrick's eyebrow slightly raised as his mind began to

wonder. *If you changed outlets, that could mean a change in price as well,* he thought. He started to continue inquiring as to what exactly she had done, but the soft buzzing from his cell phone distracted his train of thought. "If you'll excuse me for a minute, I have to take this call really quick."

For a little privacy, Derrick headed to his office in the back of the building. His wife Martina generally called on her first break, which most often was shortly after Derrick arrived at work.

"Hello," he answered.

"What happened to you coming back last night?"

He pulled the phone away from his ear, checking for the phone number. When he noticed there was not one present, he placed the phone back to his ear. "Excuse me," Derrick replied, somewhat confused as to what the caller was saying.

"You're excused!" she rudely replied. "You told me you were coming back last night. Now here it is a whole new day, and you're sitting over there acting like you don't know what the hell I'm talking about."

"Erica?" Derrick said, looking at the caller I.D which displayed unavailable. Being as though his wife and Erica's complaints were the same, he was reluctant to go any further with the conversation.

"What! Were you expecting it to be someone else?"

"Erica, chill, I wasn't expecting anything. You just caught me off guard with this anonymous phone call. I'm at work, right now, and I have a ton of shit that's gotta get done today. If you don't mind, I would appreciate it if we could talk about this when I got off."

Erica growled into the phone. She hated how Derrick was always able to find some way out of addressing their problems.

"See, there you go. You're always trying to put things off until later," Erica complained. She really wanted to continue to press the issue until she found out what was going on with Derrick but then again, by doing so, she might cause an argument. "If you promise you'll be by later, then this conversation can wait."

Derrick had no problem with agreeing to her simple terms. He was willing to say whatever he had to, to get off the phone. "A'ight, I promise to stop by as soon as I clock out," he finally agreed.

Business went well at Derrick's clothing store that day. Women of all ages, shapes, and sizes poured into his fine clothing establishment just to cop the latest fashions. *DF & Accessories* specialized in plus-sized women's clothing, shoes, and accessories. If women wanted something outside the norm, this was the place to get it.

As the workday finally drew near to closing, Derrick decided to work a little later than normal. April had completed the fall selection as he'd requested, and he needed to go over it with her.

"This really looks good," he stated excitedly, scrolling through page after page on his tablet. He was extremely pleased with the various stylish clothing selections April had chosen. "Even the quality of the clothing appears to be much better. I can assume this is going to come out costing a nice little extra chunk of change."

April made her way around Derrick's desk, quickly guiding him through the digital inventory, to the cost.

"Wow, you've nearly saved us thirty percent in comparison to last year's figures. Are you sure these numbers are correct?"

"I'm positive," April boasted, beaming with pride. She knew she had just made her employer a very happy man. "I checked the prices twice, that's why I ended up changing outlets."

Derrick leaned back in his leather desk chair, clearly in deep thought. "I'll tell you what, I'm going to reward your hard work with a bonus and dinner on me. That's the least I can do, especially being as though I asked you to work late after you already did such a great job."

April smiled, peering over at Derrick as she playfully patted on her stomach. "You don't even have to ask me twice. I'm hungry as hell, too, so let's go."

They wrapped up with work and hopped in their separate cars.

April closely followed behind Derrick as he zipped in and out of traffic in his SS Camaro. Regardless of how much Derrick loved to drive fast, he had a little extra fun testing the limits of how fast April was willing to go to keep up. Had he known April had a thing for speed, he might have decided to try a different test. When April was behind the wheel of her SRT-8 Jeep, she was a speed demon. Losing her in the sauce was simply not about to happen.

"Where did you learn how to drive like that?" he asked after they arrived at Sammy's Grill.

"Oh, that was nothing," she bragged. "I can drive way better than that. I bet if you let me see the keys to your car, I'll have them tires squealing as I fishtail through the parking lot."

Derrick couldn't help but laugh out loud. "Now hold on there, Speedy. That's a mighty big statement coming from a little lady such as yourself."

April squinted her eyes, looking up at Derrick as they entered the restaurant. "You shouldn't ever underestimate a woman like me. I'm full of surprises, and I can almost always back up what I say."

Derrick took April over to a booth that overlooked Lake Hefner. After the two snuggled in their seats, they ordered drinks and finally began to unwind.

"So, do you come here often?" April asked, seeing how familiar Derrick was with the waitresses and the restaurant's beautiful surroundings.

"Not really. I only come here for special occasions, or when I want to get away."

April casually scanned the area around them. "Well, you must have a lot of special occasions then," she assumed aloud. "It sure seems like everyone here knows you on a first-name basis."

Derrick smiled but quickly concealed his expression by easing his glass of Crown Royal XR up to his mouth.

"You know, I've never had the chance to ask you something," April continued.

"What's that?" he asked. "Are you married?"

"Damn! Just dive right in there," Derrick said, softly laughing. "Where did that come from, and why do you get to ask all the questions?"

April shrugged. "I was just wondering. But you can ask me whatever questions you want. I've just never heard you talk about another woman, but you move like a married man moves."

Derrick thought about what she was saying and smiled. If only she knew. "So, because I move like a married man, that makes you think I'm married?"

"No, not really. It's just a simple question."

Derrick appeared to be thinking about something then took another sip of his drink. "I'd like to ask a few questions of my own," Derrick said, trying to divert the limelight away from himself. "I know you do pretty well for yourself by working at my store, but that Jeep, those things cost a little money. Do you have a side job that you've never told me about?"

April picked up her drink and swirled it around with two straws. She too appeared to be weighing her answers before responding. "Let's just say it was a gift."

"A gift you say. So, would it be safe to assume that the gift is from the same man that put that huge rock on your finger?" He pointed over at the ring on her left hand. "I take it that's an indication of you being married. Even though you move like a married woman as well."

April giggled softly, then took another sip of her drink. "I wish I was married. I was engaged to someone who had lots of money, but I ended up having to break things off with him. He was involved in too many things that I wasn't trying to have any parts in getting caught up in. I just want to live a normal, everyday life, and I ain't got no interest in living a life that could lead to me serving prison time."

"Oh, one of those types of guys," Derrick said. "So, what, you're just wearing the ring to make people think you're married?"

"That and it keeps dudes away that's looking for someone to support them," she replied.

Derrick chuckled, "I bet you make it very difficult for the average man to approach you."

"Never that, an average man is just what a girl like me is

looking for. I want someone who knows how to handle a real woman. Not some drug selling thug. Right now, I don't need those problems and at some point, boys have to grow up."

Derrick and April went on to order food, eat, and order more drinks while continuing to enjoy each other's company. By the time Derrick realized what time it was, a waitress was making her way over towards them to inform them that Sammy's Grill was about to close.

"It's funny how time flies when you're having fun. I was so caught up in telling you my whole life story, that the entire night just slipped right through my fingers," Derrick said, pulling his credit card out to hand it to the waitress.

April nodded in agreement, then looked at her watch. "Who says our night has to end now? I mean, it's not like we're not enjoying ourselves. Hell, I have my own house, car, and everything that comes with that. So, if you're up to it, we can just take this over to my place."

Derrick peered over at April, contemplating whether he should. *Going over to her place sounds like a good idea, but what would that lead to?* he wondered.

He always kept his sex life and business separate. However, nothing April said implied that anything would come of his visit to her house, but then again, they had been drinking. It was late, and no matter how much Derrick tried to overlook it, he was very much sexually attracted to April. April was the very definition of a dime piece. She had thick, muscular, track legs, a nice, firm ass, and an eye-catching swagger. Regardless of Derrick's rules to always keep business and his sexual life separate, in the back of his mind, his curiosity was eating away at that rule.

"You know what, I think I'm going to have to take you up on that offer," he finally responded. "If we continue to enjoy ourselves a little while longer, I don't believe it'll hurt a thing."

April allowed a half-smile to grace her face. Then standing, she brushed at invisible wrinkles in her skirt allowing Derrick to admire her physique. "Yeah, I think you're right," she replied almost mockingly with a mischievous twinkle in her eye. "If we continue to enjoy ourselves a little while longer, I'm sure it won't hurt a thing." She stepped out of the booth. "Excuse me, give me a moment to go use the ladies room."

April purposefully switch bounced, rolling her perfectly round ass down the aisle. Whatever moral guidelines Derrick had before was out the window. In that very moment, Derrick sat lusting for April as he watched her stroll down the aisle, *Pound Game* had begun. The loser of this game may very well have to pay with their life.

***

Martina sat out at Lake Hefner cuddled up in Jonathan's arms. While embraced in his grip, she peered up into the stars. It was so peaceful. The view was astonishing. It was as if the entire universe was being seen through a gigantic magnifying glass like one could sit there beneath heavens' stars and have a crystal-clear view of the whole universe.

"Isn't this just gorgeous?" Martina asked Jonathan as her mind journeyed to a far, far away place filled with dreams and wishful thinking. "I wish I was one of those people who knew how to read the stars. That way I could tell my own future."

Jonathan released a soft chuckle. "You wish you could read the stars you say? What would you hope the stars might reveal to you that you don't think that I can?"

She playfully elbowed Jonathan in his stomach. "I'm serious silly. During this lifetime of mine, I'd just like to know what direction my life is headed. Like I want to know what I should be looking forward to. I'm so tired of going through life expecting the best, but somehow always coming out with the worst end of the stick."

Jonathan chuckled again. "Oh, I see where this is going. You wanna be able to read the stars so you can see where you and your man's relationship is going?"

"Do what? Where did that come from?" Martina quickly slid her feet into her flip flops and stood to leave. "I can't believe you just went there with me," she barked, looking down at Jonathan with disdain. "How could you take something as simple as talking about the stars and turn it into something that's about, Derrick?" Martina quickly spun and headed to her car.

"Babe, wait!" Jonathan said, hopping to his feet. He quickly reached out to grab Martina to prevent her from getting too far away. "I was only kidding, Babe. Are you going to allow that one little comment to be the reason you just up and leave?"

Martina glared up at Jonathan, then quickly looked away in an attempt to hide her frustrations. "That was totally uncalled for," she said, looking off into the distance, as she watched the water sparkle in the night. "I'm already going through enough emotional bullshit. I don't need someone to help remind me of just how fucked up my situation is."

Jonathan looked down at Martina with loving eyes. "I'm sorry," he said, pulling her into his arms and planting soft kisses on her forehead. "I don't know what the hell I thought when I said that stupid ass shit. Sometimes I can get so caught up on trying to make you frown upon Derrick, that I just blurt out the first thing that comes to mind." He squeezed Martina, nibbling at her neck and ear. "I hope you didn't think I was just about to let you walk out of my life, just like that?"

"Whatever," she replied, batting her eyes in a vain attempt to blink away her tears. "I don't know what you're going to do, but I do know I'm sick of being hurt. I'm tired of being lied to. And above all, I'm sick of sneaking around, and playing all of these goddamn games!"

Jonathan stepped back, now gazing at Martina with concern. "Well, if you're tired of playing games, then let's stop playing. I'm the muthafucka that's here to heal those open wounds, not him. And regardless of whatever else comes your way in life. I'm also that same nigga that's gonna be there to stand by your side." Tears now freely flowed down Martina's cheeks, prompting Jonathan to kiss them as they fell. "Fuck that nigga! Derrick didn't appreciate the blessing that he had when he had you, but I do. I'm willing to do whatever it takes to prove that to you, Martina."

Martina leaned up on her tippy toes to plant a soft kiss on Jonathan's lips. His words were healing to her broken heart. They gave her a sense of having something to stand on. "Maybe I overreacted just a little," Martina reasoned. "It's not like I don't believe every single word that comes out of your mouth. I just need some time to get a few things in order." Martina suddenly broke away from Jonathan, slowly making it back over to her car. "I'll call you in the morning, okay?"

"Damn, you're really going to just up and leave me hanging like that, huh?"

Martina looked back over her shoulder, giving Jonathan a warm smile before getting inside her car. "It's getting late, Babe. I'm not leaving because I want to. I'm leaving because I have to." She started her car as Jonathan stood nodding his head in acceptance.

"Well, make sure you call me first thing in the morning," he said, standing in the same spot she had left him, but now smiling himself.

"I will, I love you," Martina said, pulling away.

"I love you, too," Jonathan replied as Martina drove away into the dark of the night.

In the back of her mind, Martina knew the time was coming where she would soon have to make a decision, but would that decision be a choice she could honestly live with? Yes, Derrick had his secrets, but she had secrets of her own. Time and time again, she had played with the idea of coming clean, and revealing to Derrick what she knew of him, and what she was doing. *Would that make him change? How will he accept that? If he does end up stopping what he's doing, will it be because of what I hold over him, or will it be because he wants to stop?* Countless questions danced around in her mind, but the one thing she was certain of was the fact that things were about to make a drastic change, for better, or for worse.

***

Glocks on Satin Sheets

Derrick had been home for over an hour. His evening with April had turned into something neither of them ever expected. One glass of liquor turned into two, and two into three. Before either of them knew what was going on, they were both on the verge of stepping into a whole other realm filled with passion and ecstasy. Had it not been for the presence of Mother Nature's monthly visit, Derrick would have surely found himself engaged in activities he would regret later.

"I wonder where the hell she's at this time of night?" Derrick mumbled as he walked from room to room, searching for any explanation that might explain where Martina was. He pulled out his cell phone, debating if he should call her. *I can't call her, cause then it'll look like I don't trust her,* he reasoned. *But what if it's some other shit going on? What if—* "Fuck!" he yelled in frustration, realizing the foolish ideas he had been thinking. "I can't believe I'm sitting here thinking this bullshit about my fucking wife!"

He went back into the living room, where he flopped down in his favorite spot on the sofa. In an attempt to calm his nervousness, he channel-surfed, looking for a show that might consume his attention.

His cell phone rang. "About goddamn time!" He snarled, assuming it was Martina calling, but once he noticed the face that suddenly appeared on the screen, his little celebration came to an abrupt halt.

"My bad, Erica," he apologetically said. "I ended up working a little later than expected, then I came straight home because I was extremely exhausted."

"But you promised you would stop by so we could talk," Erica whined into the phone. "You flat out lied last night. You said you were coming straight back. Then you turn around today and tell me you're coming, and don't even show. How am I supposed to feel about this Derrick? You're always fucking lying to me."

Derrick rolled his eyes, releasing a soft sigh of frustration. His mind was already cluttered with the whereabouts of his wife, and now this. "Erica, now really isn't a good time for all of this. I already told you how tired I am. Not to mention I already have a ton of other things on my mind—" Derrick paused for a moment, allowing his words to sink in a little bit. "Doesn't any of this mean anything to you?"

Erica was ready to come unglued. She felt like she knew the truth as to why Derrick wasn't coming back to her home, but it was a truth that she couldn't willingly accept.

"No!" she barked. "What means something to me is how you keep putting me off. You keep fucking lying to me like we're still high school kids or something. Then you try and make it seem like I'm wrong because I want to spend a little time with my so-called boyfriend."

Derrick was on the verge of trying to get Erica to calm down, but the voice that came from behind him almost making him drop the phone stopped all of that.

"Who are you on the phone with?"

Derrick turned around to see Martina standing behind him, leaning against the wall.

"What—where—where have you been?" Derrick stuttered, getting out of his chair, and quickly disconnecting his phone call on the sly.

"*Where have I been?*" Martina repeated mockingly. "I think that's the question I should be asking you! You're the one sitting up in our living room, talking on the phone to one of your little bitches."

Derrick walked around the sofa to confront Martina face-to-face. The split second that Martina caught him off guard, startled him. He had one mission in mind and a look in his eye that said he meant business.

"Martina, I'm not going to ask you but this one last time. Where the fuck have you been? I'm not trying to hear no bullshit about me doing this and doing that. You need to blow that shit off and answer my damn question."

Martina could sense Derrick was mere inches from coming unglued if she didn't answer his question. Even though abuse had never been a part of their relationship, this could be the night if she didn't answer. "I've been all around the city looking for you," she lied. "I've been by your job. Your little friend's house. I even drove by a couple of bars, checking to see if I might see your car. But nooo, no, no Derrick. But what do I find sitting in my fucking living room by the time I get home, my goddamn husband sitting on the phone, caking with some thirsty ass bitch! Now it's your turn, Derrick. Where the hell have you been ducked off at all evening?"

Derrick was speechless. What could he ever say to that? Here he was out with another woman, and his wife was burning down the streets in search of him.

He scuffed, glaring at Martina as his mind tried to detect the slightest inkling of a lie. Martina still wore the same clothing she wore when she left for work this morning. *Wait a minute, why is she carrying her high heels, and wearing flip-flops? Did she come home after work? I thought she said she's been driving around looking for me.* Several things danced around Derrick's mind, but instead of sounding like a mad man and voicing his thoughts, he decided to just let things go.

"I had a dinner meeting with several of my employees," he finally said, brushing past Martina as he headed upstairs. "I would have called, but everything was all sort of spur of the moment."

Martina stood glaring at Derrick as he walked off leaving her standing there alone. She knew he was exposed. As much as she wanted to tell him she knew of everything he was doing, she didn't. In time, his own actions would make him have to reveal the truth. All she had to do was wait.

Adrian Dulan

CHAPTER TWO

UNEXPECTED NEWS

The next morning, April was awakened by her cell phone ringing on the nightstand next to her bed. She rolled over to answer and was caught off guard by that irritating electronic operator.

"You have a collect call from, Slim, an inmate at the—" April could have cursed herself a million times over for not looking at the caller ID before answering the call. Now she would be forced to face her demented ex-boyfriend Slim for the ill things she had done to him in the past.

"What is it, Slim?" April snarled after pressing 5 to accept the call from the Federal Facility.

"What tha fuck you mean, what is it?" Slim fired back. "My muthafuckin' bread, that's what! How you gon' catch an attitude after you done ran off with my money? Ain't that a bitch!" he cursed frustrated.

"Anyways," April mumbled under her breath, looking up into her bedroom ceiling. "Is that why you keep calling my phone because you think I still owe you some money?"

"April, I'm warning you. Girl, you better stop fucking around with my fuckin' cheddar and pay me what you owe me."

"*What I owe you?*" April repeated. "When is it going to dawn on you, if you ain't got a dime back by now, you ain't ever going to get it!"

Slim squeezed on the phone receiver, wishing it was April's neck he held in his grasp. "Bitch, I swear before God himself, when I get my hands on you, I'ma murder yo' bitch ass. Do you hear me?"

April began to mockingly laugh into the phone. "Good luck with that shit, nigga. By the way, don't you have somebody you need to be trying to find that owes you some noodles? Cause calling my damn phone at six o'clock in the morning ain't gon' get you shit but a hard dick and a dial tone. Now you listen and listen carefully this is the last time I'm going to ever tell you this again.

Stop calling my phone and stop having whoever you have stalking me to get my number, or I'ma file charges on you. Now, do you understand?" *Click!* April disconnected the call, not giving Slim the chance to respond.

In the back of her mind, she felt an urgent but nagging feeling that someday she might have to deal with Slim, because of what she had done in the past. Even though those ill thoughts danced around in her mind, she still quickly pushed them to the side and fell back to sleep.

***

It had been a long day for Derrick at *DF & Accessories*. He was mentally and physically fatigued behind all the extra stress he had brought upon himself as of lately. Trying to juggle more than one woman at a time was turning out to be more trouble than it was worth. Derrick was slowly coming to the realization that it might be time to let someone go.

Derrick sat in his office with his feet kicked up on his desk. He was just on the verge of nodding off to sleep when an unexpected knock at his office door awakened him. He looked up to see April peeking into his office.

"Excuse me, but do you have a moment so I can have a word with you?" She had a warm smile spread across her face as she entered the room.

"Sure, come right on in," Derrick said, now sitting up, and waving April in with his hand. "I was just about to go over a little paperwork but ended up getting too comfortable and almost fell asleep."

April softly laughed, making her way over to the chair that sat just in front of his desk.

"Well, for starters, I wanted to apologize about what happened last night. I wanted to let you know that I was enjoying myself and Mother Nature just so happen to make her monthly visit."

Derrick sat up, placing his elbows on the desk. Even though he and April had been working side-by-side for the better part of the day, neither of them had spoken one word about last night's events. "No need for apologies,' Derrick insisted. "It's not like any of that was your fault. Mother Nature has her way of doing things. We just probably had a little too much to drink. Then one thing turned into another, then, well, you know."

"Oh, is that what you think happened?" April skeptically asked with one eyebrow slightly raised. "I thought we might have had a good thing going on like we had good chemistry. We might have had a few drinks, but I believe that only allowed us the chance to let our guards down a little more than we would have at any other time."

Derrick readjusted himself in his chair. He felt an erection quickly coming on. April's straightforward approach was something he wasn't used to. "We did, I mean we do, have very good chemistry," he stuttered, trying to sound confident, but clearly failed to do so. "Mother Nature just got in the way, and—"

"And you're willing to allow me the chance to make it up to you?" April asked cunningly finishing Derrick's sentence as well.

"Yeah, umm, sure. I mean if that's what you want to do, that is."

April burst into laughter, having to cover her mouth just to keep from being so loud.

"I would like to make it up to you," she said still softly giggling. "I've been trying to think of something that might prove to be very entertaining," she said, giving Derrick a look that spoke volumes. "But I just haven't quite decided what I want to do yet."

Derrick ran both hands over his dreadlocks, trying his best to suppress just how excited he was. "Take all the time you need to get it together, I'm in," he replied. "You already got me over here looking forward to whatever you might come up with. Knowing you, it'll probably be steaming hot!"

April stood to leave. "Remember what I said last night," she said over her shoulder, heading towards the door.

"And what was that?" he replied.

"Never underestimate me," she said with a sly smile.

Derrick's whole world shook. He had never been with a woman that was so straightforward, sexy, and yet so damn mischievous. His wife Martina was his world, but April was very different in many ways. She had that edge on her. It was almost like she was the boss, and Derrick was her employee. Her presence demanded attention while her beauty kept it.

In that very moment, Derrick sat watching as April walked out of his office, his mind was made up. All rules were thrown out the window when it came to April. Whatever happened, once the two of them decided to cross that line, he would gladly deal with it when that time came. It was something about April, something in the way she made him feel. Whatever it was that was making him feel the way he felt, he was ready to find out.

After finally finishing up for the evening, Derrick headed out the store and locked the doors behind him. He felt like he was on top of the world. The conversation he had with April had temporarily distracted him from the stress that had been plaguing him.

As he made his way through the parking lot to get to his car, he took notice of something that stuck out as rather odd. Erica's red Nissan Altima was parked next to his Camaro. Over the past six months that he had been messing around with Erica, he made sure to keep his life a mystery to her. She knew nothing of where he worked, or where he lived. So, Erica being parked out in front of his job caught him by surprise.

"So, this is where you work?" Erica said, getting out of her car as Derrick quickly approached.

"Yes, it is," Derrick responded, sounding slightly annoyed that she was there. "What are you doing here?"

Erica peered around the parking lot of the plaza, then back at Derrick. "I was doing a little shopping and just so happened to see your car parked out here. And seeing as though you haven't been trying to answer any of my phone calls, I figured I would wait outside until you came out." She studied Derrick's face for a reaction, but there was none. "There have been a few things come up that I think you should know about," she added.

Derrick sighed, crossing his arms across his chest. He leaned against the hood of his car. "Yeah, well I have a few things that I want to talk to you about as well," he responded, sarcastically. "But seeing as though you have been sitting out here for God knows how long, I'll allow you to say what you've come to say first." Erica could sense Derrick was acting distant like he had something bad he wanted to say but hoped the news she came to share with him might get their relationship back like it used to be.

"I'm pregnant," Erica said, Derrick just stood there, staring at her as if he hadn't heard one word she had said. "Derrick, did you hear what I just said? I'm pregnant!"

Whatever little trance Derrick might have been in, when she repeated herself, he quickly found his way out if it. "I thought you were taking the pill," he asked in disbelief.

"I was, but not every time we had sex, and sometimes I simply forgot to take it."

Derrick felt faint. All types of fucked up shit danced around in his head. "*Forgot!* How could you forget to do something as important as that?" He shook his head, rubbing his temples with both hands. He felt trapped and betrayed. When they first got together, he was very clear about Erica being on the pill. For her to have made a mistake as big as that, rocked him. "Is it mine?"

Erica flinched at Derrick as if she were about to swing on him. "Nigga, no you didn't just try me like that!" She turned like she was about to leave, then spun around pointing her finger at Derrick. "You know what? Don't even worry about whose baby it is. You'll find out whose baby it is when child support shows up to your job." She turned to get in her car.

"Erica, for real." Derrick reached out and grabbed hold of her car door before she could slam it. "I didn't mean to offend you. I was just—" Derrick's head fell to his chest, hiding his shame. "You know I care about you a lot. And the reason why this shit has me so fucked up is because I'm a married man."

Erica just sat peering up at Derrick the same way he'd looked at her. Erica had always known that she was competing with some other woman. She just never knew the other woman would be his wife. "Well, I'm so fucking sorry for her," Erica snarled frowning at

Derrick. "What else do you want me to say besides that? Either way, I'm having this baby. And that's whether you or your wife like it or not!" Erica snatched her door free from Derrick's hand and slammed it. "I guess you have a lot more shit you need to start thinking about, don't you?" Erica hissed, before pulling off.

Derrick stood in the middle of the parking lot shocked. If he thought for one second that walking out of her life was going to be that simple, he had another thing coming.

CHAPTER THREE

LET'S GO KICK IT

It had been a little over a week since Martina told Jonathan that she caught Derrick slipping on the phone with another woman. Jonathan knew it was only a matter of time before Derrick totally destroyed his relationship with Martina.

"Last set," Jonathan said, standing in the mirror, trying to hype himself up. He glanced over at the weight bench behind him. "No pain, no gain." He rushed over to hammer out his last set of ten reps.

Jonathan was the very definition of a pretty boy. Cocky, very arrogant, and had the pretty boy swag to match. Standing at six-foot even, light skin, with curly hair, women found Jonathan to be a very attractive man. All throughout high school, Jonathan was the heartthrob of almost every young teenage girl at high school. Jonathan was a first-string quarterback in high school, which was how he and Derrick's paths crossed. Derrick was a star wide receiver, so with the two of them in starting positions on the team, they grew to be very good friends, and in time, best friends.

As the years came to pass, both Jonathan and Derrick graduated high school and began working to support themselves as young adults. Derrick was becoming a small business owner while Jonathan moved around from job to job, not quite sure as to what he wanted to make of himself. Even though the two worked hard, they played just as hard. Some might say they were party animals or even club hoppers. The two together damn near had their way everywhere they went.

In time, as the two continued to grow older, Derrick decided it was finally time for him to slow down and find himself a companion. As Derrick made strides to change, Jonathan still partied hard. However, at some point, Derrick stumbled across a beautiful young woman named Martina. She was his everything, and soon after, he married her. Jonathan secretly envied the life that Derrick made for himself. It seemed as if everything Derrick touched turned to gold while everything Jonathan touched seemed to crumble right before his eyes. Time and time again, Jonathan questioned himself. Was this a curse? Did God have a purpose for him, or was this lonely life the life God had chosen for him?

One day, just a little over a year ago, Jonathan decided to make a surprise visit to see his best friend. Ever since Derrick had opened his new clothing store, the business had kept him swamped. Unfortunately, Derrick had very little time to visit with his old friend like he used too.

That day, Jonathan dropped by, rang Derrick's doorbell, and then patiently waited for someone to answer. Soon after, he was greeted by a very much heartbroken Martina. She cried and cried, and cried, eventually collapsing into Jonathan's arms. Martina had just found out Derrick had been cheating on her, and for her to have to face that truth was devastating.

Jonathan stood holding Martina in a warm embrace. He knew that was what she needed. He knew the crippling void in her chest had to be unbearable. He also knew a woman such as Martina was unlike any other woman he had ever had. Jonathan had been with hundreds of women, but never one he deemed to be wife material. Jonathan lifted Martina's head from his chest and stared deep into her pretty brown eyes. As tears broke from the borders of her eyelids, he kissed each of them, giving her promise after promise as they fell. Whether it was the feeling of revenge Martina felt that made her allow him to continue doing what he was doing was something she didn't recognize. But from that moment in time, a relationship was formed. A relationship that neither had ever thought could transpire.

***

After finishing up a two-hour, extensive, workout, Jonathan picked up his belongings and headed to the showers. "Hey, what up dawg?" A voice called out, catching Jonathan's attention before he could leave the area. Jonathan turned to see Derrick quickly approaching and reluctantly spoke.

Glocks on Satin Sheets

"What up, Big Bro?" Jonathan responded, trying to sound like he was excited to see Derrick, when in fact, he was the last person on the face of the planet he was trying to see.

"Where the hell you been hiding at these days?" Derrick asked, walking up to give Jonathan some dap. "Every time I get up here, your ass is gone. I have been wondering what was going on with you. You had your boy thinking you don't fuck with me anymore."

Jonathan softly chuckled, dismissing Derrick's statement with the wave of his hand. "You know me better than that, Big Bro," Jonathan insisted. "I'ma always fuck with you. Man, I been wrapped up in so many other things. You already know how that shit goes. But anyway, what's been up with you, everything all good?"

"*Pssttt, all good?*" Derrick repeated. "Man, things have been going crazy for me, bruh. I mean shit has been so bad that I've been trying to figure out when I can get away for a little while. I'm talking like getaway and let my hair down like we used to back in the day."

"Word?"

"You damn straight,' Derrick exclaimed. "I'm ready to do it big this time. I've been on this ball and chain for the past few years, and this shit is starting to get old. I'm ready to get out and have some fun, escape from reality for a day or two. It's so much unwanted stress popping up in my life, right now." Derrick's voice trailed away as his thoughts went back to the day Erica told him she was pregnant. He tried over and over to convince Erica not to have the baby, but her decision was made. She was having the baby no matter what.

"I'm in," Jonathan said, snatching Derrick's attention off whatever was bothering him. "I can see something obviously has you fucked up in the head. So, let me know when you ready to do this."

"For real?"

"Hell yeah, for real. Just make sure Martina don't end up catching our asses, cause then we'll both be two dead

41

muthafuckas."

"Man, she ain't talking about nothing. This is for me. As long as you wit' it, I can handle the rest." Jonathan gave Derrick some dap, then checked his watch as if he had somewhere to go. "Just hit me up, Bro, when you ready to do this. I'll be looking for your call," Jonathan said, as he headed to the showers.

As his road dawg took off to the locker room, Derrick had a big smile on his face regarding the whole idea. He was on board, and he really needed to get away to just chill. He walked to the weights and began to warm up for his workout but stopped when his cell phone rang. It was April.

"Hey there, Ms. Ima, Make it up to you," Derrick said playfully, reminding April of what she'd said. "I've been wondering if you were ever going to call."

April softly giggled in the phone, "Well, we see each other almost every day."

"Yeah, but at work. When we at work, that's business. Now that we're off the clock. What's good?"

"Well, that depends on what you have going on for tonight," she said.

Derrick thought about the conversation he had with his best friend. He knew he had already made plans, so tonight might not be a good idea. "Right now, I'm at the gym, but later a good friend and I made plans to get out and have us a drink, drink, drink. Damn, damn, damn— is, is this phone tripping or what, what, what?" Derrick asked as he stood listening to his phone echoing away. But as soon as he'd made mention of the problem, the echoing suddenly stopped. "Don't know what that was about. All that interference must be because of where I'm at," Derrick said, assuming it was because of him being inside of a gym. "But like I was saying, me and a close friend are going out to have some drinks."

"Can I go?" April chimed in, sounding like an overly excited little girl.

"I'm not sure you wanna go where I'm trying to go," he chuckled. "As a matter of fact, I'm leaning heavily towards a gentlemen's club. And I'm almost certain that might be a little too much for a little lady such as yourself," Derrick said.

April had to restrain herself from laughing her head off in Derrick's ear. Derrick had apparently underestimated her, and she could see he had made a grave mistake in doing so. "I'll tell you what, if you let me treat you to the gentlemen's club of my choice, I'll promise you one of the best nights of your life," she stated.

Derrick had to think about that for a moment. That was a mighty big promise to live up to. "*A gentlemen's club of your choice?*" Derrick repeated, making sure he had heard her correctly.

"You heard right," April confidently stated. "All you have to do is tell me the time, and I'll tell you the place."

Derrick's curiosity went through the roof. All types of ideas flooded his mind, but he had to remain cool. He didn't want to get himself all worked up over something that didn't even turn out as he expected. "As soon as I'm done exercising, and I'm on my way home, I'll give you a call. That will be your cue to start getting dressed."

"Okay," April said, smiling from ear-to-ear. "Don't work yourself too hard. You might end up needing some of that energy for later."

***

Club Kavey boasted to have some of OKC's baddest strippers that the city had ever seen. If you were getting money, then that was the place for you. Ballers from all four corners of the game went there to make it rain big faces on some of the most beautiful women in the club.

"Damn dawg, how you gon' drag ya boy to the strip club and you already got someone coming here to meet you?" Jonathan complained as Derrick searched through the parking lot for a place to park.

"Come on, Bruh, you already knew I was trying to turn all the way up tonight. I don't understand why you sitting over there tripping like that? We are ten minutes from being in a room filled with nothing but naked women shaking their ass and titties all over the damn place."

Jonathan smirked, glancing through the passenger side window softly mumbling various curse words to himself. He was already hating that he had agreed to tag along on Derrick's little getaway. It made him feel like a third wheel. Had it not been for his curiosity, he wouldn't have been there. He would rather be laid up in Derrick's King-sized bed, cuddled up with Martina. That would most definitely have felt so much better.

Derrick finally found a spot and pulled alongside the building. "Trust me dawg, if this shit doesn't turn out the way it's supposed to, I won't ever ask you to roll again." Derrick pulled out his phone, quickly scrolled down to April's number, then called. "Ol' girl said she would have a surprise for us both, just chill. Tonight could be more fun than you ever expected." Derrick sat patiently listening as the phone rang. "Where you at?" Derrick questioned April, as soon as she answered the phone.

"I'll be pulling in any second," April replied. "Are you guys already there?"

"Yeah, I told you how long it would take me to get here," Derrick replied, sounding slightly agitated. "You must have still been getting dressed when I called and told you we were heading out."

"No, I was already dressed. In fact, I'm here now." Both Derrick and Jonathan looked back towards the entrance at the same time and saw April pulling up in a beautiful, black, drop-top Jag.

"Damn!" Jonathan screamed, watching April pull into the empty parking spot right next to them. "That's you right there?"

Derrick was speechless. He had never seen April commanding attention the way she was. The woman he knew was modest and humble. But the woman that was strolling around to his door was very much different. This woman lived life on the edge. She was hella sexy, and very much in control of everything around her.

"What are you doing, silly?" April said, standing outside Derrick's door, waiting for him to get out. "Are you just going to sit there all night, or are you coming inside?"

Derrick couldn't do anything but shake his head. April was a showstopper. She stood before him in a dress that hugged every curve on her body. The sides were completely transparent, revealing her nakedness beneath. No panties, no bra, completely naked.

"Damn!"

"I told you never to underestimate me," April said. "Now come on!" She took Derrick by the hand as Jonathan followed and led them right past the long line of people waiting to get inside.

Immediately, Derrick picked up on all the ominous glares from various hustlers and tricks trying to make their way inside. Unfortunately, once inside, the looks proved to be no different.

The small party of three made their way through what seemed like a sea of strippers until they finally made it to their table. As soon as they took their seats, a waitress was already at their table with a small tray filled with drinks and an expensive bottle of champagne.

"Wait, wait, hold up!" Derrick stated firmly, trying to stop the waitress from setting the drinks down. "There has been some kind of mistake. We didn't order any of this." The waitress smiled, calmly placing a glass of Crown Royal XR in front of him. "You must be, Derrick, am I correct?"

Derrick was baffled. He didn't know this woman from nowhere. He had no idea how she knew his name, or how she knew his favorite drink was XR. He started to question the young waitress but caught April giving her a wink on the sly. "Ohhh, I get it. You must have had this whole thing planned out," Derrick told April. "I guess I get to see if you'll really be able to live up to that promise you made me over the phone."

April leaned over, gently taking hold of Derrick's chin, pulling him closer. "I told you tonight would be one of the most memorable nights of your life." She slightly nodded in the direction of the bottle of champagne. "So, to start things off, there's a thousand-dollar bottle of champagne to make sure we loosen things up a bit. I seemed to have taken a liking to that monster that was awakened when you were a little buzzed the other night." April stood from the table, now peering down at Derrick with her sensual eyes that were filled with seduction. "I'm going to have a little fun," she said. "Those sexy women up there dancing on the stage are calling my name." Derrick sat gawking as April made her way up to center stage, dancing, and tipping the two strippers as well.

"Damn, Bro, you did that," Jonathan said, giving Derrick his props on hooking up with such a beautiful woman. "Where in the world did you come up with her?"

Derrick took a sip of his XR, hearing Jonathan, but not really paying any attention at all to him. April had his undivided attention. She had a certain air of mystery about her that seemingly helped draw Derrick all in.

"I thought I was hooking up with one of my employees from the job," Derrick finally said, sounding distant, as his mind seemed to clearly be in another place in time. "But I don't know who the hell that gorgeous muthafucka is right there!"

Jonathan nodded in agreement. "She works for you?"

"Pssttt, you damn right she does. And from now on, she's about to be getting so much overtime that everybody else might as well quit." Jonathan held up his glass for a toast.

"Cheers to that, my nigga. I feel you on that."

An hour flew by filled with several rounds of drinks, loud laughter, and lap dances for everyone. Derrick was without a doubt having the best night of his life. While Derrick and April both seemed to be consumed with entertaining one another, Jonathan's cell phone was blowing up. Usually, when Derrick was away, Jonathan would be with Martina. But seeing as though, Jonathan was so curious as to what type of life Derrick lived outside of his marriage, Jonathan hadn't talked to Martina all day. "Say, Bro," Jonathan said, nudging Derrick in the arm. "I'm fixing to go use the restroom real quick, I'll be right back."

"Do ya thang, baby boy," Derrick replied, chuckling from feeling the liquor that surged through his system. "I ain't going nowhere. I'll be right here when you get back."

Glocks on Satin Sheets

Jonathan smirked at Derrick as he turned and headed towards the restroom. Jealousy reeked from the pores of his skin. Why he had grown to become such a hater, he might never be able to explain that, but as Jonathan snaked his way through the crowd, his anxiety grew. He couldn't wait to tell Martina everything her husband was out doing. *Maybe this might be the straw that breaks the camel's back,* he thought. Maybe after tonight, he would finally have Martina to himself.

Making it inside the privacy of the restroom stall, Jonathan quickly pulled his cell phone out and called Martina. "Hey, Babe. My bad I missed all your calls earlier. I was—"

"You was what, Jonathan?" Martina snarled, stopping Jonathan mid-sentence. "Out doing the same damn thing Derrick does to me every night! I've been calling your phone all day. Now you're just finding the time to call me back?"

The sound of the restroom door opening startled Jonathan. He cautiously peered through the stall door, peeking to make sure it wasn't Derrick.

"Martina, relax, I came out with Derrick to this strip club called Kavey. I saw him at the gym, and he invited me out for some drinks. If I weren't so caught up in trying to prove to you how much you didn't need this bum ass nigga, I wouldn't even be here."

"Oh, so you're back hanging out with Derrick again?"

"Naw it ain't nothing like that, Babe. I'm just here so I can give you the inside scoop on what's really going on with this dude—" Jonathan paused for another second, making sure that the coast was clear before he continued, "Martina, I'm just going to tell you like this, you need to be very careful if you're still having unprotected sex with this fool. All these dirty hoes this nigga be messing around with. He'll fuck around and give us both something." Jonathan spent the next five minutes replaying everything that had gone down up until that point. Even though what he was doing was nothing more than a hater move, he was still willing to do whatever it took to ensure that Martina would be his. "Babe, listen, I gotta get back out there before this nigga come in here looking for me. I'll call you back in a little while, okay?" Jonathan stood, listening for a response, but when none came, he glanced at the screen and noticed Martina had already hung up. "Fuck!"

He could only assume she was hurting and needed some time alone. But then again, she could have been on her way up there. He nervously tucked away his phone while rushing out the restroom. Immediately, he encountered a small group of thugs, openly mean-mugging him.

"Look at this bitch ass nigga," a short chubby man uttered to one of his friends that stood nearby. "I bet they probably got his bitch ass licking asshole or sucking dick!"

Jonathan tried to act like he didn't hear anything as he passed by, but his ego wouldn't allow him to. "Excuse me?" he barked, stopping and sizing both men up. "Who tha fuck are you talking about, Bruh?"

Before Jonathan realized what type of situation he was in, he was surrounded. A dark-skinned goon with long dreadlocks and gold teeth was in his face while two others followed up from behind.

"Who tha fuck you think we was talking to?" the goon snarled. "You got something on your chest you trying to get off."

Jonathan made a quick glance over his shoulder, then felt something hard being shoved into his lower back. It was a gun. "I ain't come here for no problems," Jonathan said, raising his hands. "I'm just trying to get back over there with my peoples."

The short chubby man came alongside Jonathan and chuckled, "What happened to all that big boy shit you was poppin' a second ago? You wasn't trying to get back to your peeps when you stopped and got to bumping yo gums."

Jonathan glared at him. He could see whoever the man was, obviously was the crew's leader. His neck was iced out with the initials

C.M. in diamonds hanging from his chain. "Let this punk ass nigga make it," he ordered. "But before you go, you and your man's better be careful who you fuck with around here. Just cause that pussy looks good to ya, don't mean that hoe is good fo' ya. Feel me?"

Jonathan nodded in understanding and quickly broke free from the small circle that surrounded him. He made up his mind to share with Derrick everything that happened, but by the time he made it back over to the table, there was a beautiful redbone that looked identical to Lisa Raye sitting there.

"It took you long enough," Derrick exclaimed, peering up at Jonathan with a devilish smirk on his face. "This is Juicy, she's going to be rolling with us tonight." Jonathan looked down at the beautiful woman, who was peering back up at him with lust-filled eyes. As much as he wanted to get to know her, the words that man had just said to him rang out loud and clear in his mind.

"Naw I'm straight, Bro," Jonathan said, nervously looking back over his shoulder for the group of thugs that had just threatened his life. "That's all you for tonight. I'm just ready to get back to the crib because I got a lot of shit I gotta do."

Derrick looked up at Jonathan somewhat confused. One minute he was mad because Derrick had a date, and he didn't. Now he was ready to go home. But if he wanted to head home and miss out on all this action, then that was on him. Derrick had his own ideas of what he had planned for the two beautiful women.

***

Mob stood along with several members of the Goon Squad, watching as Jonathan and the small group he came with prepared to leave. Every muscle in his body screamed for some action, but Mob's boss Slim had given him specific instructions. He told him to be patient and find out everything he could about April and the people she was with. It seemed like it had taken Mob forever to find out where April had been hiding out, and now that he had found her, it was time for a little good old-fashioned payback.

Mob was one of Slim's top hitters from the Goon Squad. Mob had been employed as a hitman long before the majority of the C.M. members were even thought of. By rights, he should have been the one in charge in Slim's absence, but he was a killer. He loved his role of being the man behind the man. Mob had been down with Slim since he first started the Crimson Mafia.

When the Crimson Mafia was nothing more than a bunch of Blood niggas trying to get on, Mob watched as the C.M. transformed from a gang to a powerful organization. When the money came rolling in, along came the ticks and fleas as well. That's when Slim met April.

Mob witnessed Slim go from a boss hog, fucking every woman his heart desired, to a one woman's man. He watched reluctantly as the woman his boss so dearly loved took advantage of him. Time-after-time, Mob tried to warn Slim that April simply meant him no good, but Slim refused to listen. He was blinded by her snake ass ways and her lying tongue. April was such a cold piece of work. Mob played with the idea of killing her on many different occasions. The way she was working Slim made Mob think she might have been working for some other crew.

Money suddenly came up mysteriously missing, and packs would come up short. All the while, April and her small crew of thirsty ratchets stayed shining. When the police came knocking to lock Slim up on a weak murder case, April did what any low-down snake would do, she bit him. April stole two hundred and fifty thousand and disappeared in the city streets.

For the past couple of years, Slim all but went crazy trying to bounce back after taking such a huge loss. April took half of his stash, almost folding Slim's whole crew. But being the real nigga that Slim was, being held back was something that was simply not about to happen. He was well connected, and his click was a crew of diehard go-getters. Now that the money was back to rolling in, and he was stronger than ever, it was nothing for him to put a price on someone's head.

"Listen up," the chubby man known as Staxs said to his squad. "I want you to follow them and find out where they're going. Make sure you stay far enough behind them, so you don't get spotted."

Mob just stood glaring at Staxs with obvious contempt. It was no secret that Mob hated taking orders from Staxs, but he knew he had to continue to play his position. Mob was a straight-up killer and the leader of the Goon Squad.

The Goon Squad was a small crew of killers inside the C.M. Before one could ever become a boss or the head of the Crimson Mafia, they had to put in work and show where their loyalty lay. Even though Staxs was a boss in the Crimson Mafia, he didn't gain his position because his murder game was official, he bought it.

Staxs was one of those loud, flamboyant hustlers. Even though he was truly about his paper, he was too flashy for Mob. Mob was the quiet low-key, murder ya whole click type of nigga. While Staxs was the type that sat around talking cash shit all day. He hid behind his money, allowing the Goon Squad to put in all the work.

Mob ice grilled Staxs before walking off, leaving him to think he was running something more than his mouth. If Mob's loyalty to the Crimson Mafia didn't run so deep, he would have been body rocked Staxs to sleep.

"That fool better watch himself," Staxs growled to Devil, which was the goon that stepped to Jonathan and checked him. "That nigga looking all upside my head like my heat don't clap back!"

Devil only stood listening, giving no indication as to how he really felt about what Staxs was saying. He too was one of Slim's top hitters, but there was one big difference between him and Mob. Mob had brought Devil into the family, therefore his loyalty was with Mob without a doubt.

***

Derrick held tight to April's waist while he long stroked her from behind. Every time he hit that spot it made her cry out for more. That spot also made her moan and forced her to run her face further into Juicy's fat pussy.

"Ummm shit—I'm cumming!" April moaned between licks of Juicy's pussy.

"Are you cumming for, Daddy?" Derrick questioned April, as he watched her juices began to cover his rod. "Tell me you're cumming for, Daddy," he instructed, but only so he could hear just how much he was pleasing her. Now instead of taking his time, he switched gears and pounded away with solid thrusts.

"Yes!" April cried out. "Yes, Babe—I—Babe wait—Babe wait," April stammered, struggling to catch her breath, struggling to keep from screaming, but struggling to continue enjoying the ride.

Derrick's dick felt so amazing. He constantly kept switching gears, fast to slow, hard to soft. Derrick palmed both of April's ass cheeks, spreading them far apart to watch as his dick slid deeper and deeper inside of her, with every stroke and every cry, Juicy lustfully watched Derrick, wishing she could feel his big, black dick up inside of her. Now instead of enjoying April's soft tongue dancing around her clit, Juicy was forced to watch April get her back blown out.

"I can't take it anymore!" April said, sounding winded, and crawled from between Juicy's legs.

Derrick softly chuckled as he watched April slide to the edge of the bed to rest. She had bitten off more than she could chew, but lucky for her, it was someone else in the room that he could get his rocks off on.

"Lay back," Juicy instructed Derrick after April had gotten up from the bed. "I hope you don't think I'm about to run from this dick like she did." Juicy straddled Derrick, thumping the tip of his dick against her already swollen clit. Slowly, she ran the tip of his dick between her pussy lips to lubricate it before guiding it up inside of her. "Ssss- damn," she groaned, as she now ground on his rod, finding her rhythm, then bouncing her fat ass on him.

Clap! Clap! Clap!

The sound of their bodies colliding together filled the room. Instead of being concerned with making April jealous, Derrick turned it up another notch. Derrick fucked Juicy with short, quick thrusts, causing her to cry out and loudly moan.

"Uhhh!" Her head rolled around, now singing songs of love to the ceiling. Her plump breasts jiggled with each thrust, causing Derrick's mouth to water. Taking hold to one breast with one hand, he nibbled at her nipples, flicking his tongue at it, then sucking it.

"Bite it," Juicy whined, towering above Derrick, greedily welcoming the pain. "Bite it. Ohh—sss-yessss!"

Finally feeling the slight sting of jealousy, April crawled back into the bed. She gently massaged Juicy's back, then her waist, planting soft kisses on her neck. "It's my turn now," April said, peering over Juicy's shoulder.

Derrick couldn't do anything but look up at April and smile. He would have never suspected April to be the freak that she was. But now that he knew, he figured it was something he could get used to.

Juicy slid off Derrick and got down on all fours between his legs in the doggy style position. Lifting his dick, she began to lap at the juices that covered his long thick rod. At first, Derrick paid no attention to the sight of April taking her position behind Juicy, but when Juicy cried out a loud scream of pleasure, he was all eyes. It was April's turn to fuck. Whatever she had strapped on, she was running it up in Juicy, and she was clearly about to make her lose her mind.

Clap! Clap! Clap!

Adrian Dulan

CHAPTER FOUR

THE TRUTH

Derrick stumbled into his home the next morning, not giving a damn what Martina or anyone else might have suspected of his whereabouts from the night before. The only thing Derrick seemed to be concerned with was getting some rest. He had been sucked, fucked and completely drained dry. Even if Martina wanted some dick just to keep them from arguing, he couldn't give it to her. April had served him up with a double shot of some good pussy. It was over for him, a wrap! He needed to get some rest.

As Derrick stumbled across the kitchen floor, slightly tipsy, he failed to take notice of Martina sitting at the dining room table smoking a cigarette.

"Why didn't you come home last night?" she angrily asked.

Derrick stopped in his tracks, turning towards the voice. He already knew an argument was coming, but after what he had experienced last night, he was in no shape for it. "I ain't trying to do this, right now," he firmly stated, giving Martina a look that said now was not the time. "We can talk about this, and whatever else you wanna talk about after I get some rest.''

Martina's head snapped back as she quickly snipped out her cigarette in the ashtray. "So, now we're not communicating anymore?"

Derrick released a loud sigh of frustration. "No, I'm just tired, and I don't want to spend the rest of the morning explaining something to you that you'll never understand."

Martina frowned, stood up, and made her way over to Derrick. Her eyes roamed over his body from head to toe as if she were able to find traces of another woman. "How do you know I wouldn't understand?" Martina fired back. "Just tell me why you didn't bring yo' ass home last night?"

Derrick rubbed his tired eyes, turned as if he were about to walk away, and then stopped. His patience was wearing thin. He wasn't sure if it was because he was extra tired, or because of the liquor that still flowed through his system. Either way, if Martina kept on, she was subject to a rude awakening.

"Maybe I didn't come home, because of this! I'm sick of walking in my own goddamn house and being questioned like I'm some little kid." He headed towards the staircase.

"I've done everything I can think of to try and make you happy!" Martina yelled after him. "But for some reason, you wanna dog me out. I'm sick of being treated like shit, Derrick! I'm sick of it!''

Derrick stopped once again, glaring at Martina. "I told you I wasn't trying to go there with you, right now. But seeing as though you don't know what tha fuck, *Wait until later* means there goes the door." Derrick pointed towards it. "Lock my shit back after you leave!" He stormed up the stairs, leaving Martina to gather her thoughts. Even though he knew he had taken things a little further than he had intended, at least he would finally be able to get some rest.

"You know, it took a moment to shake off that hurtful ass shit you just said to me," Martina said, walking into the bedroom behind Derrick while he quickly undressed. "I would have never thought you would have ever said something like that to me."

Derrick sighed. "I'm tired, Martina. You just keep going on and on, and I'm fucking tired!" He climbed in the bed, getting comfortable under the covers.

"I can see you're real tired, Derrick. That's why I came up here to tell you to pack your shit and leave."

Derrick began to chuckle. "Oh, my God," he exclaimed through his hands that were now covering his face. "I see you've lost your mind, haven't you?" Derrick removed his hands from over his face, peering over at Martina. She stood with her hand resting defiantly on her hip.

"This is my shit! The house, the cars, hell even the clothes you got on your goddamn back are mine! I guess you done forgot who moved who in from their parents' house." Derrick rolled over, covering his head with the covers.

"Is that how you wanna play this little game?" Martina

quickly dug through one of the dresser drawers, pulling out a DVD. "I wonder whose house the judge is going to say it is after I show them this!" she shouted and placed a DVD into the DVD player before pressing play. Instantly the room filled with the sounds of someone making love. "Uhhh! Derrick—yesss. Ohhhh, Babe yessss!"

Derrick immediately flung the covers off his head, recognizing the cries of one of his past lovers. "When, where, and how did you get this?"

Martina smirked, stopping the DVD, and ejecting it.

"We're not doing any communicating, remember?" Martina tossed the remote to the television onto the bed, heading towards the bedroom door. "Either you can leave, or I can call the police. And I'ma tell you this much after I show them this DVD and the pictures of you leaving the club with them stank ass hoes last night, there is no way in hell they're going to side with you!"

***

It's funny how things appear when everything seems to be going your way, and everyone seems to cater to your every need. It's also funny how drastically everything can change in the blink of an eye. One moment, you might be the prized trophy that everyone is fighting to obtain, and in the next, you're nothing more than an opponent in the same competition.

It was 3:00 a.m. and Derrick peered up into the ceiling of his small hotel room. His thoughts danced from one extreme to the next, all the while listening to *Tank & Wale's 'You don't know'* streaming through his iPhone. Derrick struggled to figure out how he had allowed himself to end up in this type of situation. One minute he felt like he was the king of the world, and the next he lay alone in a small hotel room. He felt confused, alone, and as if he had no one he could open up to or explain some of the many things that were going on in his life.

Derrick tossed and turned, trying to will himself to fall asleep, but he couldn't. His mind wouldn't shut down without figuring out a way to solve his problems. He needed a way that might put some order back in his life. By the time Derrick was finally able to doze off, his alarm on his cell phone had come to life, announcing yet another new day. Grudgingly, he rolled out of bed and began preparing himself for work. Regardless of what went on at home, he still needed to make sure he handled his business.

As Derrick walked out of his hotel room that morning, reality hit him like a ton of bricks. He had always had a habit of trying to avoid the truth, and the truth was he might be a father soon. Derrick thought about Erica on the stand telling the court about their secret love affair, and their unborn child. He even thought about those pictures Martina claimed to have taken the night before.

Did she have someone following him this whole time? What made her put a camera in their bedroom? What else did Martina know? Would she file and try to take half of everything he owned?

Millions of questions seemingly flooded Derrick's mind at the same time. But surprisingly enough, in that same moment, he was searching for clarity, he spotted Erica coming out of McDonald's while he sat in the drive-thru waiting to receive his morning coffee.

Honk! Honk! Derrick tapped his horn a few times trying to get Erica's attention. When Erica failed to take notice of Derrick's attempts to get her attention, he quickly rolled his passenger side window down and called out her name.

"Erica! Erica!"

Erica stopped just before reaching her car, staring over in his direction. As soon as the realization of who it was calling her name registered, she quickly blew him off and got inside her car to leave. Derrick immediately slammed his car into park, leaving it blocking traffic. If he ever planned to get some order in his life, this was a good place to start. He ran over to stop her from leaving.

"What do you want?" Erica snapped through her partially cracked window.

"I just wanted to apologize for the way things have been going here lately," Derrick said, slightly winded from his quick dash across the parking lot. "I never meant for things to turn out the way they have. I just fucked around and got myself off in some shit that I don't know how to get myself out of."

Erica appeared to think about it for a moment, then shrugged it off. "So, what are you saying, Derrick? You want me to help you figure out how to tell your wife that I'm pregnant?"

"Naw, I ain't tripping about what she thinks, this is about us," Derrick stated convincingly. "I need to have a talk with you about this baby, our future, and everything." Derrick kneeled closer, speaking through the small crack with pleading eyes. "Can we talk later? I really need to see you, Erica."

Erica sat seemingly weighing her options. But truth be told, it was all a front. She was willing to do whatever it took to get Derrick back in her arms, even if it meant dealing with another woman.

"Call me when you get off work," she said, putting her car in reverse. "But if you even think about standing me up again—" She pulled away, leaving Derrick to put the pieces of that puzzle together.

In the back of his mind, he knew he was wrong for continuing to play games with Erica's heart. But he needed to do what he had to. There was no telling how far Martina was willing to take things.

***

Monday nights at Club Kavey were one of the slowest nights of the week, but tonight, big spenders lined up and down the sidewalk waiting to get inside. Big Bruce, a 6'4, 320- pound bouncer, stood guard at the front doors, making sure all the female dancers made it safely inside. Club Kavey was inside of a small plaza with no parking in the back. Everyone had to make their way inside through the front doors.

"Yo' back tha fuck up!" Big Bruce yelled while Cinnamon, one of the club's star strippers, struggled to make her way through the crowded entrance. "If one of you bum ass niggas try to grab another tittie or one more piece of ass—I'ma start flatlining shit out here."

A few guys waiting in line cried out in laughter. Everybody knew Big Bruce was just putting on a show. No one would dare touch even the shadow of the dancers. Security was most definitely on deck, and half of them were on some goon shit.

Jeremih's 'Worthy', featuring *Jhene Aiko*, blared through April's speakers as she whipped into the parking lot. Every person waiting outside fell deathly quiet as she pulled her drop top jag right up to the front doors.

"Damn!" That's all you could hear as April stepped out of her car and gently closed the door behind her. Her skintight black tights showed every curve of her thick thighs and legs. While her loose-fitting, see-through top exposed her cleavage. The whole crowd was so quiet that you could have heard a pin drop, but instead, the sound of her red bottom heels clicking across the concrete-filled the air.

"Right this way, Ms. Jordan," Big Bruce said as he personally guided April through the crowd and into the building. You might have thought April was the owner, or even a star stripper by the way everyone catered to her, but in reality, she was a bartender there, this was her second job, her third hustle.

"April—April," Juicy called out as soon as she spotted April coming through the doors. "Girl, I've been calling you all day. I know you saw me calling. Oh, so now that you got a new little boyfriend, you can't fuck wit' a bitch no more?"

April softly laughed, dismissing Juicy's assumption with the flick of her wrist. "You know I got that other job. Then after I leave there, I gotta get home and try and get some rest for this nonstop party here."

Juicy glanced back towards the entrance as the two made their way to the dressing room. "Where's that fine muthafucka, Derrick? I see you rolled up in here by yourself tonight. Why you didn't bring his fine ass back with you?"

April stopped dead in her tracks, eyes bulging, looking as if she had something big to tell her. "Girl guess what happened today at work— tell me why a sheriff came up to the job and served Derrick with some papers?"

Juicy frowned, having no idea what type of papers April could have been talking about. "*Papers*! What kind of papers?"

"Divorce papers!"

Juicy gasped. "That nigga is married?"

"Was he! You should have seen that stupid ass look he had on his face when they served his ass."

Juicy burst into loud laughter.

"That nigga looked like he was about to start crying."

Juicy doubled over, having to hold her stomach from laughing so hard. "You ain't say nothing to him about it?"

"Did I," April continued, "That nigga is making that good money. I'm talking legit shit. I'm trying to get his ass. I was like— Babe are you okay? Do you need to stay at my place until you can get back on your feet? Girl, I was riding that nigga shit so hard, he couldn't see past me even if he wanted to."

They stood just outside the dressing room discussing Derrick's situation. Big Bruce felt sorry for whoever this poor soul could be. He already knew the two women together were a cold piece of work. If a man wasn't careful, the two could easily scam a man out of house and everything he owned.

"Y'all call me if you need me." Big Bruce said, cutting in on their storytime. "I see you two are back up to your old tricks."

Twenty minutes later, April stepped out of the dressing room wearing some super low-cut booty shorts and a black Club Kavey t-shirt. She quickly made her way through the club over to the section of the bar that she would be working. But as April drew closer to the bar, she took notice of a man sitting at the bar that she remembered seeing the other night.

"Can I get you something to drink, or have you already been helped?"

The man sat quietly, watching April as she made her way behind the bar.

"Yeah, I'd like to get a double shot of that," he said, gesturing at April's fat ass with a glance and a slight head nod.

April cut her eyes over towards the man, giving him a half-smile. She didn't do chubby men at all. Had it not been for the big dumb ass diamonds all over his chain, April would have surely gotten someone else to help him.

"I'm sorry," April replied apologetically. "I don't think I'm going to be able to fit all of this into one of those tiny little shot glasses." She gestured to her lower body.

"Well, let me get a bottle of the house's best champagne." The man softly chuckled.

April immediately headed over to where they stored the champagne, "Will you be drinking alone, or shall I bring glasses for two?" she asked as the man appeared to have forgotten something.

"Now where the hell have my manners gone tonight?" he exclaimed. "You had me over here stuck in my own little world. I almost forgot that I'ma need two more bottles for my two little niggas."

April paused for a moment, looking back over at the man. Whoever he was, he must have had his bread right. Each bottle of champagne was a thousand dollars a pop.

"I'm sorry, I didn't get a chance to get your name," April said, quickly bringing three gold bottles back over to where the man was sitting.

"Staxs, and these two right here this is, Young Syke, and the other is Puncho. These are my up and coming hitters of the Goon Squad," the man replied, holding out his iced-out wrist to shake April's hand.

April immediately picked up on the name, *Goon Squad* but she couldn't remember where she had heard it before. There were so many clicks and crews circling throughout the Oklahoma City streets, so it was hard to keep up with all the names. April stole a quick glance at the two young hitters that Staxs spoke so highly of. The one named Young Syke stood ice grilling her so hard she couldn't tell if he was trying to intimidate her or if he was about to attack her.

"You alright?" April asked, trying to get a better feel for the situation.

"Is you alright?" Young Syke fired back, looking as if he was ready to take flight.

"Easy, easy now," Staxs warned his young hitters that were quickly growing antsy. "You'll have to forgive me, please. I'm not supposed to give them no food, or anything to drink after dark." He laughed at his own comment.

"Well, are you sure you still want to keep giving them something to drink? It already looks like they've had enough," April said, skeptically looking back over at Young Syke.

Staxs smirked, giving a slight head nod to his young hitters to fall back. "Give me a minute so that I can holla at Babe real quick."

Both young men walked away, glaring at April as if they were ready to kill something. Her gut told her that something was very wrong with the situation, but for some reason, she was unable to identify what that something was.

"Them two niggas might need some type of counseling," April said, wiping down the bar where the two young men had sat.

"Don't pay them little niggas no attention. They just don't take well to strangers," Staxs replied, softly chuckling. "But fuck talking about them, what's good with you for tonight?" Staxs pulled out a massive wad of nothing but big faces and counted out the money for the drinks.

"I have to take my ass home and go to bed. I have two jobs. One at night, and one that I have to be at in the morning," April said in a serious manner. April scooped up the small stack of bills Staxs had placed on the counter. After counting it and recounting it, she glanced over at Staxs slightly puzzled. "You know you gave me too much money, right?" April held a thousand dollars in one hand and three thousand in the other.

"What, you don't think I know how to count? The extra is for you," he bragged. "You out here working all hard. A nigga like me trying to see you shine."

April gasped, holding the money close to her heart as if it held some sentimental value to her. She was a certified actress. She knew how to get whatever she wanted out of anyone. "Awww, this is so sweet of you. Do you mind if I come around there and give you a hug?"

Staxs smiled, waving her over. He knew if he continued to bait his trap with cheese, he was bound to catch a rat. "There's plenty more where you got that little change from," Staxs whispered in April's ear as they embraced.

April slightly pulled away, now staring deep into Staxs' eyes. "You doing it like that, little daddy?" she asked.

Staxs smirked, then reached over and took a sip of his champagne, "Come fuck with a real nigga, and you'll find out!" Staxs and his boys finished off what they could of the three bottles he purchased waiting for April to get off.

April followed behind Staxs as he navigated her through the Mission Hills houses. The lakeside views and beautiful landscaping that could be seen in the darkness of the night were but a telltale sign of some of the many luxuries to come.

April's anxiety slowly began to rise as they passed by house after house. Her thoughts journeyed back to a time when she and Slim did the same thing. A time when life was all good and money meant nothing to her. So many times, before, April wished she had made better choices with the opportunity that Slim had given her. She wished she had spent her money wisely, instead of carelessly tossing it into the wind as if this moment in time would last forever.

April spent the last few years bouncing from one relationship to the next. She was searching for the man that could fill the shoes of her notorious ex, but she fell short and only came up with men that proved to be nothing more than a thorn in her side.

Eventually, April found herself needing a source of income, which in time lead her to *DF & Accessories*. Derrick's new women's clothing store had given April a platform that she could build from. In time, she became the store manager. Even though the money April brought in was enough to pay her bills, it was a far cry from what she was used to. Just to be able to live in the shadow of the life she once had, she still needed to figure out a way to make more income.

April went back to the nightlife, but this time she worked as a bartender at Club Kavey. Instantly, the money started rolling back in.

Tricks that never would have had a chance with a dime as bad as April happily showered her with money. Even though that too quickly grew old, for the time being, it would do. April knew if she kept searching for a little while longer, she'd find the man she was looking for. Was that man Staxs, or could it have been Derrick?

As Staxs tapped on his brake lights to turn into his driveway, April's hungry eyes looked through every window of her car, trying to take in the magnitude of his home. "This is gorgeous," April confessed, taking in the newly built home.

Bright lights lit up the interior, causing her to wonder if Staxs really lived there alone. Staxs pulled his white Range Rover in front of the middle door of his three-car garage. After hitting the button, the door raised up.

"You go ahead and park inside," he said through his partially cracked window. "I'll leave my truck parked outside for tonight."

April pulled inside, parking between a brand-new Corvette and a candy apple red Porsche Cayman GTS. *I see lil' daddy wasn't lying about his paper,* April thought. *I might just have to give him a little drink from the fountain of* youth.

"Can I get you anything to drink?" Staxs asked April, after leading her inside. He then allowed her to roam freely around his spacious home.

"Whatever is fine with me," she responded, taking in the beautiful paintings that decorated his walls. "Do you live here alone? I've never seen a man put his home together with such an even balance. This looks like it might have had a woman's touch to it as well."

Staxs chuckled to himself. "I don't have many visitors. I try to keep people as far away from me as I can and out of my business. So, to answer your question, yes—I live here alone." Staxs poured two glasses of Vodka and then grabbed a bottle of cranberry juice out the fridge and added it to the glasses.

"So, I should feel lucky that you've brought me to your home tonight?"

Staxs smiled, then walked back over to April with the drinks he had just made. "Why wouldn't you? I work hard for mines, unlike some of these thirsty ass muthafuckas out here." Staxs passed April one of the drinks. "Let's make a toast, shall we?" Staxs lifted his glass in the air. "To new beginnings."

"To new beginnings," April repeated, then took the drink straight to the head, right along with Staxs.

"Ergggh!" April growled, holding her chest. "You must have put too much liquor in mines. That was way too strong!"

Staxs stood watching April's reaction as the poison he'd put in her drink flowed through her system. "Ohhh, is that what that burning is?" he snarled.

April's eyelids fluttered as she quickly began to feel dizzy. "What did you just give me," she cried, stumbling forward, reaching out to grab Staxs, but fell to the floor.

"Bitch I ain't had the chance to give you what I want yet!" Staxs said, towering over her. "But after me and my nigga right here get done with yo' ass that little pussy gone be busted up!"

April struggled to lift her head from the floor to see who Staxs was speaking of. At first, she couldn't see anything, but doubles of Staxs. Yet, as her vision slowly came in, and quickly went back out, she realized who the other person was.

"Devil," April cried out as tears instantly welled up in her eyes. She knew Devil was one of Slim's top hitmen, and she also understood what he was there to do. "I was going to pay," April struggled to speak, but suddenly collapsed. The negative seeds she had planted years before had finally grown and came back to haunt her.

CHAPTER FIVE

URGENT MESSAGE

Derrick awoke early Tuesday morning to a hot cup of steaming coffee, and the daily newspaper which was waiting for him on the kitchen table. Derrick ended up staying the night at Erica's, so the two of them could get an understanding as to where their relationship was headed regarding their baby.

"I hope you remember what you promised me last night," Erica said, walking into the kitchen while taking a spare key off her key ring.

"I remember what I said," Derrick stated, looking up from the newspaper. "But can you promise me you'll be the understanding person that I'm going to need you to be? I'm going through a separation with my wife, and I'm going to need you to be strong."

Erica squinted her eyes, shooting daggers at Derrick for even mentioning his wife. "Haven't I always been understanding?" She slammed the key down on top of the table and turned to leave for work.

"Umh!" As bad as Derrick wanted to pick that key up and give it right back to her, he couldn't. He still needed to make sure he kept everything peaceful on this side of the playing field.

Derrick picked up his phone, checking for recent updates, but the first thing that caught his attention was an urgent message from April that said, *//: I know you're receiving this message on rather short notice, but I won't be able to make it to work today. My mother is very sick, so I'll be spending some time with her today. Give me a call when you have some time.*

"What type of shit is this!" Derrick yelled. He couldn't believe April didn't show him any consideration or give him any advance notice.

Now that the store hadn't been opened, he was afraid that the other employees or customers might have left due to the doors being locked.

***

After the workday had finally come to a close, Derrick walked through the store and thanked everyone for the tremendous effort they put forth.

"I don't know how we made it," Derrick said to his Assistant Manager, Georgette Clark. "April didn't show, then we had two other people turn around and go home."

Georgette gave Derrick a quick nod, then finished counting the money out of the cash register. "I don't know how we made it either," she said, putting the money in a paper clip, then stuffing it into a money bag. "You're lucky we have such loyal, hardworking people here, because if we didn't, we sure as hell would have been in a lot of trouble." Georgette placed the moneybag on the counter for Derrick. "Have you had the chance to talk to April since you received that text this morning?"

"Not yet. I was going to give her a call before we left work this evening," he said.

"Please do, I hate hearing stuff like this happening to good, hard-working people. She does a lot for this store you know?"

"Trust me, I know firsthand what she does for this store," Derrick replied, turning to head back to his office. "Oh, before I forget to ask, I need you to do me a really big favor." He looked at her before adding, "I need you to step up and handle April's position until she gets back. You know all the day-to-day functions. Plus, I know that I can count on you."

Georgette was twenty years older than Derrick. She had a keen sense for business, and her age gave her a certain degree of guidance that no one else had yet. "I'll be more than happy to help you. I'll make sure that I'm here a little earlier tomorrow morning."

Derrick smiled, sliding the key to the front door on the counter. "You take this so that you can get in tomorrow morning, and I'll finish up around here. How does that sound?"

"Sounds like I'll be seeing you in the morning," Georgette said, scooping up the key and heading to the back to grab her things. "Tell April, I hope her mother gets to feeling better. I'll see you tomorrow. Bye-bye!"

Before pulling out his phone, Derrick watched and waited around for everyone to go home for the evening. He was slightly anxious to hear from April.

"Hello, hello, hello." Derrick snatched his phone away from his ear, glaring at it because it was echoing again. "April, pril, ril, il can, can, can you hear, hear, hear me? I, I, I don't know what's going on with my phone, phone, pho—but I was just calling to check, heck, eck on you."

April sat listening as the phone echoed his words to her. As bad as she wanted to cry out for help, the Glock Devil held pressed against her temple held those spontaneous actions in check.

"My mother is sick," April firmly stated, hoping that Derrick might suspect something by the firmness in her voice. "She has cancer, and I'll be out of town for a few days."

Derrick sat, struggling to make sense of all the echoing going on over the phone line. Even though it was hard to get a clear understanding as to what was being said, he did hear something about cancer, and a few days.

"Take all the time you need!" Derrick yelled into the phone as if the problem was due to a lack of being able to hear one another and not the echoing going on. "I'll give you a call back when this phone isn't tripping so much." Derrick disconnected the call, making a mental note to contact his cell phone company first thing the next morning. It was the second time his phone acted up. If his cell phone company couldn't figure out a solution, then it might be time to get a new phone.

After finishing up for the evening, Derrick locked up the store and headed out to his car. As Derrick made his way through the parking lot, he took notice of a black Crown Vic facing his direction. Derrick squinted his eyes, straining to get a good look at the people inside. But due to the jet-black tint that covered the car's window, his efforts were in vain.

"Damn detectives!" Instantly, Derrick's mind went back to the day he had been served with divorce papers. He assumed it might have been how Martina was able to keep such close tabs on him. But to have detectives sitting outside his place of business made him furious.

Derrick stormed over to his car and quickly climbed inside. Regardless of whatever evidence Martina claimed to have had against him, that still gave her no right to spy on him. Derrick pulled out his phone and called Martina. When his phone call was forward to voicemail, he made up in his mind that he needed to stop by and pay her a little visit.

***

"Uhmm, yes," Martina cried out as she lay with her legs pinned back, watching Jonathan's big dick plunged deep into her wetness. The mere sight of his stomach muscles tightening and glistening from their hot sweaty sex was just enough to push Martina closer to her climax. "Hit that shit," she moaned, reaching down and slowly rubbing her tingling clit. Martina's back arched as she delicately closed her eyes to slip away into pure bliss. The way Jonathan pounded away on her pussy she couldn't do anything but confess her loyalty to him. "This is your pussy, Fuck me!" Martina's warm cum oozed from her pussy, coating Jonathan's shaft. As it slid down the crack of her ass, it formed a puddle on the bed. Her legs trembled and quaked as she felt another orgasm quickly coming on. "Yesss, Babe—oooh yes!" Martina rubbed her clit faster and faster with each bed shaking thrust Jonathan dished to her. While opening her eyes to witness the magic Jonathan performed on her pussy, she caught sight of a menacing set of eyes watching her every move. "Derrick!" Martina cried out, pushing Jonathan to the side so he could get off her. "What are you doing here? Get out! Get out!"

Jonathan, being startled by Derrick's name alone, immediately rolled out of bed and quickly reached for his clothing to try and cover himself.

"Naw nigga don't stop now! You wasn't worried about me watching when you was up in my shit, fucking my goddamn wife!"

Martina could sense things were on the verge of turning into something very serious. The look Derrick had in his eyes was unlike any look she had ever seen him give anyone before. Martina quickly rolled out of bed, wrapping the sheets around her naked body to cover herself.

"If you don't get the hell out of here, I'm calling the police," Martina yelled, giving her best attempt to try and distract Derrick.

Derrick turned his attention back to Martina, glaring at her with all the hate his mind and body could muster. The sheets she had used to try and cover herself were filled with huge wet spots from her cumming all over them.

"Bitch you should have already called them muthafuckas when you first saw me."

Bam! Derrick hit Martina so hard that her body went flying into the wall. She slid to the floor, resting peacefully.

"You didn't think I was going to find out, did you?" Derrick screamed, turning his attention back to Jonathan. "And to think, you was supposed to be my best fucking friend."

Jonathan spared a quick glance over his shoulder, frantically trying to wiggle his feet into his shoes. Just as he was finally able to get one foot in, Derrick charged him. Jonathan did everything he could to put up a good fight against Derrick. But Derrick's fight was fueled by rage, he was simply no match for him.

"Was it, worth it nigga?" Derrick roared, peering down at Jonathan. "Was that pussy good to you?" With each antagonizing question, Derrick slammed his fist down into Jonathan's face. "I hope you muthafuckas know you ain't getting shit from me. Do you hear me? Nothing!"

Derrick walked back across the bedroom, where he left Martina resting peacefully on the floor. Reaching down and grabbing a fist full of her hair, he lifted her head up, hoping to awaken her.

"You thought you were going to be able to move this clown ass nigga up in my shit, didn't you?" Martina's eyes fluttered as if she were beginning to awaken. "Well, you can have that nigga,"

Derrick barked, spraying spittle into Martina's face. "Do you understand me, you nasty ass bitch? You can have him!"

Boom! Derrick slammed her head back into the floor in disgust. The faint aroma of sex still lingered in the air. While the cum soaked sheets wrapped around Martina, further enraged him.

"Sweet dreams, Bitch!"

CHAPTER SIX

FORCED IN THE GAME

For the last several days, Staxs held April captive in his basement. The knight in shining armor April thought Staxs could be was nothing more than a wolf in sheep's clothing. Time-after-time, Staxs forced himself on April, having his way with her. For days she was forced to endure the sexual abuse and mental anguish he continually brought upon her. Silently, April made a vow to kill Staxs for everything he had done to her. No matter how bleak her situation may have appeared, she would still find a way, somehow.

April wasn't always the sweet, innocent woman that so many people made the mistake of thinking she was. She was a thorough go-getter. She was down to push that bag state-to-state, and 100 percent about that action, if that's what it took to get that money. Slim withheld no knowledge in grooming his queen to be. He had given April the game on so many different levels that she alone could have run the Crimson Mafia in his absence. Not only was April laced up with hella game, but she was also a trained shooter as well. D-boys from all over the city longed to have such an asset as a part of their squad. If you had someone as valuable as her on your team, the possibilities were endless. April was down for whatever, as long as the end result was her collecting some bread.

The sound of the basement door creaking, as it opened, alerted April that someone was entering the room. Quickly scrambling across the floor, she put her back to the wall. Fear held a tight death-defying grip on her mind. She was tired of being taken advantage of, tired of crying, and tired of wishing that she could do something about it. The basement light suddenly popped on, blinding April. She cowered away in the corner, shielding her eyes with her hands. The smell of Staxs' stinky cigar, assaulted her nostrils, as he and Devil came towering over her.

"Look at this trout mouth having ass bitch," Staxs spat, glaring down at April, who sat balled up trembling on the floor. "I don't know why you are sitting there looking like you so scared. Don't nobody want any more of that week old, stank ass shit you working with."

April peered through the small cracks of her hands, as tears now poured down her cheeks. "Well, what is it that you want from me then?" she asked.

Staxs chuckled, "You have something of ours that doesn't belong to you. And we want it back."

April's head fell to her chest, as she began to sob. She knew exactly what they wanted, but she didn't have the means to give them the money back. April had stolen two-hundred-fifty thousand from Slim when he got locked up. When word spread that he would be serving life in the penitentiary, she used half of his money as a down payment on a new life.

"I told Slim that money was gone a long time ago," April cried. "But you can take everything I own. My condo is paid for, and I have two cars that are both paid for as well."

Staxs looked down at April as if she was the scum of the earth. "Bitch, does it look like I need that cardboard box you live in? Now here's the deal, so listen up. From now on, you are fixing to be working for the C.M. until you get that debt paid. For whatever reason the boss wants me to keep your stinking ass alive. I have the slightest clue as to why, but from this point on, that's how this shit is going down."

Instantly, April's mind began to run wild with all types of ideas. She knew very well how Slim and his crew operated. They were a small crew of killers that supplied bigger crews or organizations with kilos of cocaine. Why they wanted April working for them, after she had already proven that she'd take from them, was unclear, and April had no clue either. But if this was what they wanted April would be more than happy to sting their asses again.

Staxs began shaking his head at April as if he had read her thoughts. "You is one thirsty ass bitch, ain't you? You think niggas don't know what yo' stupid ass is thinking, right now?" Staxs peeped back over his shoulder at Devil. "Give her the envelope!"

Devil stepped from behind Staxs wearing an all-black hoodie looking like the angel of death in the flesh. Glaring down at April with his eyes filled with hate, he hurled a small envelope over at her, hitting her in the face as photographs spilled everywhere.

"After you check those pictures out, there's a fresh change of clothes and some food upstairs," he said with a menacing tone. Devil turned to take his place back behind Staxs but suddenly spun around as if he had forgotten something. "Tomorrow you'll be hitting the highway, so you'll need to be ready and get plenty of rest tonight. If by chance, you even think about going to the police, every last muthafucka in those pictures will be dead before the sun sets."

April peered around at the many pictures scattered about the floor. The thought of looking at the pictures had never crossed her mind until Devil made the threat of killing someone. April quickly scooped up a handful of pictures and immediately began thumbing through them. Each photograph was a picture of her immediate family. Her mother, father, sister, even her younger brother. They had pictures of her family at work and at home. From the images, there was no telling what they knew about April and or her family.

"If you go anywhere near my family, I'll—"

"You'll what, bitch?" Devil pulled his Glock from underneath his sweatshirt and placed the barrel against April's forehead. "Bitch I'll blow yo' whole fuckin' face-off, then murder your entire family because the shit makes my dick hard."

Oh, how April longed to get a grip on that gun Devil held ever so tightly in his hands. If somehow, she could strip it away from him, she would end the nightmare right then.

Staxs chuckled, kneeling beside April. He knew what types of thoughts were running around in her head. Slim had warned him to be cautious of her. April wasn't the innocent, weakling she put on to be.

"So, do you want that burger or not?" Staxs sarcastically asked. "You can either go upstairs and eat a nice, juicy, bacon double cheeseburger and get ready for tomorrow, or you can go talk to Jesus about the dumb ass choices you've made in life. The choice is yours."

The next morning, April was awakened to Staxs tapping a 9-millimeter against her forehead. "Wake yo' scandalous ass up!" he sang in her ear as if today was yet another beautiful day in his neighborhood.

"Get that gun outta my face!" April screamed, quickly becoming agitated with all the childish games Staxs continuously played. "I already agreed to do whatever you wanted me to do. All this other bullshit is uncalled for."

Staxs cocked the hammer back on the Glock, slowly running the tip of the gun from her head to her cheek, and then to her mouth. April tried to move, but Staxs pressed the gun into her mouth, forcing her to freeze. "*Uncalled for*," he repeated as he kneeled down, using the barrel of the gun to remove the sheets from off her. "I run this shit around here," he hissed, now pressing the gun against April's crotch. "Who tha fuck is you to try and tell me what's called for, or uncalled for? You just worry about doing whatever the fuck I tell you. Do I make myself clear?" Staxs smiled, as April now ice grilled him. He knew he had her exactly where he wanted her. Now it was time to put her to the test. "Here," Staxs said, putting the gun on the floor right in front of her. "Now get tha fuck up and get ready!"

April instantly snatched the gun up off the floor, pointing it right back at Staxs. "Now who's running shit!" *Click*! *Click*! *Click*! April squeezed. *Click*! *Click*! *Click*!

Staxs couldn't control himself any longer. He burst into loud laughter, spraying spittle into April's face. The gun he had thrown on the floor was empty. He had just given it to her as a small test, to see what she would do. "I'm still running this shit, you dumb ass bitch! You thought I was going to be stupid enough to put bullets in a gun when I already know you wanna kill me?" Staxs stood from his kneeling position, wiping tears of laughter from his eyes. "The first time is on me. But the next time is on you. I think you need to remember that you have a family that can lose their lives if you fuck this up." Staxs dug in his back pocket, pulling out the clip to the gun. "You'll need this for your trip," he said, tossing it on the floor in front of her. "But when you make it back, be sure that you got that tight pussy of yours ready to go. I'm sure I'll be looking for another round with yo' ugly ass." Staxs turned and went back upstairs, leaving April almost drowning in tears. As bad as she wanted to load that gun up and kill Staxs, she couldn't. Her family was in danger and she needed to make sure she paid the debt off.

April sped down I-35 showing little regard for any police, or governing agency that could pull her over, and find the three kilos of cocaine stashed in various compartments throughout the car. Her mind was elsewhere, replaying each time Staxs put his filthy hands on her. Tears clouded her vision, forcing her to quickly wipe them away. She was slowly slipping away into a dark, evil place. A place where revenge had given birth to murder and hell had become her destiny.

The sound of '*My Main*', by *Milla J,* came blaring through her cell phone, indicating she had an incoming call from Juicy. It had been several days since April had the chance to openly talk to anyone, and that small amount of freedom made her want to cry more.

"Hey girl," Juicy said when April answered the phone. "I haven't heard from you in the last few days. I figured I had better give you another call to make sure you were alright. Everybody has been asking—"

"Juicy," April cried out, stopping her from saying anything else. "Something bad has happened."

"Oh, my goodness, are you okay?" she gasped. "Do you need me to come get you?"

April shook her head, having to wipe her face again. It took a moment for her to finally get her thoughts together. But when she finally did, she told Juicy everything that Staxs and Devil had done to her.

"Do you want me to call the police?" Juicy asked, sounding genuinely concerned. "I know exactly where he hangs out." Once the police go to arrest his ass, they'll make sure your family is safe."

"No!" April sternly exclaimed. "I can't risk anything happening to my family behind some dumb ass shit I did in the past. I only, only, only told, told you, you, you because" April frowned, pulling her phone away from her ear to look down at it. This was the second time this had happened in the last couple of days.

"What's wrong with your phone?" Juicy inquired.

"I, I, I don't know, know, know," April replied quickly becoming frustrated with all the echoing going on. "I'll call, all, ll, you, ou back, ack, ck." April disconnected the call, feeling relieved she had finally told someone about her twisted situation. Now that someone knew what was going on with her, if something did by chance happen to her, the police would know who to blame.

***

"It's almost two o'clock!" Cakes yelled, checking out his watch. "Where tha fuck is this punk ass bitch at?" Cakes' nerves were on edge. He paced back and forth from the kitchen to the front door. Occasionally, he would step out on the front porch, glaring up and down the block. But no matter what he did, the situation he was in had yet to change and April was nowhere to be found. "Call her phone one more time," Cakes instructed one of his young lookouts. "If she doesn't pick up this time, I'll call that nigga Staxs and find out what tha fuck is going on." In the back of Cakes' mind, he began to wonder if something had gone wrong. Not once in all the time since he had been buying from the C.M, had they ever been off schedule. For him not to receive his package today, could mean things were over for him. Cakes had exhausted all his leads, and he was clean out of options.

Cakes was a young hustler from the Northside of Wichita Kansas. For the last few weeks, his luck had gone from sugar to shit. He had seen a lot of misfortune and had experienced loss after loss. First Cakes suffered a thirty-thousand-dollar loss after getting robbed, then turned right around the next day and the drug task force raided his main stash house. Cakes was left to try to make a come up off a few bogus jack moves. When that proved to be fruitless, his sights fell on the plug. No matter how good business had been in the past, it was either him or them. Someone had to be the one taking the loss and seeing how he had already taken his—it was time for someone else to take theirs.

Six, a young eighteen-year-old lookout, repeatedly called April's cell phone, only to be forwarded to the voicemail. He knew how much Cakes needed this lick to stay afloat. So, he did whatever he could to try and make this lick happen. "I don't think she's coming," Six mumbled reluctantly after his call was forwarded for the fifth time. "I think she just cut her phone off. Now instead of the phone ringing, it just goes straight to voicemail." Cakes growled, slamming his fist into the palm of his hand. He was on the verge of snapping when he caught sight of the 760 Staxs told him April would be driving.

"There that bitch go," Cakes hissed, watching as April pulled in the driveway, parking. "Now remember what tha fuck I told you. Stay tha fuck out my way until I tell you I need you." Six nodded then ran to take his position in front of the television.

***

April got out of the car, stretching her legs, after a long non-stop drive. The neighborhood she had been instructed to deliver the pack to was none other than the slums. Some of the residences were small duplexes that were obviously vacant, while others bore the signature of local gang graffiti and trash everywhere. As April wondered if there was some kind of mistake with the address, the sound of a screen door slamming jolted her out of her observations.

"You're late," someone barked. "What took you so long?"

April turned towards the voice, glaring at the man as if he had shit all over him. "And you are?"

Cakes came around to the driver's side of the car, matching April's evil glare. "I'm Cakes!" he arrogantly exclaimed. "I have been blowing your phone up for the past hour. You left a nigga to think something had happened to you."

April's head snapped back, twisting her face up with the most scornful expression she could conjure up. "Nigga I ain't gotta answer my phone," she snapped," I told you I was on my way. All that calling my phone ain't about to make anything happen any sooner."

Cakes glared at April, wanting to slap bark from her ass. He couldn't stand females like her. Cute with a banging ass body, and a dope boy bag. He figured she was so slick at the mouth because she was connected to the Crimson Mafia. Boy did he have a surprise for her. "Yeah, you're right Shorty. Whatever you say, now you go ahead and grab that work out of the car, so we can go in here and weigh that shit up."

April smirked, rolling her eyes, glancing down the block as if the sight of Cakes disgusted her. "Nigga you know how this shit goes," April snarled. "First I count the money, then we can start weighing shit up."

The way April was snapping made Cakes take a good look up and down the block. *I wonder if she's alone, or if she has someone lurking around? This bitch might be strapped, too?* Cakes glared over at April, giving her a thorough once over. She wore skinny jeans, an oversized red sweatshirt, and some Nikes. From what he could tell, she didn't have a bulge to indicate that she was strapped, and there were no other cars on the block, other than the norm.

"A'ight, you win," Cakes conceded. "I'm trying to handle this business. So, all this back and forth between us, we can just let all this bullshit go!" Cakes led April into the small dusty old house that he was using as a meeting place. Once inside, he instructed her to have a seat while he ran to the back to grab the money.

April reluctantly walked over to an old, wornout recliner, and took a seat. Judging by the way Cakes was dressed, and her surroundings, April wasn't so sure that Cakes could afford the packages hid outside in the car. Most dealers that bought weight usually wore nice clothing, or even wore a little jewelry. But not

Cakes, he wore a pair of cheap, tan Dickies, with a white t-shirt. His hair looked like it was well overdue for a touch-up and his eyes told a story that she couldn't trust.

April peered around the small living room as a feeling of urgency grew ever so fast in her chest. Something wasn't right, and she could feel it. A young kid was pounding away on an Xbox controller and not once had he looked up to acknowledge her presence. April could remember talking to the same young kid on the phone earlier, but now he acted like he didn't even see her. April thought back to an important rule Slim had taught her, long ago. He said, *Always, pay attention to your instincts. That soft voice will always be there to help guide you. If ever that muthafucka tells you to go, then go. You might not ever get a second chance if you don't.* Just as April made up her mind to get the hell out of that house, someone grabbed her by the hair, snatching her out of the recliner, causing her to scream!

"Shut tha fuck up!" Cakes drug April into the center of the floor, where he brought his knee crashing down into her chest. "What's up with all that shit-talking now, bitch! You still tough? Are you still tough, bitch?" Cakes wrapped his hands around April's throat, trying to crush it. She squirmed beneath him, clawing at his arms and hands. She couldn't break free he was just too powerful. April's strength was quickly fading as she fought for oxygen. She was slipping away into darkness. "You gon' tell me where that pack at?" Cakes released his grip when he saw April begin to stop moving.

She coughed and gasped for air. More coughs. April lay coughing on the floor almost to the point of vomiting. "You-you can have it!" she cried out, before going into another long coughing spat. April tried to roll over on her side, so that Cake's knee wouldn't be pressing down into her chest, but he wouldn't allow her to budge.

"How do I unlock the secret compartments?" Cakes hissed, grabbing a fist full of April's hair, yanking her head off the floor.

"I'll tell you whatever you want. Just get your goddamn knee out of my chest."

Cakes glared down at April with a sinister smile starting to form on his face. Snatching April to her feet by the hair, he sent his young lookout into action. "Go grab the duct tape and trash bags out the back," he ordered Six as he brought April's face alongside his. "Better yet, just bring the whole duffel bag!" Cakes turned his attention back to April while gripping her hair tightly in his hand. "Now where tha fuck is that shit at bitch!"

Tears streamed down from the corners of April's eyes. She was blinded by rage and filled to the brim with hate. Had Cakes known everything she had been through he might not have been so quick to try and rob her. "It's right here!" April snarled, pulling her gun from underneath her sweatshirt, jamming the barrel under Cakes chin.

Boom! She fired as his brains and blood splattered all over the ceiling like a scene out of a horror movie. When Cake's body dropped to the floor, April quickly squeezed two more rounds into his lifeless body. One for Staxs, and one for Slim.

Just as the smell of gunpowder had begun to settle in the room, the soft patter of feet hitting the floor caught her attention. April looked up just in time to see the young lookout standing in the hallway. He had a mixed look of surprise, confusion, and hatred all tied into one. Forcing himself to take his eyes off his fallen leader, he looked up just in time to see several sparks flying from the end of April's gun.

"Wait!"

Boc! Boc! Boc! Bullets ripped through his young body as if he were being used as nothing more than target practice.

Glocks on Satin Sheets

CHAPTER SEVEN

GOOD NEWS

Slim got down on the floor of his cell, hammering out another one hundred straight push-ups. His mind was on full tilt as he thought about the ups and downs of the past few years. For so long, the taste of revenge had been nothing more than a dream to him. But now that the tables were starting to turn in his favor, those dreams were now becoming a reality.

"Ain't no fun when the rabbit got the muthafuckin' gun is it?"

Slim's celly Wayniac looked up to see Slim pacing back like a hungry lion. He couldn't tell if Slim was having another one of his violent mood swings, or if he was finally open to having a conversation with him.

"Hell, nah, it ain't no muthafuckin' fun," Wayniac replied. "Especially seeing as though the rabbit runs fast as hell." Wayniac sat up in his bed, watching Slim as he picked up a water bag and began curling it. "Everything all good with you, big man?"

Slim softly chuckled. He knew Wayniac must have been scared. The whole time the two of them had been confined to their cell, Slim only had a few words for him. "I'm always good fam. Now that this one situation I've been planning has finally fell through—man, shits about to turn up around this bitch." Slim walks over to the small desk in the corner of their cell. He pulled a letter from a stack of papers and handed it to Wayniac. "Read this."

Wayniac peered down at the letter, unsure as to why Slim wanted him to read his legal mail. He didn't want to be the one Slim took his frustrations out on, but now he had no choice. Wayniac slowly read over the small letter, and everything Slim had said earlier suddenly made sense.

"Damn big dawg, this says here that you're going home."

Slim looked over at Wayniac, giving him a mischievous smile. If only Wayniac knew what horrors lay in the near future for certain people, he might not be so happy about the government releasing him.

"Yeah, I'm about to finally get some action back at the streets," Slim said, pacing back and forth. "But this time a few things are gonna be very different."

Wayniac bobbed his head up and down, appearing to be glad to hear some positive news for a change. "So, what's gonna be so different this time?" he asked, without giving any thought to what Slim said earlier.

"Let me just put it to you this way," Slim said, stopping and glaring at Wayniac. "Fuck everybody!"

***

"I'm going to have to advise you two to stop seeing one another." Attorney Ryan Zackery says to Martina while she and Jonathan sat in his office going over her pending divorce case. "I'm not saying that this should be permanent, but I am saying at least until everything is final—" Ryan paused for a moment, allowing his advice to sink in. "If it ever comes out that you two were seeing one another—we could be in a world of trouble."

Martina sighed, she was frustrated with trying to get her attorney to approve of her and Jonathan's relationship. "Me and Jonathan got together after I made Derrick leave," she argued. "What I'm doing now has nothing to do with what Derrick was doing while we were together."

Ryan nodded. "I understand your situation," he stated. "But I still think you're missing the point that I'm trying to make. I believe Derrick's argument is going to be that you two have been fooling around for a while now. He's going to try and make that his excuse for him seeing other people."

"There's no way he can do that," Jonathan chimed in, quickly becoming just as frustrated as Martina.

Martina was irritated at the thought of Derrick finding a way out of their situation without paying up.

Ryan leaned back in his office chair, turning his attention to Jonathan. "Judging by the looks of things, I'd say we don't know exactly what, Mr. Walker can do – do we?" Ryan pulled off his wire- rimmed frames, tossing them carelessly on the desk. "I want you two to understand something critical. We can't make any moves until all the facts are in. Everything that we talk about, we talk about using an open mind. Neither of us truly knows what Derrick's argument is going to be. But we do know that each and every move counts."

"So, what am I supposed to do? Just stop living my life because Derrick knows I'm with Jonathan now?"

"Once again, I'm not telling you that at all. All I'm trying to say to you is you need to use a little more discretion. Tell me do you want the court to believe you were faithful the entire time you were married to Derrick, or would you rather the judge doubt, you?" Martina appeared to give his question a little thought, started to reply, but Ryan held up one hand, silencing her. "Sounds like a no-brainer, right? Well, that's exactly the point I'm trying to make," he continued. "If you don't make better moves, you might as well throw all of our hard work out the window."

Martina glanced over at Jonathan with loving eyes, reaching out to take his hand. "He's right," she admitted, gently rubbing the back of his hand. "If the court doubts me for one minute, everything we've worked for will be gone."

Jonathan leaned closer, staring into Martina's eyes. "Whatever you feel is best, I'm all for it. But I think our relationship has nothing to do with anything."

Ryan cleared his throat to regain Martina's attention. "Mrs. Walker hear my words and trust them. Let me do my job because I know what I'm talking about. You only stand to lose more if you don't."

Martina nodded her head in understanding, while her eyes began to tear up. She couldn't stand the thought of being alone. But with everything she stood to lose, she had no choice. "We'll do it your way. I believe you."

***

Erica put together a delicious homecooked meal for Derrick that night. Smothered pork chops, corn on the cob, shells, and cheese, and green beans with buttermilk biscuits to top it off. Erica sat at the end of the dining room table, sipping on a glass of wine, watching Derrick as he picked through his food. Her gut told her that something was weighing heavy on his mind. But whatever that something was, Derrick wasn't trying to talk about it.

"Babe, what's wrong?" Erica asked, genuinely concerned as to what could be bothering Derrick. "You haven't eaten one bite since we sat down. Care to talk to me about what's going on in that head of yours?"

Derrick sat his fork down and gently pushed his plate away. He dabbed at the corners of his mouth with a napkin before tossing it on the table.

"I'm sorry, Erica. It's just that my mind has been on this rollercoaster ride for the past several days." Derrick sighed, sitting up at the table, cradling his head in both hands. "It just feels like I'm flying from one extreme to the next. No soon as I see an end to one problem, another problem pops up." He stood, walking over to peer out of the dining room window. He thought about talking to Erica about finding out his best friend had been fucking his wife but quickly decided against it. The last thing he needed was someone trying to rub something in his face.

"If you don't talk to me about what's going on, how will I know how to help you?" Erica set her glass down and went to stand behind Derrick, giving him a warm embrace. "I'm here for you, my king. Whatever is going on in that head of yours, you can talk to me about it." Erica kissed his back, inhaling his Polo Blue cologne. She just loved everything about him. Burying her face in his shoulders, she smiled at the thought of just being able to hold Derrick in her arms forever.

Derrick gently tugged at Erica's fingers, unlocking them from around his waist. He needed some time to think things through, maybe even a little space. "I need to go outside and get some fresh air," he said, walking away, leaving Erica staring at him in disbelief. "Maybe I'm bugging out because I've been at work and in the house all week. I might just need to take a ride and enjoy a different scene for a change."

Erica smirked at Derrick, not liking the idea of where this could be headed. In the back of her mind, she assumed Derrick might be getting homesick.

"So, you're just going to keep what's bothering you bottled inside?" Erica seriously asked. "How is that fair to me, when I'm the one that has to deal with you while you're on this emotional roller coaster?"

Derrick stopped just before reaching the front door. "I'm not forcing you to put up with anything," he stated. "We decided to make this relationship work together! How fair is it to me that you're trying to force me to open up about something I'm not ready to talk about yet?"

Erica was on the verge of barking back a slick rebuttal, but Derrick had already left. Even though she assumed Derrick might be getting home sick, she figured that as long as she was having his baby, he would never go too far without her.

Derrick sat on the hood of his car, caught up in the beauty of the dark blue sky as the sun began to set. He thought about everything that had transpired in just a matter of days and had to shake his head in disappointment. "What am I going to do with myself?" he said out loud, staring into the heavens above. "I got a wife sleeping with my best friend. And some other woman claims to be pregnant with my child."

The thought to just hop in his car and go for a long drive suddenly crossed his mind. But just as quickly as the idea entered his head, an even better one popped up as well. Club Kavey had proven to be one hell of a stress reliever the first time he visited it, so why not go there. Now that he was visiting alone, he wondered would it still prove to be just as effective.

***

An hour later, Derrick sat quietly listening as Juicy told him everything about what April had told her earlier. Derrick had his doubts as to whether he should believe her or not, but the fact that Juicy was so relentless in her efforts to get him to believe her did make him somewhat curious.

The sound of *Wiz Khalifa's 'Lit'* featuring *Ty Dolla $ign* banged through the club's speakers. Juicy informed Derrick that it was her cue to perform and quickly hurried off. Derrick couldn't help but admire the

way Juicy took control of the stage, commanding the crowd to splurge by the simple sway of her body. Juicy was no doubt good at what she did, in fact probably one of the best Derrick had ever seen. Thoughts of the night he and April shared her in a threesome crossed his mind. That night was picture perfect, all the way down to the smallest detail. Derrick thought about the promise April made, stating that that night would be one of the most memorable nights of his life.

April had to have known Juicy before that night. Derrick thought to himself. Regardless of how sophisticated April might have seemed, that night revealed another side of her.

The song Juicy was doing her performance to finally ended. She quickly scooped piles of money into a small bucket, then hurried backstage to get dressed. Derrick had just ordered another round of drinks when he caught sight of a small group of men eagerly watching him from the corner of the room. At first, he tried to dismiss the idea of someone watching him. But when he looked away for a moment, then took a casual glance back at them, he saw them headed in his direction.

Derrick picked up his small glass of cognac, swirled it, and then took a sip. He tried his best to appear unmoved by the menacing glares etched deep in their faces. But something in each of their eyes spelled trouble. It was something that couldn't be ignored.

"What it do, fam?" Staxs said as he walked right up in front of Derrick, blocking his view. "You here to see somebody?"

Derrick glared up at Staxs, ready for whatever. He was far from a punk, but he was no fool either. There were three other goons behind him, and each of them reeked of death.

"This is a strip club," Derrick finally replied sarcastically. "I'm just sitting here minding my own business. I'm trying to check out these beautiful women."

Staxs chuckled softly, pulling up a chair next to Derrick to take a seat. "Minding your own business, you say? From what I hear, you like fucking around with other niggas hoes. Is that what you also call your business?"

Derrick rolled his eyes, quickly becoming agitated with whatever this man was trying to get at. He had no idea what he could have been

talking about. But whatever it was, he needed to voice it and move the fuck on.

"Other people's hoe's—" Derrick said, pausing for emphasis. "is none of my business and is not one of my businesses—" Derrick paused again, giving Staxs a forced smile, then continued, "It's none of anybody else's business either."

Staxs burst into loud laughter, mimicking Derrick who sat poised, and quite unfazed by him or his men. "Check this out, fam—fuck all the bitch ass, read between the line games, you trying to play. The bottom line of this conversation is April Jordan is off limits! I know you and that trifling ass bitch been fucking around. And that shit ends here tonight."

Derrick smirked, not taking Staxs words too kindly. He set his glass on the table, turning his attention to Staxs with a menacing glare of his own. "Or what?" he growled tauntingly.

"Or I'ma blow yo muthafuckin' head off nigga, that's what!"

Derrick slid to the edge of his seat but quickly became aware of the deathly silence that lingered in the air around him. Everyone was watching him, seemingly waiting for something to pop off. At first, Derrick wasn't aware of just how close to getting killed he actually was, but as he looked back, he saw it. Staxs's goons had guns out, waiting on the word to unload on him.

"Hold tha fuck up," Big Bruce's voice boomed, instantly drawing everyone's attention. "What the hell is going on over here?" Big Bruce eyed Staxs's and his men who now had their guns out. "Ain't nobody killing shit up in here. If you niggas got a problem with this nigga, take that shit down to them white folk's club. Y'all niggas better go shoot they shit up. Don't have this spot hot just because you niggas don't know how to act!"

Staxs smiled, giving his men a nod to head out. "Fuck you talking about, fam? Ain't nobody fixing to die. We were just leaving."

Derrick stood watching as the small group of goons made their way through the club and out the front doors. Whatever doubts he had earlier about what Juicy was trying to tell him, had just been erased. There was something going on with a good friend of his, and whatever that something was, he was going to be there to help her through it.

***

Staxs and his small entourage of goons mobbed through the front doors of *The Lounge* and headed to his office in the back. Staxs scanned the dimly lit room in search of Devil, who had called him earlier, relaying the news about what happened to April on her first trip out of town. Although Staxs could care less if April lived or died, he did care about the three kilos that were supposed to be delivered to Cakes that had mysteriously come up missing.

Staxs walked into his office and immediately spotted April standing over by his desk in tears with Devil standing across from her. The thought of just taking off running, jumping through the air and kicking April dead in her throat flashed across his mind, but the fact that it was a place of business, quickly made him decide against doing that in public.

"What tha fuck is you up in here crying for?" Staxs growled, slamming the door closed behind him.

"This is not for me," April cried. "I don't think I can continue to do this anymore."

Staxs walked around his desk and took a seat. Devil stepped over and had a private word with Staxs and then quickly left.

"So, tell me what happened while you went to make that little move?" Staxs said, leaning back in his chair to intently watch April.

"I-I did what you told me," she stammered, taking a seat in a chair across from Staxs. "I took it straight to Cakes like you said. But when I got there, some guy named T pulled out a gun and started asking for the dope."

Staxs chuckled softly and leaned back in his chair as he peered up at the ceiling.

"Bitch you lying," he barked, glaring at her. "Do you want me to tell you how I know you're lying?"

April shrugged, trying to appear confused like she had no clue as to what Staxs was talking about. "You ain't know that nigga Cakes, or that fool T until I sent you to meet Cakes. You want me to believe some

dumb ass nigga jumped out with a gun, demanding that you hand over the dope. But before he left, he told you his name."

April's head fell to her chest as she sobbed. On the outside, it appeared as if she was mentally distraught. But on the inside, her mind was working as quickly as possible to come up with her next response.

"I swear," she cried. "They took all the dope. And then when whoever that nigga T was, left the house, Cakes tried to kill me."

Staxs sat glaring at April seemingly unfazed by her plea. Even though his gut told him that April was lying, there was some truth to her story. Staxs' out of town resources told him Cakes and one of his lookouts were found dead up in one of his spots. So, despite what his heart told him, he did have to believe her to an extent.

"I'm telling you like this, if I find out you're lying to me, I'ma murder your whole fucking family. And the fucked up thing about it all is, I'ma tie yo' scandalous ass up and make you watch me murk they ass one-by-one."

April covered her face, playing her role to the tee. There was no way in the world anyone would ever find out if she was lying or not. That would just be another secret she would take to the grave with her.

"I'm telling the truth," April exclaimed. "I wouldn't dare do anything that could put my family in harm's way. All I want to do is pay back what I owe and get back to living my life."

Staxs smirked, quickly pulling out his cell phone to call Devil. There was nothing he could do about his assumptions but wait. Sooner or later the truth would come out. When it did, she would wish she had never heard of a nigga named Slim.

"Take this bitch back to my crib so she can get her shit and get tha fuck out!"

April sat glaring across the desk at Staxs as he barked his orders to Devil. As much as she wanted to hurl her own insults back at Staxs for continuing to disrespect her, she kept it to herself. Staxs' time was coming, and she couldn't wait.

Staxs ended the call, leaned back, and watched April closely. He didn't want to allow April to leave and go home, but then again, he had a job to do. *The Lounge* was jammed packed, full of people having a good time. Seeing as it was Slim's business, Staxs was also left in charge of the day-to-day functions of it as well. A soft knock at the door stirred Staxs from his thoughts. Devil entered with two other goons and ordered April to follow them.

"One more thing before you go," Staxs said to April, who already had one foot out the door. "Remember I got eyes on your people. Any funny shit and everyone dies."

April ice grilled Staxs just before turning to leave. She was mere inches from saying something that might very well cost her life, but she held firm. In time Staxs would get what he had coming to him. She just needed to be around to make sure he got it.

Later, that night, Staxs sat in his office with the lights dim, and *Tank's 'So Cold'* streaming through his office speakers. Chocolate, a young dark skin waitress, knelt before him, giving him head. Staxs palmed the back of her head, grinding his dick as far as he could down her throat.

"You is cold wit' that shit," Staxs growled, watching as Chocolate devoured him. Her warm saliva ran down his dick, where it came to rest deep inside his boxers. He gently massaged her shoulders, feeling the nut beginning to build. "Turn around," he instructed Chocolate, wanting to feel his dick sliding in and out of her pussy.

Chocolate slurped and sucked on his dick one last time. She already knew how Staxs liked it. Ever since Staxs hired her from day one, she had been one of his private sex toys. Staxs always made sure to put a few extra hundred on her check, so in return, she gave it to him just the way he wanted it.

Staxs bent Chocolate over the desk, thumping his thick dick up against her ass. "You ready for this dick?" Staxs growled, running the tip of his dick between her ass cheeks to slowly guide it to her pussy.

"Yes," she moaned as he slowly pushed up inside of her. "Staxs," she cried out more so out of showmanship than actual feeling.

He grabbed her by the ponytail, pulling her head back so as to kiss her.

"Fuck me," she hissed, staring back at him with passion burning brightly in her eyes.

Staxs sunk his teeth into her neck, grinding his dick up inside her. When he was sure her pussy was wet enough, and her body was ready, he pounded away.

Clap! Clap! Clap!

"Oh, baby yessss!" she moaned.

As Staxs stood behind Chocolate pounding away, the door to his office quietly opened. Several goons were led into the room, following closely behind their fearless leader.

"You having fun with ya new wifey?" A man asked, but Staxs never heard a thing. He continued to drive deeper, pounding harder and harder. Just as he felt his dick began to swell threatening to release his load inside of her—he looked up spotting the men in his office.

"Slim," he barked, recognizing his boss. "Oh, shit my bad. Hold on fam."

Slim stood glaring at Staxs while Mob made his way to flip on the lights. "So, this is how you been spending your time while I've been away?" Slim snarled, watching as Staxs and Chocolate hurried to get themselves together.

"Nah, fam, I was just having a little fun with Babe."

Slim's calculating eyes roamed over Chocolate's thick thighs as she struggled to squeeze her curvaceous body into her jeans. "Babe?" Slim repeated mockingly. "Nigga you around here calling these busted up looking hoes, Babe?" Slim turned peering back over his shoulder. "You, niggas trying to get your dick sucked?"

They chuckled.

"That ugly ass bitch gotta pay to suck this dick," Young Syke quipped.

"Fam-o is outta line for sitting up in here barebacking that bitch."

Chocolate looked up slightly surprised to hear them talking about her like she wasn't even in the room. She had heard stories of how grimy the C.M. could be towards women. So, instead of taking the time to get her shirt completely on before leaving, she hurried out the room only half-dressed.

"You know if you wasn't so worried about getting ya little dick wet, you might be able to tell me why we getting so hot in the streets." Slim walked over to his old desk, gazing down at it like it was infected with some kind of disease. His thoughts ran wildly. But there was one thing in particular that stood out in his mind. "Where is April?"

Staxs felt as if he wanted to curl up and die right there on the spot. He knew Slim to be a highly intelligent individual. For one to try and play on his intelligence would surely warrant death. "I-I sent her home an hour ago," Staxs stammered. "I didn't know what you would want me to do, being that she had to—"

"Murder some niggas," Slim said, finishing Staxs' sentence. "How did you know?"

Slim gave Staxs a menacing once over. "Ain't too much that goes on in my city that I don't know about," Slim stated firmly. "But enough talk about all this simple ass bullshit you be on. It's time to take care of business. I want you to round up every top-ranking member of The

C.M. and have them in this office in an hour. Whichever

muthafucka don't show up to this meeting, consider their ass out!"

Staxs nodded in understanding, quickly trying to make his way to the door. He expected to hear his death sentence being handed down for the foul shit he had done to April. But no, soon as he was safely out of the office, he knew he had made it. Now all he needed to do was make sure what he had done to her remained a secret, even if that meant blackmailing April.

Adrian Dulan

CHAPTER EIGHT

SURPRISE PARTY

Agent Luther McCracken stormed into his office, slamming the door behind him. Word that the leader of the Crimson Mafia had been released just touched his ears, making him furious. Just as things were beginning to appear as if the Feds were gaining some leeway on operation, *Slim Pickings*, the courts released Slim from prison. Now everything the FBI had come to understand about the Crimson Mafia would surely change. There was no telling what changes Slim would make now that he was out of prison.

McCracken spun his chair around peering out his office window into downtown Oklahoma City. His light blue eyes danced wildly over the many rooftops, wondering, what might come of the city now that a notorious killer had been released back into society again. McCracken released a loud, frustrating sigh, as he sat rubbing his tired eyes. He was finally ready to admit that he was tired. Finally, able to say he had had enough, and finally came to the point of being willing to call it quits.

McCracken had been working for the FBI for more than twenty years. He was known throughout the bureau for always finding a way to catch the big fish. But the years of late nights and early mornings had definitely taken its toll on him. His once broad shoulders, now sagged heavily, seemingly weighed down from years of stress. His face bore the deep lines of worry. He now had sad deep-set eyes and a head of hair that was mostly filled with gray. The some odd years he had been on this earth had been a long hard half a century. Now that he was drawing ever so near to his retirement, his only desire was to crack this one final case and retire.

A soft tap at the door stirred McCracken from his thoughts. He turned to see Agent Stevens, the top DEA assigned to operation, *Slim Pickings* walking through the door. Stevens was also in his early 50s, but his fifty some odd years hadn't been as long and dreadfully hard as McCracken. Stevens was a married man with kids, and he was also a proud grandfather. Although he too was nearing retirement, his drive to crack this one last case wasn't like his partners. He had come to be content with the accomplishments he had made throughout his career.

"Just the man I was hoping to see," McCracken stated, standing, giving Stevens a firm handshake, then taking his seat. "I was wondering what type of recent information we have on Emanuel *Staxs* Brown?" Stevens took his seat across from McCracken, opening a small manila folder.

"Well," he began, quickly thumbing through several papers. "The last thing I can remember is April Jordan was seen leaving Club Kavey with him after work."

McCracken crossed his legs drumming his fingertips across the tip of his chin. "Do we still have eyes on, Staxs?" Stevens slowly shook his head, apparently consumed by some report he was reading.

"Well, we're going to need eyes on Staxs and April Jordan as soon as possible." Stevens glanced up from the file, picking up on the urgent tone in McCracken's voice. "I just found out this morning that they released Slim from prison yesterday."

"*They what*! You're kidding," Stevens exclaims in disbelief.

"Oh, how I wish I were," McCracken assured him. "And the killer part of it all is, no one said anything about him even having his appeal in the court system. They just let the son of a bitch out. Then expect us to magically build a case against him and arrest him." Stevens rubbed the back of his neck as if the pressure of the job was weighing on him.

"This could be bad," Stevens said, sounding disappointed. "Once Slim finds out April is hanging out with Staxs, we all know what he's going to do next." McCracken nodded in agreement, then quickly picked up his office phone.

"What are you doing?" Stevens asked, watching McCracken with a puzzled expression.

"I need to see if we can get eyes on April immediately. I have a crazy feeling that there is more to this story than what meets the eye. Staxs nor April is crazy enough to cross Slim and for them two to be hanging out only spells trouble!"

***

"Ladies! Ladies! Good morning to you all," Derrick announced as he strolled through the front doors of his store. "Is everyone doing alright today?"

Cynthia, one of Derrick's new employees stood nearby struggling to set up a display she had been instructed to put up. "I guess I'm doing okay," she replied halfheartedly. "Although I would be doing a whole lot better if I understood exactly how, Ms. Jordan wanted me to set this thing up."

Derrick waved over another employee to assist Cynthia with her problem. Outwardly, he appeared calm, cool, unbothered by the fact that one of his new employees didn't know how to set up a simple display. But inside, he was bubbling forth with excitement. Happy to be at work today and glad to know that April was back at work as well.

After leaving his newest employee with a few encouraging words, Derrick quickly made his way to the back of the store. No matter how hard he tried to conceal his excitement, he simply couldn't. Curiosity about the secret lifestyle April was living only made him want to learn more about her.

"Hello, Mr. Walker," April said as soon as she noticed Derrick standing in the doorway watching her intently. She had been working alongside Georgette. The fall selection had just arrived, so the two loaded small carts for the other employees to push out front.

"April, Georgette," Derrick responded with a slight wave and a warm, welcoming smile. "Is everything all good in here?" April timidly nodded while Georgette continued to pile up another cart full of clothing. She knew Derrick knew the truth as to where she had been for the past week. All she wanted to know was how he felt about her now that he knew the truth.

"Everything is just fine," Georgette reassured Derrick, after sitting another stack of shirts on the cart. "Now that April has finally returned, maybe we can get things back to normal."

Derrick softly chuckled, spinning on his heels to leave. "April, when you get a second of free time, I'll need to see you in my office."

Instantly the butterflies that had been resting in the inner deepest parts of her stomach swarmed to life. She thought she could hear a tinge of disappointment in Derrick's voice, but then again, she wasn't sure. The thought of being fired suddenly flashed across her mind. But as she pondered Derrick's intentions, the memory of how he stood behind her watching intently, popped up in her mind.

Maybe he doesn't want to fire me. April reasoned. *He very well might want me to stick around for a little while longer.*

Derrick sat at his desk. *Knock! Knock!* He looked up to see April standing in his doorway with eyes filled with worry.

Before he could offer his words of comfort and understanding, April was already begging for his forgiveness. "Derrick, I am so sorry you had to find out I'm involved with such crazy people," she started. "None of this would have ever happened if it wasn't for my crazy ex-boyfriend."

Derrick stood from his seat, making his way around to April. Tears could be seen filling the borders of her eyelids. Derrick could only assume there had to be more beneath the surface than she was willing to talk about. "Did they hurt you?" Derrick asked walking up and taking her by the hands.

She never responded, but accidentally allowed a soft cry to escape from her lips.

"April, you've got to talk to me. You had everyone around here worried sick about you."

April gazed into Derrick's eyes. "I'm sorry—I didn't—I just—" She melted away in Derrick's open arms, sobbing uncontrollably. "There is so much that I need to talk to you about," she cried. "But I don't want to drag you or anyone else into this mess that I've gotten myself into."

He gently rubbed her back, allowing her to cry on his

shoulder. "You're not alone," he tried to reassure her while holding her tightly in his arms. "But in order for me to help, you have to talk to me."

April slightly pulled away from Derrick gazing up at him with a look of surprise. "You're not mad at me? I thought that you would hate me."

"Hate you," Derrick repeated, almost shouting. "I have no reason to hate you. I'm too busy trying to understand what's going on in your life so that I can help you. You've given me no reason to want to hate you." April looked away, as if Derrick may suddenly see the horrible secrets she had been forced to keep embedded in her mind.

"I would like to talk, but just not here," April admitted. "If you have time to stop by after work, I'll gladly—"

"Be there," Derrick chimed in, filling in April's sentence with his response. "Even if you hadn't offered, I'd already made plans to stop by."

***

A couple of hours had passed since Derrick left work for the evening. The feeble roadblocks and constant whining Erica used to try and keep Derrick from leaving, proved to be to no avail. He now stood just outside April's front door, nodding to the sounds of Avant, which April had playing on her home stereo.

"That's my shit—" Derrick sang while bobbing his head to the beat. "I wonder if she knows anything about that." He pressed her doorbell, ringing it several times. He was excited to be off work, and just as excited to finally be able to talk about what was going on in April's life.

"What are you doing, Mr. Impatient?" April said, opening her front door. "You standing out here pressing on my doorbell like a wild man." She playfully grabbed him by the shirt and snatched him inside.

"Pssttt—what do you think I'm doing?" Derrick responded. "I'm trying to hurry up and get in here to you. Look at this place, it looks amazing!" Derrick stood peering around April's cozy condo while she wrapped her arms around him in a warm embrace. "What is that smell?" he asked, sniffing the air.

"That's a T-bone steak, along with all the trimmings. I lit a Midnight incense so that it might smell fresh in here as well."

Derrick nodded in approval. He appreciated what she had done to make his visit comfortable. Little did she know, he needed her comforting attention just as much as she needed his.

"I like this whole mellow mood thing you've got going on," Derrick admitted. "Candles are burning, soft music playing in the background. Hell, you've even got the back-patio door slightly open, allowing the moonlight to shine in. This looks and feels really amazing."

April leaned up on her tippy toes, giving Derrick a passionate kiss on the lips. "We have so much to talk about," she whispered. "We can either talk about it now, or we can talk about it after we eat."

Derrick ran his fingertips down April's waist and continued to her thighs. She wore nothing but a long white t-shirt with no panties and no bra. Her nipples were already hard and pressing against her t-shirt.

"Yeah, we do have a lot to talk about," Derrick said, planting soft kisses on April's cheek, then her neck, and finally her shoulder. "But I'd rather we talked about everything later. We have a whole lot of catching up to do."

***

Slim sat listening to the soft rumble of Mob's car speakers as he and two of his goons drove to pay a visit to an old friend. From the time April had run off, disappearing in the city streets, Slim made a vow to get even with her. At one point, Slim's love for April ran deep. In fact, his love for April ran so deep that the money she had taken in the past would have meant nothing as long as she had stayed by his side when he needed her.

But when April left Slim for dead, forcing him to face his

worst nightmares in the belly of the beast alone, his love for her turned to hate. Hate that was so utterly strong, he was willing to do anything to ensure April suffered as he did.

"That's her car right there, Blood," Mob announced as he pulled up to the curb, parking in front of April's condo.

"And that looks like that nigga's car she was fucking with at the club," Young Syke added.

"Looks like fam-o still creeping around with ole girl, even after we told his bitch ass to fall back."

Slim glared through the dark tinted windows on Mob's 4 door GMC truck. He already knew the car Syke was talking about belonged to Derrick. Slim was thorough in his research of everyone April was involved with.

"Yeah, that's that nigga's shit," Slim snarled. "You two gon' ahead and strap up. We about to push up in this scandalous ass bitch's house and throw these two love birds a surprise party."

***

Clap! Clap! Clap! Clap!

Derrick had April doggy style, cornered in the middle of the sectional sofa. Even if she wanted to try and run from the dick, she couldn't. Derrick had her jammed in a tight squeeze, head down, fucking the dog shit out of her.

"Uhhh! Please yes," she cried out as Derrick hammered away.

Derrick had never asked April one single question. It was almost as if he was fucking April so good that she told him everything he thought he wanted to know without even asking.

"I've been so bad Daddy fuck that pussy! I've been so baaddd."

Derrick's cell phone suddenly rang, slightly throwing off his rhythm. Whoever the caller was, it wasn't someone he had stored in his phone call log. All his contacts had their own, special ring tone. "Hold on, I need to answer that," Derrick said, stopping to reach for his cell phone. "This call might be important."

April looked back at Derrick, welcoming the time-out. The

dick was without question some of the best she had ever had. But they had already been at it non-stop for over an hour. She was drained and needed a break.

"Hello," Derrick answered, trying his best not to sound winded. "Are you almost finished yet?" the caller asked.

Derrick frowned, peering down at the number. He couldn't recall ever seeing it before and wondered if it was this game Martina was playing. "Excuse me, what did you just say to me?"

"Nigga, I said is you almost finished yet!"

Derrick glared back over at April, who sat watching him curiously. He didn't want to ruin the mood by allowing his temper to get the best of him. But it was already too late. Whoever had called, had the intention of rubbing him the wrong way, and they needed to be checked.

"Nigga," Derrick barked, repeating what the caller said. "Don't call my phone with these childish ass games you trying to play. Who the hell is this?" The phone line fell silent for a moment. But as Derrick sat listening close for a response, he could have sworn he heard whispering and snickering going on in the background.

"Ain't nobody playing on your phone. I called this number to talk to, my bitch! Now put that stank ass hoe on the phone."

Derrick pulled the phone away from his head, peering over at April. He started to hand the phone over to her but stopped himself. He didn't want the caller to think he had gotten the best of him.

"Check this out, Bruh. I don't know who you are, or who the hell you think you are. But don't ever call my phone again. Do you understand me?" The phone line went dead, leaving Derrick standing there butt naked, glaring down at April, "I don't know what type of crazy-ass shit you have gotten yourself involved in, but you had no right to give my number to anyone!"

April gasped, pulling her white t-shirt over her body. "I haven't given your number to anyone," she fired back. "Why would I give—" The sound of the patio door sliding open caught both of their attention. Three men dressed in all black, quickly filed inside taking positions on both sides of April's sectional. "Didn't I tell you to put that hoe on the phone?" Slim barked. Derrick started to respond with something even more sarcastic, but the fact that Slim's goons already had their guns out, made him think twice.

"What the hell is all this about?" Derrick asked, raising his hands. "If it's money you want, take my wallet out of my pants. I have a few hundred in there."

Slim made his way around the sofa scooping up Derricks clothing off the floor.

"Shut tha fuck up, and get dressed," Slim yelled, tossing Derrick his clothes. "Do it look like we here to rob you for that chump change?"

Derrick quickly began getting dressed while Slim and his men stood quietly observing him. "He doesn't have anything to do with what me and you have going on," April said, looking over at Slim with pleading eyes. "Let him go. I've already agreed to do everything you wanted me to." April's statements caught Derrick by surprise.

"You know these people?" he asked in disbelief.

"Muthafucka don't worry about who the fuck she knows!" Slim barked. "Just put your fucking clothes on like I told you before I make a decision that might not work out in your best interest—" Slim paused to give Derrick a few moments to get dressed before continuing. "I'm going to let you walk out of here alive tonight. But if I ever even hear about you creeping around fucking with this bitch, right here—" Slim cut his eyes over at April, then turns his attention back to Derrick. "You're a dead man."

Derrick looked down at April, then back over to Slim. April was obviously involved in something that was so serious it was actually life-threatening. Whatever kind of trouble that was, he didn't want any parts of it.

"Look, Bruh, I hope whatever differences you have with her, won't cause you to do something crazy to her. But on the other hand, you don't ever have to worry about seeing me again. So, if it's cool with you—" Derrick gestured towards the door. "Can I leave?"

Slim studied Derrick for a brief moment as if he was having second thoughts. Derrick didn't go to the police when Staxs pressed him at the club, so he could only hope he wouldn't go now. "Go on and get tha fuck up outta here," Slim spat. "And remember what I told you fam—don't fuck with this bitch again!"

Slim walked closer to April, now towering over her. He could see the fear creeping into her eyes because he knew that he was the last person she could have ever expected to see. "Well, well, well—look what tha fuck I done finally stumbled upon." Slim blew into his hands as if they were cold. "What's up with all that shit you been talking over the phone? I bet your sneaky ass never thought you'd see me face-to-face again."

April sat looking up at Slim terrified. She struggled to pull her t-shirt over her legs to cover herself better. "Just do whatever you came here to do. I'm not going to sit here and allow you to patronize me. I'm still not afraid of you."

An evil smile spread across Slim's face. "Oh, I know you ain't afraid," Slim said mockingly. "And trust me I'm about to." *Smack!*

CHAPTER NINE

PUT MY MIND AT EASE

Several months had flown by since Slim was released from the penitentiary. Now that he was back on the streets, he held April on an incredibly tight leash. Her innocent, but beautiful face was being used as the new face of the Crimson Mafia. Everyone except Slim's closest business associates assumed he was still in prison. By Slim using April as someone to handle all his dirty work, that minimized his chances of ever going back to jail again.

April was awakened bright and early to the sound of Slim turning on the shower in the bathroom. Being that April was now the new face of the C.M., Slim forced her to come and live with him. Not only was she being used for the sole purpose of handling all Slim's dirty work, but she was also everything Slim imagined her to be. Slim made sure he got as much as he could for his buck. He promised to make April suffer hard, and now it had become her harsh reality.

April grudgingly rolled out of bed and headed downstairs to make Slim's morning coffee. Her daily routine consisted of the same tedious, mentally draining chores: have the house cleaned before noon, get a daily drop off/pick up list from Slim, and hit the streets in that order. Everything was set up so that nothing she did would ever draw any attention to Slim.

Ding Dong!

The unexpected sound of the doorbell caught April by surprise as she quickly made her way to the kitchen. No one ever came by this early in the morning, unless they notified her, or Slim said it was cool.

Ding Dong!

Cautiously April crept closer to the door, peeking through the stained-glass windows to see who was outside.

"Damn," April cursed, spotting Staxs outside the door. She could only assume Slim knew he was coming, so she opened the door, allowing him inside.

"Damn, a nigga can't get no good morning? No hey, how you doing, Mr. Staxs? No nothing! You just going to stand there with ya face all screwed up?" Staxs walked by April, eyeing her from head to toe. Her red silk nightgown clinging ever so tightly to her body while her red headwrap gave her eyes that chinky eyed look. Staxs was digging all that.

"Slim will be out of the shower in a minute," April snapped, rolling her eyes at him. "You can either go wait in the living room, or you can go back outside to your car. I really don't give a fuck." April slammed the door behind Staxs and tried to scurry off to the kitchen to continue with her duties.

"Naw hold tha fuck on," Staxs hissed, snatching April back to him by the arm. "Did I tell you that you could leave? Because I really don't recall the words *'Get tha fuck outta my face'* coming outta my mouth. Do you?" Staxs spun April around, wrapping his arms around her, and grabbing a handful of ass. "Did you miss me?"

April dug both elbows deep into Staxs chest, trying to break free. "Get the fuck off me!" she growled through clenched teeth. "If Slim comes out of that bathroom and sees this, we're both as good as dead!"

Staxs chuckled softly. "Does it look like I really give a fuck about dying?" he asked, pulling her gown up, then roughly clawing at her ass cheeks. "I have been fucking you for a while now. This is my pussy, and ain't a damn thing you, him or anyone can do about it." Staxs slid his hand around to her crotch, working his fingers feverishly to get inside her thong.

"I said get off me!" April shouted, shoving Staxs back into the door. "I'm sick of your fat, nasty ass touching me! You can do whatever you feel you need to do, but this bullshit stops now!"

Staxs stood glaring at April as she shot up the stairs to her bedroom. He wouldn't dare try to excite the situation any further, Slim still knew nothing of the dealings he had with April. Staxs managed to manipulate things so that April still believed he would kill her family.

Staxs pulled out his cell phone, instantly ready to make

someone an example. He knew he couldn't touch April's family or even Derrick. Slim had given him a pass, and if he killed her family, he would surely find out what had been going on. As Staxs stood pondering who he could hit that would send a clear message regarding the fact that he wasn't to be fucked with, immediately the memory of the first time he laid eyes on Derrick came to mind.

"Oh, I know who'd be the perfect example," Staxs said out loud, remembering Derrick's best friend. "I bet by me murking that pretty ass nigga, she'll get the message."

***

April headed out that evening to do her daily rounds of collecting and handing down orders. The '*To-Do List*' Slim had given her was a rather short one. Surprisingly enough, one of the top names on the list was none other than Staxs. April knew Staxs would probably still be mad about the way things happened earlier. Regardless of how he felt, she was tired. Tired of being mistreated and tired of him thinking he could continue to have his way with her. If push came to shove, April was fully prepared to put an end to her problems with Staxs, if he continued to press her.

April whipped her Srt-8 Jeep into the parking lot of an old abandoned warehouse. It was the designated meeting place for top-ranking members of the C.M. to drop off money. It was in a safe, quiet, and very discrete location. The warehouse had been purchased by some of Slim's connections. So, the threat of police showing up was never a problem. April drove around to the back of the warehouse where trucks normally unloaded or received orders. Staxs was parked in the far corner of the parking lot against the warehouse's huge metal fence. Had someone just so happen to stumble across them while they were conducting business, they probably wouldn't have paid them any attention. That's just how low the area was.

Staxs flashed his headlights several times, indicating that he wanted April to come over to his truck. April was slightly reluctant to get out because there was no telling what Staxs would do. April exited her Jeep, knowing his eyes were glued to her every move. She wore red high heels, with white tights. Her red top bore the initials DF in white letters and was cut short to show off her perfectly flat stomach. Her gold hoop earrings swayed back and forth with every step while her Chanel frames concealed her evil intentions.

"You dressed up all fly and shit for me?" Staxs questioned April as she opened the passenger door to his white Range Rover.

April rolled her eyes, smacking her lips. She hated Staxs with a passion. He assumed everything in life was made or done specifically for him. "No, I didn't put this on for you," she snarled, sounding very much annoyed to even have to explain anything to Staxs. "I got dressed so I can get out and handle my business. Now, do you have the money that I was sent here to pick up?"

Staxs head snapped back as if April's words were a sharp slap to his face. "Bitch miss me with that sucka ass shit you just came up with. My money straight every time. Let's not forget I used to run this whole organization."

April glared over at Staxs, then quickly dismissed the idea of popping off something slick. It was obvious Staxs just wanted a reason to argue. It was better for her if she didn't entertain his childish fits and stayed focused on the reason she was there in the first place.

"Well, if you don't mind—I'd like to go ahead and get the money so I can leave."

A mischievous smile cut across Staxs' face. "I'll give you the money," Staxs said, staring down at April's thick thighs licking his lips. "But what are you going to give me in return."

April shook her head out of frustration. No matter what she did to get Staxs to back up off her, he wouldn't. There was only one solution to this problem, and if Staxs continued he would no doubt force her hand. "I ain't got shit else for you, Staxs. That bullshit you have been putting me through is over. Enough is enough! I refuse to sit here and continue to play these games with you."

Staxs bobbed his head up and down, peering out the driver's

side window. "Well, I guess it's curtains for your man's people then."

April looked back over at Staxs, who was now frowning. "What man? I don't have any man."

Staxs chuckled softly. "Pretty boy with the green eyes ain't your man?"

April's mouth almost fell to the floor. "What did you do?"

Staxs shrugged as if April's question meant nothing. "I made sure that you'd get the message. Ain't nobody fixing to be playing these tough girl games you trying to play."

Instantly tears of regret began to well up in April's eyes. Neither Derrick nor his friend had done anything to deserve the violence that had come into their lives because of her.

"What is it that you want from me?" April yelled.

"I want you to get cho' muthafuckin' ass in the back seat and put my mind at ease," Staxs spat. "Maybe if you make it feel real good to a nigga, then I won't have to murder your man's family, too." Staxs opened his door, stepping out as if he was king of the world. He slowly scanned the parking lot, adjusting his Gucci frames before getting in the back seat. "You just gon' sit up there and cry me a fuckin' river, or you gon' get yo' black ass back here and suck this dick!"

April opened the passenger door wiping away the tears that rolled down her face. What she was about to do, should have been done a long time ago.

"Come on and get in," Staxs said, watching April as she stood with the back door open, staring at Staxs like he was crazy. "I promise it won't take as long as it did before. As good as you looking today, hmm you got a nigga already about to bust."

April ice grilled Staxs so hard there should have been no misunderstanding as to what her real intentions were. Staxs unbuckled his jeans, opening them. Then pulled out his dick through the small slit in the front of his boxers. He softly pulled on his dick, making it hard.

"Nigga you thought I was gon' suck yo little ass dick!" April pulled a chrome 380 pistol from the small of her back and pointed it at Staxs.

"What am I supposed to be scared or something?" Staxs said tauntingly. "Did you forget you done already pulled a gun on me before? I told you last time that time was on me. But this time—" Staxs looked down the barrel of April's gun, then back up at her. "You gon' make me fuck tha shit out ya momma with a butcher knife. Bleed that bitch out, then make ya daddy suck her stankin ass pussy."

Pop!

"Ahhhh!"

Pop! Pop! Pop! Pop!

Staxs fell against the back door, taking shots to his dick, thigh, stomach, and throat. When he felt the bullet enter the side of his neck, his reflexes made him reach for the wound. He frantically fumbled with the back door, struggling to get it open. When he was finally able to get it open, he stumbled out, falling. "Urgghhh!" he grunted when his body hit the ground.

"You still want some of this pussy, nigga?" April calmly strolled around the truck to where Staxs lay bleeding to death on the ground. Blood poured from the corners of his mouth while his dick dangled from the slit in his boxers by a thin piece of skin. "Looks like you are going to need a little help if you ever plan on getting some pussy again," April snarled with an evil look spreading ever so quickly across her face.

Staxs's bottom lip trembled as if he were trying to say something. "Fffuck—you—bitch!"

April softly giggled. "*Fuck me?* No- fuck you, nigga."

Pop! Pop!

April sent two more shots to his dome, leaving him slumped on the ground. She then did a quick search of his truck for the 88 bands she had been sent to collect. "I guess you won't be needing this anymore," April said, lifting a small duffel bag out the back of Staxs' truck. "You should have learned to leave well enough alone, and maybe you wouldn't be laying there dead with ya dick hanging out." April strolled back over to her Jeep and got in. Now that Staxs had been eliminated, all she had to do was finish her business with Slim, and this nightmare would finally be over.

***

"I'm going to be a father!" Derrick cried out to no one in particular as he ran alongside Erica who was being rushed to the delivery room. "Breathe Erica, you've got to breathe. Do you remember how they taught you to do it?"

Erica quickly nodded as she was hit with another wave of contractions. "Ahhh, Derrick," she cried.

"Babe you can do this, just stay focused."

Derrick stopped following Erica when they reached the delivery room. He didn't have the stomach to see a child being born, let alone witness all that pain and blood. Derrick paced nervously around the waiting room for what seemed like an eternity. Every five minutes he took a casual glance at the clock, wondering if his child had been born yet.

"Derrick, I'm so sorry I'm late. Have they come out and told you anything yet?" Derrick spun around to see Georgette headed in his direction with a bag full of goodies.

He had called Georgette as soon as Erica started having her first contractions. Georgette had been so helpful around the store that she and Derrick's bond had become stronger. She had also managed to earn the new title of God Mother.

"No, not anything yet," Derrick responded, sounding disappointed.

"Well, how long has she been back there?"

"It's been every bit of two hours. My feet hurt, and I feel like I'm about to go crazy out here."

Georgette took Derrick by the hand, guiding him over to several empty seats. "Let's have us a little sit-down, shall we? You've been walking around all this time and you need to sit down and relax."

Derrick flopped down in the chair next to Georgette and ran his hands through his dreadlocks. "I wish there was something I could do. I feel like I just left her to go through this all alone,"

Derrick solemnly explained.

Georgette gave Derrick a warm smile, softly patting him on his knee. "My husband was the same way when we had our first child," Georgette admitted. "Some men have the stomach for it." She slightly shrugged. "And some don't. Don't allow yourself to get caught up in the minor things. A blessing has been given to you. You have better things to start thinking about."

Derrick nodded in agreement, then sat back and took a deep breath. The next several hours flew by with Derrick having an eye-opening look at what the next eighteen years of his life would consist of.

"Congratulations, Mr. Walker! You have a beautiful baby boy waiting for you in the next room."

Derrick peered up at the doctor, but he couldn't find the words to convey anything he was feeling right then. It was almost as if the whole world stopped and all he could see was this older white man in scrubs, staring at him with a huge smile. Derrick peered back over at Georgette who also sat frozen in time. Nothing felt real. He felt like he was the only living human being moving around in a world that was completely frozen.

"Derrick! Derrick!" Georgette's soft voice broke the deathly silence that engulfed his mind. "It's time, this is what we've been waiting for."

He quickly shook his head, shaking free the tears that were building in his eyes. He had no idea he was crying until Georgette dabbed at his tears with a napkin.

"I'm a father now," he exclaimed. "I never thought I would see this day coming."

Georgette stood him up and gave him a warm embrace. "You are a father," she stated. "Now let's get in there so I can see this beautiful child you've created."

He was led down the hallway to a room where Erica and the baby were located. When he stepped into Erica's room, his heart instantly melted away at the sight of Erica cradling his son.

"You did such a good job," he said in a voice that cracked as he struggled to hold back more tears. "I want to thank you for giving me this opportunity to be a father and live my life again through his eyes." He leaned over and kissed Erica ever so softly on her forehead. "Can I hold him?"

Erica peered up at him with tears streaming down her face as well. She could see how happy Derrick was about the baby she held in her arms, but Erica had a few secrets. Secrets that were now in the open. Secrets that she didn't have the heart to explain.

"Oh, my god," she cried, handing Derrick the baby.

"Erica are you alright?" Derrick asked.

The doctor quickly made his way over to Erica's bedside, checking several monitors. "She's probably just tired," he said softly. "She's still heavily medicated, not to mention she's exhausted from having the baby."

Derrick held his little boy in his arms and looked down at him. He recognized Erica's nose, her eyes, but those lips— "Look at my little man, he's got my big ole fat lips!"

Erica felt like she wanted to die. How could she continue to let things go on any further? Erica loved Derrick with all her heart and wouldn't dare dream of ever doing anything to hurt him.

"I want to name him after me," Derrick insisted, rocking the baby gently in his arms. "We'll name him after me. I think the other little girls his age will love it." Derrick glanced back over at Erica expecting to hear or see some kind of response, but to his surprise, Erica appeared to be dozing off. "You go ahead and get some sleep, my love. I know you've got to be very tired."

Tears of regret continued to roll aimlessly down Erica's face. She was plagued by thoughts of the day when Derrick found out the truth, but she couldn't picture her life going on any further without Derrick in it.

"I love you," she whispered softly.

"I love you, too," Derrick responded. "Now get you some rest. I'll be right here."

***

"Blood, this muthafucka is overheating," Young Syke shouted

when he spotted a stream of smoke pouring from under the hood of Puncho's box Chevy.

"Fam, we all good. We just gotta—" Puncho pumped vigorously on the gas pedal to no avail, his car still sputtered, coasting to a stop in front of the curb. "Damn!"

"Nigga I knew we shouldn't have driven this raggedy-ass car on this mission!" Young Syke glared over at Puncho, who continued pumping the gas pedal in an attempt to restart the car. "Dawg we can't be sitting here stuck on the side of the road in this piece of shit. We have to get over there to that mark ass nigga's house so we can handle our business."

Puncho cut his eyes over at Young Syke, releasing a soft growl. That last remark about his car struck a nerve. "You just gon' sit over there and talk about Stunna like she can't hear you?" Puncho asked Young Syke seriously. "Everything was all good when we were riding around bump'n that 2 Chainz. Now my shorty done ran a little hot, niggas be hatin'".

Young Syke couldn't do anything but shake his head in disappointment for taking such a risk. He knew better. No matter what, this mission had to be completed or there would be hell to pay. "Check this out fam-o, I'ma take these next few blocks on foot. A nigga gotta make sure we get this job done."

"Why you can't wait a few more minutes until my shit cool down blood? By the time you make it to the fool's house, my shit gon' be up and running again."

"Shit!" Young Syke sucked his teeth, shaking his head.

Puncho just didn't get it. Here sat two young black males, in their early 20s, dressed like thugs. Both wore snug fitted baseball caps that were pulled down around their heads. And both wore Crimson colored t-shirts. They looked every bit the part of the notorious gang their organization was built from.

"Fam-o—you ain't got no L's. Your tag light is out, and ain't a hubcap within a mile of this muthafucka. We got guns in the car, and we look like we up to no good," Young Syke reasoned with Puncho. "We going to jail if them people come through here fam-o."

Puncho shook his head, still not having any understanding of what Young Syke was trying to say. The mission would have been his first body, his first chance to show the C.M. what he was made of. There was no way he could allow Young Syke to leave him out on this mission. "They gon' think we just some young niggas having car trouble,"

Puncho explained, "Look at us dawg we young."

Young Syke wasn't trying to hear it. True, both of them were young. Puncho was 21, stood 5 feet 8 inches, and weighed 140 pounds. Syke was 24, stood 5 feet 11 inches, and weighed 165 pounds soaking wet. But the rollers wouldn't see it as two young men having car trouble. They would see two possible gang bangers in an upscale neighborhood looking for trouble.

Young Syke quickly hopped out of the car. He knew what he had to do. Arguing with Puncho wasn't getting the job done. "Blood, when I hit your phone, you need to have this muthafucka running again so you can come get me."

"But what about—"

"No buts," Young Syke barked, cutting Puncho off mid-sentence. "Do what the fuck I'm telling you fam-o. I have already wasted too much time explaining myself to you."

***

"Martina, we've come too far for you to up and want to turn back now. Where is all this sudden change of heart coming from? Everything seemed to be going perfect. Now all of a sudden you want to change it." Jonathan kneeled in front of Martina with pleading eyes.

"I don't know where it's coming from," she replied sniffling, dabbing at the tears that rolled down her cheeks. "I still have feelings for Derrick, but here I am trying to have a relationship with you. I thought it would erase my feelings for him."

Jonathan's head fell to his chest. It was not what he expected to hear.

She sighed before adding, "I don't want to hurt you, Jonathan.

I'm just trying to figure out a way to move forward in life, but I can't! For some stupid ass reason, I can't get my husband out of my head."

Jonathan stood and turned his back to Martina. He slammed his fist into the palm of his hand. "So, what am I supposed to do?" he questioned, throwing his hands in the air, spinning back around to face her. "Stop trying to be with you because you're the one that's confused?" he shouted, answering his own question.

Martina folded her arms across her chest and brought one hand to the bridge of her nose. "I don't know Jonathan. I have no idea what you should do. All of this hopping around from one relationship to the next is only making things harder for me."

"So, what are you saying?"

"I'm saying we need to slow down. I'm saying I'm not sure I even want a divorce. I'm saying—" Martina broke down crying uncontrollably. The pain she was putting Jonathan through was visibly etched deep in his face.

"Babe it's okay," he said, kneeling back in front of her. "I understand this can be hard, but I'm going to be here every step of the way to help you get over him." The sound of someone knocking at the front door distracted Jonathan momentarily.

"Are you expecting anyone?" Martina asked.

Jonathan shook his head while standing to answer the door. "You know I don't ever have people just pop up. They must have the wrong address."

Knock! Knock! Knock!

Jonathan hurried down the hall into the living room and over to the front door. "Who is it?" Jonathan asked, peering through the peephole as he waited for a response, but was met with nothing more than silence. "Who is it?" Jonathan asked again, this time much louder, but when he still got no reply, he unlocked the bolt to peek outside into the darkness.

Bok! Bok! Bok!

Young Syke dumped slugs through the door as soon as it began to open. When he noticed the door was only partially open due to the chain lock, he kicked it in to find Jonathan crawling across the floor covered in blood.

"Please—I don't have any money," Jonathan weakly pleaded as blood rolled from the corners of his mouth.

Bok! Bok!

Syke emptied two more rounds into his body, leaving Jonathan's brains scattered around the living room floor.

Syke peered around the living room, debating if he should do a quick search for anything of value, but the sound of several feet shuffling around in the apartment prompted him to abandon that idea. The police would surely be there at any moment, so it was in his best interest to get the hell out of there.

Adrian Dulan

CHAPTER TEN

A MATTER OF TIME

Ever since Staxs's body was discovered behind the abandoned warehouse, Slim had been forced to keep April on an even shorter leash. Slim had suspected April of being the one who killed Staxs, but with little or no proof, he had to let his assumptions go. Yet, with three kilos missing from the first mission April was sent on, and now eighty-eight thousand floating around in the streets, the shady jack moves that weren't adding up before were starting to add up now.

Slim sat at home in his oversized leather office chair. He was in deep thought as he realized that there was something definitely going on with April, something that could be seen in her eyes and felt in her presence. The woman that once used to back up and bow down to the slightest menacing glare, now stood strong with a killer intensity that matched Slim's. Something was going on that had boosted her confidence. Something that even made her confident enough to stand defiantly against Slim.

Slim was by far no weakling. He stood 6'2 with 235 pounds of solid muscle and was highly favored as a look-alike of Treach from the old-school hip hop group *Naughty By Nature*. He was convinced that for April to be standing up to him, she had to have done something to make herself believe she had somehow established the upper hand. He watched April on his security cameras as she quickly finished with her morning duties. He froze the camera on a frame that only showed April's face and stared into the monitor, gazing deep into her eyes. Her eyes told the story of someone else that he knew, a person he had only come to know when he looked at himself in the mirror.

"Do you need anything?" April asked, slipping into Slim's home office from the doorway. "Because if you don't, I'm about to lay down and watch my morning shows."

Slim unfroze the camera and turned his full attention to April.

"Naw, I'm good," he replied." But I do need to bark at you about some important business."

April sauntered into the office like she was auditioning for the next *Hood Top Model*. She wore flip flops and extra tight low-cut booty shorts with a white wife-beater on. Had Slim not been a man that was so in tune with running his business, he could have easily been distracted. April was very skilled in the art of manipulation. One would surely have to know what to overlook, or they could get caught up in something they might never find their way out of.

"I want you to go down to *The Lounge* this evening and meet up with some of Staxs's old crew. I'm putting you in charge of them. I figured it would be best if you got a little more involved in the action and got to know them."

April frowned. "Why I gotta fuck with Staxs' people?" she snarled, thinking it was Staxs' people that killed Jonathan, and Staxs's people that also scoped out her family. "I hate them dusty ass Eastside niggas. They always be on some ole scandalous ass shit!"

Slim studied April for a moment, remembering what he had been thinking of her earlier. *This bitch sure must be feeling herself to be snapping like this,* he thought. *I wonder what she has done, or what the fuck she got up her sleeve?*

"Well, it's not like I can just go out and hire someone off the streets to pick up where Staxs left off," Slim explained. "The game don't work like that. Now seeing as though you were Staxs's go-to person, I'm putting you in charge of that nigga's people as well. If you got a problem with that, deal with it! This ain't about you, and you ain't running a muthafuckin' thing around this bitch."

April sensed his whole demeanor change. One minute he seemed to be calm, cool, collective, and in the next, he seemed to be ready to get dead off in her ass.

"So, this is how it's going to be in order for me to pay my debt?

You're just going to keep putting me in these fucked up situations until something really bad happens to me?"

He chuckled. "This isn't about trying to figure out a way to put you in some kind of twist. Don't you think if I wanted to off you, I could kill you right now, seeing as though you sitting right here in my shit?" He paused, allowing the reality of the situation to settle in. Unbeknownst to April, her slick comments weren't doing anything but bringing her one step closer to death. Slim wasn't about to keep playing games with her. "Now that we have an understanding, in order for us to get this money out here, we gotta move like we wanna get this money out here."

"Since when did this thing become a thing about *us* getting money?" she asked. "I thought I was only around to pay off a debt. I damn sure haven't been making any money."

Slim grabbed a blunt out the ashtray, leaned back, and sparked up the blunt. "It's always been a *we* thing," Slim replied. "You was just too consumed by your own selfish desires. You got greedy and stole from a nigga. You made the savage come out a nigga and show you who the fuck you was fuckin' with."

April broke eye contact with Slim, knowing in her heart that he spoke the truth. She wouldn't dare continue taking Slim down memory lane out of fear of what he might do. "So, when am I supposed to start making some of this money, you're speaking of? Seeing as though I'm putting in all of the hard work?"

"Immediately," Slim exclaimed. "Your debt to me will be considered paid as long as we can both walk away from this game as very wealthy people."

April appeared to give thought to Slim's offer, but something wasn't quite adding up. "Why me? Why not one of them other niggas out of your circle?"

Slim took a long hard pull from the blunt and inhaled a cloud of white smoke through his nostrils. "Because I can't watch them other niggas like I can watch you," he replied. "The feds are looking for me to show my face back in them hot ass streets, but I ain't ever gon' do no dumb ass shit like that. I'm moving everything through you from now on. That's the plan, and that's the way this shit is going down."

April couldn't do anything but look at Slim with newfound respect. Slim had this whole thing planned out since day one.

While everyone was sitting around thinking Slim would get out and try to control the game the way he used to, Slim switched everything around. Now no one would ever see him coming, or better yet, see him leave when the game was over.

"I'm in," she stated firmly. "If this plan of yours gets my debt paid, and my family off the hook, why not. But there are a few things that I feel like I'm being forced to do that I shouldn't have to do if we're partners."

Slim smirked at April, then blew a huge cloud of smoke across his desk, into her face. "Some things are nonnegotiable. That pussy down there between your legs belongs to me! And you still gotta stay here with me and move the way I tell you to move."

April stood, obviously frustrated, and started out of his office. "Don't you see I'm still fuckin' talking to you?" Slim barked.

April stopped mid-stride and glared over her shoulder with that menacing look Slim had begun to notice on her more and more. "Are you finished yet?"

Slim released a forced laugh. He knew in his heart what he would have to do. April was a killer now, and there was only one way to deal with a killer when you could no longer control them.

"Yeah, I'm done, bitch. Go on and watch ya little punk ass shows. I'll have that list ready in a minute, then you can get out there and collect my money."

***

It had been two dreadfully long weeks since Martina walked into the living room and found Jonathan's brains blown clean out of his head. The mere sight of small chunks of gray matter scattered around the living room floor almost pushed Martina over the edge. She needed to talk to someone and fast. The horrific visions that plagued her mind made her feel like she was losing touch with reality.

Martina sat outside in her car, staring down at her cell phone. She had been contemplating whether she should contact Derrick or not. The loss of Jonathan only intensified her desire to want to be back with him. At times, Martina called Derrick's phone just to hear his voice. For some reason, whenever she called, he fussed about someone that was supposedly stalking him. Martina had the slightest idea who the stalker could be. Her only concern was listening to his voice. After finally building up the courage to call Derrick once again, she sat silently and listened as he yelled at the top of his lungs.

"Hello! Look you crazy, peeping Tom ass, black mutha—"

"Derrick!" Martina's sweet voice could freeze the hardest man's heartbeat. He was speechless, surprised that Martina had contacted him. "Do you have a minute so that I can talk to you?" The phone line was so deathly quiet that Martina had to check the duration of the call to make sure the timer was still running. "I know you're probably mad as hell at me, right now. You might even want to call me all kinds of bitches and hoes, but I need you, Derrick. I can't continue to live another day without you in my life."

He sat silently on the other end of the line, choked up. He struggled to formulate the words that might express the way he was feeling, but nothing came to mind.

"I'll understand if you don't want to talk to me," Martina continued. "If you'd like, I'll hang up and do my best to try and never call you again."

Derrick continued to remain silent for a little while longer. Just as Martina started to hang up the phone, Derrick spoke, "How have things been going for you?"

Those seven little words meant so much to Martina that she softly cried, fighting with all her might to try to hold herself together.

"I've been—" She started but stopped when she heard Derrick's son crying while he rocked him gently in his arms. "Is that a baby I hear?" she questioned, puzzled as to why a baby was anywhere near Derrick. He damn sure wasn't anyone's daycare worker, nor did any of his friends have kids.

"Yes, it is a baby you hear," he stated firmly. "I have a son. His name is Derrick Jr."

Martina almost fainted and hit her head on the steering wheel. "You had someone pregnant while you and I were together?" she asked in disbelief.

"I didn't know she was pregnant," Derrick explained. "All of this is something that kinda just happened. There is no way I would have ever planned to have a baby. I didn't know I was even ready for a baby—" He paused for a moment, eagerly waiting to hear Martina's response. When the phone line remained silent, he continued explaining how it all happened, but the phone vibrated, indicating that he had a new notification. Martina had disconnected the call.

"I wonder why she's calling all of a sudden?" Erica asked, startling Derrick as she walked up behind him with a bottle in her hand. "Does she know about me?"

"Wow!" Derrick exclaimed, spinning around. "So, we're eavesdropping on each other now?"

Erica kissed him on the lips and scooped the baby out of his arms. "You're my man now, and she already had her turn."

Derrick couldn't do anything but chuckle softly. Erica had found herself a permanent place in his life. But even though Erica was now the mother of his child, Derrick still secretly missed his wife.

***

Electronic bells sounded, indicating someone had just entered Derrick's store. "Good morning," Cynthia greeted from the checkout counter to someone she believed to be just another customer. "Welcome to *DF & Accessories*. Is there anything that I can help you find today?"

Martina made her way over to the checkout counter. "Yes, is Derrick available?"

"He sure is, but I'm not exactly sure where he's at in the store, right now. Who should I tell him is asking for him?"

Martina gave her best *bitch please, you should know* look. "My name is Martina, I'm Derrick's wife," she explained.

Glocks on Satin Sheets

The young clerk hurried off to locate her boss. In the back of Martina's mind, she began to wonder had Derrick possibly slept with the beautiful young clerk as well. She was pretty, had long hair, and even reminded her of herself when she was a little younger.

"Ahem!" Derrick cleared his throat as he walked up behind Martina, letting her know he was present. "What are you doing here?" he asked curiously.

"I had to talk to you face-to-face," Martina explained. "Us talking over the phone just wasn't good enough."

"For what?"

"So—" Martina's words trailed away into the silence. She could sense how standoffish Derrick was, but what could she expect. It's not like he didn't have a lot to be angry about. "So, we can talk Derrick?"

Derrick's olive-green eyes roamed over Martina's body from head to toe. Flashbacks of Jonathan nailing her danced around in his mind. He fought with everything he had to keep from blacking out and going ape shit.

"Follow me." He battled with his mixed feelings as he led her through the store to his office. On one hand, he was a happy father and proud to be in a position to raise his child. However, on the other hand, he still had some serious issues he needed to deal with. "Please come in and have a seat," he told her as he strolled in the office and made his way around his desk to his chair.

Martina sat down across from him. "I don't want to continue to go forward with the divorce," Martina stated confidently. "I love you too much. I'm willing to do whatever it takes just for us to get back together." Her cheeks began to tremble as she tried to hold herself together. "I need you back in my life. I can't go on living like this anymore," she said breaking down and crying uncontrollably.

Derrick was out of his chair and at her side in a flash. "I understand, Martina. I feel the same way, too," Derrick admitted, lifting Martina's chin and resting his forehead against hers. "But do you really believe we can make this thing work, in light of everything that happened?"

She slightly shook her head, pulling away from Derrick. "I wouldn't be here if I didn't," she said with tears streaming down her face. "But do you think we can?" she questioned. "You're the one that has to believe."

Derrick stood from his kneeling position and pulled Martina into his embrace. "I once read a book that said if you have faith, you can do anything."

Martina giggled softly peering up at Derrick with loving eyes. "What book might that be? I've never known you to be the type to read the Bible."

He chuckled before giving her a long passionate kiss. "Just because I've never really believed in the Bible, doesn't mean I didn't have faith."

***

Smack!

"How dare you!" Erica yelled, after reaching back and slapping Derrick as hard as she could. They stood in the bedroom with Jr. sleeping "Do you think you can just walk in and out of my life? You promised me and your son a life together, and now all of a sudden you're trying to back out on us!"

Derrick ran his fingertips over his lips, checking them for blood. "I know what I promised you," he stated firmly, taking his lick in stride. "But when I made those promises, you knew I was very vulnerable."

Erica shook her head in disbelief. "Nigga you must be smoking crack! What type of man wants to be with a woman who's been passed around between his so-called homeboys?" Derrick glared at Erica, furious that she would go so far as to bring up something as hurtful as that. "If you wanna leave, then leave! But know that you're not only walking out on me, but you're also walking out on your son as well."

"You're crazy as hell. You can't come between me and my son. If I want to see my son, ain't a damn thing you can do about it."

"Keep thinking that nigga. You really don't know what type of bitch you fuckin' with."

Derrick smirked and spun on his heels to leave. He had no patience for entertaining idle threats. Jr. was his son, and no one on the face of this earth could come between them.

"Hey little man," Derrick said, looking down into his son's crib. "Did Daddy's little power ranger sleep well?" Derrick scooped his son out of his crib and planted small kisses on his forehead.

"Give him to me!" Erica yelled, startling Derrick and the baby. "I told you if you walk out on me, then you walk out on him, too. Now give me my goddamn child!"

Derrick looked on in disbelief, surprised that Erica would do this in front of the baby. "You've really lost your mind," he said, passing the baby over to Erica. "You would act an ass in front of the baby like this?" He shook his head in disappointment. "I will be the bigger person and just leave. I see you're obviously not in your right frame of mind, so I'm out!"

He left the apartment determined to go somewhere and just chill. He had overheard several of his employees talking about a laid-back spot called *The Lounge*. In light of everything that was going on, it was a perfect time to venture out to try something new. Now that Erica was acting out, showing her true colors, it made his transition back home a whole lot easier.

Twenty minutes later, Derrick was pulling up to *The Lounge*. Just by his brief observation of the outside of the building, it appeared to be a nice place. The majority of the cars parked outside were nice. There was nothing that screamed ghetto, and the building itself looked like it was recently built.

This might be alright, he thought while getting out the car. *A nice little spot that I can duck off too and nobody will know where I'm at.* He went inside and strolled over to the bar.

"Can I get you anything to drink?" A young white female bartender asked Derrick as he took a seat.

"Let me get a double shot of Crown and Coke with a double of

1800."

"Will you be ordering anything to eat with that?"

Derrick scanned the bar, looking for a menu. "I will, can you bring me a menu?"

The bartender left to make the drinks and returned with the drinks and a menu. Instead of scanning through the menu and placing his order, Derrick took the double shot of 1800 straight to the head. The warm sensation going down into the pit of his stomach proved to be just the remedy he needed. "Thank you," he said, peering up at the bartender with grateful eyes. "I really needed that." Just as Derrick scanned the menu, he felt someone intentionally bump into his chair.

"Ooops! I'm sorry, I didn't see you sitting there," a woman's voice said behind him.

He turned to see a familiar face he hadn't seen in quite a long time. "April how-how are you?" he stammered. "What are you doing here?"

April gave him a sheepish smile, then walked around his chair and took a seat on the other side of him. "I'm just here enjoying a little music and getting some alone time."

Subconsciously, Derrick scanned the dimly lit room, looking for anything or anyone that might scream danger.

"Relax," April said, placing her hand on top of his. "There is no one here but me. I've been meaning to call you so we could talk about what happened the last time we were together, but I just couldn't bring myself to do it. I can just imagine how disappointed you were with me."

Derrick took a quick sip from his glass. "You would think so, right?" he said mockingly. "So, what was all that about anyway? That was some real fucked up shit. I really didn't know what to think or do."

April took a deep breath and went on to explain everything in depth that had happened in the past and caused her to be in her current position. The puzzled expressions that continually flashed across Derrick's face told her everything she needed to know. He was definitely disappointed with her.

"My heart goes out to you," he said, skeptically eyeing April. "Why haven't you gone to the police? Why do you keep putting up with all this bullshit?"

"I see you've forgotten just that fast," April said. "They'll send someone to kill my family, just like they did with your best friend." Derrick glared over at April, obviously having no idea what she was talking about.

"What friend?" Derrick snapped.

April looked over at Derrick somewhat surprised. "You don't know?"

"Know what?" Derrick barked. "Stop playing these guessing games with me and tell me what the hell you're talking about."

"They killed your friend, the one you brought to the strip club that night."

Derrick was speechless and began to feel nauseous. He didn't know what to think or say. Was this why Martina had come running back to him? Was Jonathan a message for him to leave April alone? Whatever the case, Derrick knew in that very moment that he needed to get the hell away from April.

"Look, I gotta go," Derrick said, standing up, pulling out his wallet to pay his tab.

"Derrick don't just up and leave. Everything has already been taken care of."

Derrick slammed a 50-dollar bill on the counter, overpaying his bill, then turned to leave. "Whatever you're involved in, you're in it way over your head. I can't risk losing my life or my son's life fucking around with you. Stay the hell away from me!" He stormed out *The Lounge* with April hot on his heels. Had either of them known that they were closely being watched, the little conversation they just had might not have ever taken place.

"Did you see where she went?" Slim asked Puncho, who sat in a small booth in the far corner of the room.

"Yeah, she just ran outside behind dude. I didn't go outside after her because I figured she might see me."

Slim sat silently trying to visualize the situation. He couldn't believe April would have the nerve to try to cross him after the opportunity he had just given her.

"Are you sure it was the same guy from the strip club?" Slim continued.

"I'm positive," Puncho exclaimed. "I know it was that nigga because me and Young Syke had to ride with Mob to follow dude home that night."

Slim released a loud frustrating sigh. April held no respect for his authority and neither did Derrick.

"I guess them two love birds gotta learn the hard way," Slim spat. "I'll bark at you in a minute." Slim disconnected the call and immediately dialed one of his most loyal and trusted killers. Whenever Slim needed to be sure a job was done and done right, he called on Devil.

"I'm listening," Devil said, answering his phone in a deep menacing voice.

"Remember dude I was telling you about that we threw that little surprise party for not too long ago?" Slim said, pausing for a moment to allow everything to register. "I need you to pay fam a little visit. That nigga's pass just got revoked."

"Say no more, it's done!" Slim disconnected the call with a sinister smile quickly spreading across his face. Derrick would soon be dead, now all he had to figure out was how he was going to deal with April. She had taken his kindness for weakness, and by doing so, she crossed the line for the last time.

***

It was close to midnight and Agent McCracken was still on the job going over phone records that had been taken from Staxs' phone. From everything that McCracken could gather from Staxs' text messages, Staxs was doing a drop off the morning of his death. McCracken then compared that knowledge to information regarding the whereabouts of the rest of Slim's immediate circle at the time of Staxs' death. For the most part, Slim's hitmen were untraceable, but records showed April leaving the house forty-five minutes before Staxs' body was found. McCracken remembered a text he had just read stating, *//: She'll be there in a minute.* Now he had a name to put with that *'she'.* Now McCracken would just have to dig a little deeper to make sure that what he was on to was, in fact, the truth. He called Stevens into his office and the two of them began combing through various reports.

"Do you think she had something to do with helping them run the organization this entire time?" Stevens inquired.

"It sure would make sense if she was," McCracken stated. "That would explain her sudden interest in Emanuel Staxs Brown."

"Unbelievable, this whole time we've been looking for one of the C.M.'s key players to make a move, and they switched the entire way they move around. They made someone we would never suspect a key player, then made it look like it was all about some secret relationship."

"Do we have that tail on Ms. Jordan yet?" McCracken asked.

"Not yet. It's been hard to get anything approved, seeing as though we haven't produced any solid evidence."

McCracken fell into a moment of deep thought before stating, "I don't care what it takes, we need to make that happen."

"Do you think April might have something to do with Staxs being murdered?" Stevens asked curiously.

"It's possible. But I don't want to jump too far ahead. First, we need to make sure what we've assumed up to this point is factual, then we can go forward from there."

***

'Fly Shit Only' by Future pounded away in April's home stereo while Derrick held her in a 69-position terrorizing her pussy. Derrick had both arms wrapped around her waist with a firm grip on her ass cheeks. He slowly rocked her back and forth, running his tongue in and out of her pussy. He made sure to take his time, occasionally sucking and nibbling at her tingling clit as she struggled to give him head. Every time she lapped at the pre-cum on the tip of his dick, he sent her over the edge with pleasure

preventing her from doing anything more. Every time she tried to suck it he ran his tongue so deep inside of her that all she could do was moan. The end result was April laying her head on Derrick's leg and planting soft kisses on his thigh.

"Fuck me, baby!" she panted.

Derrick ran his tongue up and between April's ass cheeks and gently nibbled at her thighs. April felt like she was being eaten alive and nearly lost consciousness because of how good it felt. She peered over her shoulder to get a glimpse of just what Derrick was doing to her, but simply couldn't see. He was down there going ham! She ground her body into him, trying to force every inch of her throbbing pussy into his mouth.

"Eat that shit, Daddy. Eat it! Derrick!"

He sat up and flipped April on her stomach so he could fuck her from behind. Her pussy was so wet that he slid right in.

"Derrick, get up!"

Derrick pounded harder and harder causing April to cum. He watched as his dick disappeared into her pussy, growing whiter and whiter with every stroke. April was cumming so hard, her juices oozed out, smearing all over her ass cheeks.

"Derrick get yo nasty ass up!" he heard a familiar voice bark.

He grudgingly opened his eyes to see Erica standing over him with Jr. in her arms. "That don't make no goddamn sense!" she yelled. "How you gon' be laid up in my house, on my fuckin' couch, dreaming about fucking some other bitch?" She glared down at him with all the hate her little body could muster. "Give me my goddamn key back!"

He looked down to see his dick had made it through the small slit in his boxers. "Damn." He grabbed the covers, trying to cover himself. "It's too early in the morning to be coming in here with this bullshit. If you really on this trip about me leaving, don't think that it's a problem. I can sure make that shit happen."

She sucked her teeth and rolled her eyes in disgust. She really didn't want Derrick to leave. She was only trying to say something crazy, hoping he might fight to stay.

"What time is Jr.'s doctor's appointment?" Derrick asked,

sitting up to wrap the covers around himself.

"Why?" Erica fired back. "It ain't like you have to go with him. I'm his mama and his daddy, he doesn't need you for anything!"

Derrick smirked while standing and brushing past her to go to the bathroom. "I see you stay on ten with all the bullshit," he said over his shoulder. "He's my son, too. I'm going to be at every last doctor's appointment he has until he's grown!" He walked into the bathroom and slammed the door behind him. If Erica insisted on continuing with all the whining and sarcastic remarks, Derrick had made up his mind that he would be leaving a lot sooner than later.

***

Later that morning, Erica rode with Derrick to Jr.'s doctor's appointment. All she could think about was how quickly things had changed just after one brief phone call. One-minute Erica had what she believed to be a happy little family, the next she was on her way back to square one. She was used to having setbacks, but now there was a child involved, a child that might not ever get to know who his real father was.

Erica and Derrick barely said a word to each other during the ride and avoided so much as looking at each other as they walked into the doctor's office

"Yes, my name is Erica Lamberg. I had a ten o'clock appointment." Erica told the older white women that worked at the reception desk.

"You're late," she replied nonchalantly after checking her computer. "Dr. Rosewood wouldn't normally see you if you're late, but seeing as though this appointment is for a newborn, I might be able to get you in."

Erica glared at the old woman, contemplating if she should respond sarcastically. Today was not the day to be told about what Dr. Rosewood would normally do. Erica had already woken up to her man dreaming about fucking another woman, not to mention he then threatened to leave.

"Whatever," Erica mumbled, turning to find an empty seat for them to sit in.

"Do you all do paternity testing here?" Derrick asked, stepping up to the counter while Erica went to find a seat.

"We sure do," the nurse said. "You'll just have to speak with Dr.

Rosewood when he calls you back for your appointment."

Erica almost broke her neck trying to hurry to get back over to Derrick. "What, now you don't think that he's yours?" she nervously asked.

"Naw it ain't nothing like that," Derrick responded. "It's you acting like I'm not going to be able to see my son if me and you don't stay together. If I go ahead and get this test done, then I'm sure the courts shouldn't have a problem with allowing me to remain in my son's life."

"Derrick, I was just upset," Erica said apologetically. "I would never come between you and your son. Let's just talk about this later. I don't want us out here discussing our business in front of all of these people."

Derrick skeptically peered over at Erica. "Now you wanna talk like you got some sense. I'm telling you, if I hear any more bullshit about me not being able to see my son, I'm hiring an attorney."

She nodded in agreement. Even though her relationship with Derrick was on the rocks, Erica still felt she had a chance. A chance to be in Derrick's life for as long as she continued to keep her darkest secret, a secret.

CHAPTER ELEVEN

GOODBYE ERICA

Derrick drove home from Jr.'s doctor's appointment in total silence. In the back of his mind, he felt something brewing. Something just wasn't sitting right with him. Derrick thought about the DNA test that he had scheduled for the next visit. *Am I really doing the right thing? Do I need a blood test?* Thoughts of Martina and Jonathan suddenly flooded his mind. *What happened? How did April's ex even know anything about Jonathan?* There were a million questions weighing heavy on his mind that needed answers. But even beyond that, something was wrong. Something Derrick had not been able to figure out.

"Do you want me to stop somewhere and get you some breakfast before I drop you off?" Derrick asked, but Erica was still in no mood to talk. All she did was sit on the passenger side, acting like Derrick hadn't said one word to her.

Ever since Derrick asked for a DNA test on little Jr. Erica had made a vow to keep her mouth shut. All her comments had done up until that point was get her into trouble.

"I take that as a no," Derrick replied. "Seeing as though you're not going to answer my question."

By the time Derrick finally pulled up outside Erica's apartment, Erica was boiling mad. Derrick's nonchalant attitude had her ready to blow a gasket. One minute he claimed to be madly in love with her, and the next he was trying to walk out of her life.

Boom!

Erica slammed Derrick's car door so hard that Derrick thought she had surely broken something.

"See I'm not about to keep putting up with all this extra bullshit," Derrick growled, slamming his car in park and hopping out to get Jr.

"I got him," Erica snarled, strutting around to the driver side where Derrick unbuckled Jr. from his car seat.

"Man back the fuck up," he snapped. "I'm telling you Erica, you better chill the fuck out with all the bullshit."

Erica smirked. "Or what, you gon' leave us and go back home to your little cheating ass wife?" She walked up to the front door and unlocked it for them to go inside. "You ain't going to do nothing but run your ass right back to me once shit goes wrong," she was fussing so much that she initially didn't notice a man sitting in the living room with a gun pointed at them.

"Come right on in," Devil said, flashing a wicked smile full of gold teeth. "Make sure you close and lock that door behind you."

Derrick's mind reeled trying to figure out what was going on. *Man, are we being robbed? Is this somebody that Erica could possibly be messing around with?* Even in light of all the other questions that suddenly popped up in Derrick's mind, one stood out as clear as a hot summer's day, *or does this have something to do with April?*

"What's this about?" Derrick inquired as Erica closed and locked the door as she was told. "Whatever you want, just take it and leave. I have a newborn baby in here, and I don't want any problems. I'm begging you, bruh, don't do this in front of him."

Devil stood from the sofa and slowly made his way over to a standing Derrick. Just as Devil came face-to-face with Derrick, he brought the butt of his gun crashing down on Derrick's forehead.

Smack!

Erica screamed out in fear as Derrick's knees buckled. "Derrick!" Erica yelled once he hit the ground. She rushed over to help him, but Devil wasn't having it. He caught Erica mid-stride and hit her so hard that the sound of her jaw breaking echoed off the walls.

"Please stop," Derrick pleaded, cradling his son as a steady flow of blood dripped into his face. "I'll give you whatever you want. Just please, don't do this."

Devil glared down at the crying infant Derrick held tightly in his arms. "Nigga if you don't shut that little punk muthafucka up, lil daddy gon' get some too. Now go have a seat in one of those chairs over there." Devil turned his menacing gaze on an unconscious Erica. "Bitch wake yo ugly ass up," he snarled, reaching down and grabbing Erica by her collar. "I'm trying to have a little fun with you like ya mans over there did with, April."

Derrick's heart felt like it skipped a beat when he realized why it was all happening.

"I swear, I haven't seen April since—" Derrick paused thinking about his encounter with April at *The Lounge*.

"Last night," Devil said, finishing Derrick's statement as he pulled Erica across the floor. "I already know, that's why I'm here."

***

Slim sat in the comfort of his home, bored to death. He wanted to be out in the streets, but with everything he had going on, he couldn't allow himself to be seen anywhere other than where he was right then.

He flipped from one channel to the next while April sat on the other side of the bed trying to read a book. He could tell April was catching an attitude about something, but whatever it was, it couldn't have been too bad because she simply kept huffing and puffing and smacking her lips like somebody was getting on her nerves.

"Could you please stop doing that?" she snapped, tired of sitting there listing to Slim turn the television from one channel to the next.

He smirked at her and turned the volume up. "Ain't nobody making you stay in bed. You can always get up and go find something else to do." His throw away cell phone rang, and he pulled it out before tossing the remote between the pages of the book that April was trying to read. "Take that and see if you can find me something to watch while I take this call."

Grrrrr, I hate him! April thought, snatching up the remote and immediately turning the TV to the news. Before she could drop the remote on the bed, she noticed a news reporter standing in front of an apartment building that look like it had Derrick's car in the background. She drew closer to the screen and strained to get a better look. "Oh, my God! It is his car." She hopped off the bed in a flash while turning the up the volume.

"This evening police responded to what they assumed to be a home invasion. But when they arrived on the scene, they found it to be much, much more. Sources say that police were called to 2201 North Penn when neighbors heard the cries of a man and a woman calling for help. Shortly after authorities arrived on the scene, they heard a small child crying in the apartment. After several attempts to get someone to open the door, police finally broke the door down, stumbling on something they never expected. The child's father had been brutally beaten, shot, and left for dead while the child lay crying merely inches from where its mother lay dead."

April gasped. *How could this have happened?* April thought. *Did Slim find out I saw Derrick at The Lounge?* All types of questions flooded April's mind as she scrambled to get to her phone. After a quick search of all the hospitals in the metro, she knew exactly where Derrick was.

"If all of this is because of me," April said as she fought to control her emotions. "I'll never forgive myself."

***

Agent McCracken stood in the middle of a gruesome crime scene, peering around at the carnage that had been left behind. Erica's body lay naked on the floor before him, with her face so badly beaten she was unrecognizable. A foul odor of human feces lingered in the air. McCracken gagged and quickly pulled out a white handkerchief to cover his mouth and nose.

"Whoever did this wanted to make a public announcement," Stevens said, standing just behind McCracken scribbling down various notes. "But what surprises me the most is they killed her, but not Mr. Walker. Either it was a crazy ex-boyfriend wanting to get revenge, or it was some sicko out to make a mark in the art of killing. Either way, the homicide detectives will have their work cut out for them."

McCracken shook his head and glanced over to where they found Derrick tied up on the floor. A huge blood stain covered the floor, where his body once lay. The police had no leads as to who would do such a thing, or why. But as McCracken stood tossing different scenarios around in his mind, the perfect piece to this puzzle suddenly materialized.

"Someone wanted Derrick to suffer," McCracken stated softly, still peering at the huge blood stain in the carpet. "They wanted Derrick to see his girlfriend get raped and murdered. They wanted to torture each of the victims until their bodies gave out."

Stevens appeared to be struggling to give any credit to McCracken's line of reasoning. "But why would they do that?" Stevens asked, looking at McCracken curiously. "We're dealing with your average everyday hardworking people. What on earth could they have done to someone to warrant this?"

McCracken slowly shook his head. "It's not what they could have done, it's what he—" McCracken gestured over to where Derrick's body once lay. "Might have done. Think about it, why are we here?"

"Because we're investigating Derrick due to his dealings with—" Stevens gave McCracken a look of surprise that indicated he now understood. "April!"

"That's right," McCracken agreed. "Ever since Slim was released from prison, look at what's been going on. Derrick's best friend gets killed. Now his girlfriend and almost him. To anyone on the outside looking in, they might not be able to understand what's going on. But seeing as we knew the sky would rain down blood once Slim was released— it's safe to say it's raining now."

Stevens pulled at his necktie, loosening it. The air in the room suddenly felt hot to the point of being suffocating. "So, what do you say we do now?"

"I say we—" McCracken was distracted by a young female agent quickly approaching.

"Excuse me," she said in a hushed tone. "Sorry to interrupt you. I was just informed that April Jordan just walked into the hospital where Derrick Walker is. Seeing as though we haven't been able to get eyes on her up until now, what do you want me to do?"

McCracken glanced over at Stevens and gave him a look that said the news had just made his day. "I don't want you to do anything," McCracken stated. "Agent Stevens and I were just on our way over there. If anything, have whoever has eyes on April ensure that she doesn't leave."

***

April sat alone on an empty row of chairs, crying her eyes out. The harsh reality of where her life had ended up came bearing down on her conscious relentlessly. People all around her were dying or at risk of losing their lives. The negative seeds she had planted in the past had grown and were now choking out the good progress she had made in her new life.

As she sat alone in the lobby of the hospital, she said a silent prayer in hopes that Derrick would live. He didn't deserve anything that happened to him because of her. He was a hardworking man that had simply gotten involved with the wrong woman.

"Excuse me, April Jordan is it?" April looked up to see two unfamiliar, middle-aged white men standing over her.

"And you are?" April asked.

"My name is Luther McCracken, and this is Agent Stevens from the

D.E.A. I was hoping I could have a word with you? That is, if you have a moment."

April nervously glanced back and forth between both men. She knew trouble was brewing but did her best to keep her composure. "What can I do for you?"

"Well, for starters, what is your relationship with Mr. Derrick Walker? I can see that you appear to be very much emotionally attached to the man. Wait, excuse me, the married man."

"Derrick was my boss when I worked at his clothing store. We grew to become good friends, and to learn that something as crazy as this has happened to him and his family, literally breaks my heart."

McCracken smirked at Stevens who seemed to be studying April's every move. "When you say good friends, is that like BFF or I'm sleeping with the boss type of friend?" McCracken continued.

April cracked a half smile instantly picking up on McCracken's sarcasm. "Would one of you mind telling me what my relationship with Derrick has to do with what happened here?"

McCracken burst into laughter in April's face. "Ha! You can't see how this has anything to do with you?" he asked in disbelief. "You are unbelievable. Let me be clear with you about something, Ms. Jordan. I hate to play games with people. Now, I have dead bodies popping up all over the city, and in one way or another, they are all connected to you. If you wanna stand here and act like you're the slickest fox in the whole wide world, I'll gladly throw your slick ass in jail. Until we have this whole thing all figured out, I'm onto you. And once things come to light, I'm going to go slap your dope dealing boyfriend with this pretty little indictment called R.I.C.O." McCracken drew one step closer to April, who rose to her feet looking nervous. "Now I'm giving you one chance and one chance only—get to talking!"

April took a nervous glance at everyone who sat scattered around the lobby. She was no dummy when it came to playing chess against the feds. Almost every man she had been with in the past were either ballers or niggas with the feds on their heels for one reason or another.

"Look you can ask me whatever questions you wanna ask me, but first I'm going to need to call my lawyer. And second, you'll probably need to go ahead and get that indictment."

McCracken flinched as if he were about to do something that would surely land him on CNN news. "Okay, smart ass," he spat. "You wanna play games with the big boys? We'll be in touch," he stated as he and Stevens walked off.

April was left standing in the middle of the lobby clueless as to what had just happened. The feds knew her by name, and somehow, they had put together a story linking her to the killings that were going on around the city. Her first thought was to take what little she had and leave Oklahoma City for good. The thought seemed like it would be a pretty good idea, but the feds knew her by name. She would have to talk to Slim to see if he could figure out a better way to deal with the problem.

***

"Ahhhh!" Derrick awoke screaming at the top of his lungs from what he thought to be just another nightmare. He struggled to sit up and a pain shot through his head, causing him to wince. He squeezed his swollen eyes shut as he attempted to block out the pain.

"Babe you're going to hurt yourself so lay back down."

He opened his eyes, instantly recognizing his wife's voice. "Martina," he whispered, barely able to speak." What happened? Where am I?"

"You're safe now," she assured him. "You pulled through this thing exactly like I knew you would. Now everything is going to be alright."

He slowly looked around his hospital room, trying to remember how the hell he ended up there. He had no memory of being brought to the hospital. Nor did he have any idea he had been shot and beaten within inches of losing his life. All he could remember was Jr.'s cries echoing in his mind.

"Where's my son?" he asked with fear in his eyes as his memory returned. "Where is he?"

Several nurses suddenly rushed into the room to calm him. They gave him a shot and then left Martina to explain to Derrick what had occurred with his son.

"I was trying to tell you they had him in the West wing, but you didn't give me a chance," Martina said, looking at Derrick with loving eyes.

"I'm sorry I yelled at you," Derrick explained. "I was just

afraid something might have happened to Jr." Derrick sighed, relaxing a bit as the medication he had just been given flowed through his system.

There was a soft tap at the door followed by, "Mr. and Mrs. Walker, my name is Agent Stevens, and this is Agent McCracken from the F.B.I. I know that right now is a very difficult time for the two of you. But it is very important that we have a word with you."

Martina glanced down at Derrick who appeared to be barely hanging on to consciousness. "Can't this wait? Can't you see my husband has been through hell and—"

Derrick took hold of Martina's hand and gently squeezed it. "It's okay," he says in a raspy voice. "I can do this."

Adrian Dulan

CHAPTER TWELVE

IS THAT THE FEDS

"What makes you think I'ma just up and walk away from everything I worked my ass off to build?" Slim questioned April, who
had pleaded with him for the past week to leave the city. "Fuck them bitch ass crackers! We've been laying low for a whole week. Ain't shit happened, so I think it's time for us to get back on our grind. If them muthafuckas ever come and try and shut us down, at least we'll be caked the fuck up and ready for whatever!"

April glared at Slim. "Fine, if you feel it's in our best interest to get back out in them hot ass streets, it's your fuckin' call!" she yelled.

She stormed upstairs to get ready to leave. She knew in her heart that she hadn't been completely honest with Slim about everything he needed to know. She was damned if she did, and damned if she didn't. Slim wouldn't have any mercy on her if he found out she had told Derrick everything about him.

After April was finally dressed and ready for the day, Slim gave her a quick rundown of everything he needed her to do. Even though something deep down inside her was telling her to make a run for it, April quickly pushed those thoughts out of her mind. She had a job to do, and nothing would come between her making sure that her family remained safe.

April took her instructions, slid her sunglasses on, and hit the streets. After being cramped up in the house for the past week, it almost made her feel good to be on the grind again. As she weaved in and out of traffic to get to the first thing on the days to do list, an all-black Impala suddenly caught her attention. It was initially about four car-lengths behind her, but the further she drove, the closer the car crept up on her until it was finally directly behind her. *FEDS* was the first thing that popped into her mind. She started to call Slim to tell him just how real shit was but wondered how he would react.

What would Slim really think? she thought. *Will he think the feds were on to them, or that the feds were just on to me?*

She made a sudden exit off the highway, hoping to lose her tail. She peered up into her rearview mirror and exhaled with frustration when she saw that they were still there. Panic ran rampant through her veins. Not only were the feds on her ass, but they made no attempt to hide it. She drove down Kelly Avenue until she had almost reached 36th Street. She turned into the Park Estates Housing Addition, concocting a plan to put distance between her and the car following her. She pulled up and stopped at a stop sign where a group from the Steady Grinding Boyz crew stood skeptically eyeing her Jeep. She hoped their attention would be drawn to the black Impala behind her, but each of the young goons stood eyeing her suspiciously. She had become their supplier after Staxs was killed, and the fact that it wasn't a collection day had the Steady Grinding Boyz wondering why she was creeping through their hood.

April drove on, going deeper into the Park Estates Addition when the car behind her suddenly sped up. It aggressively pulled up to her bumper and then swerved to the outside lane like it was trying to drive around her. She pulled over to the curb, hoping whoever was inside the car kept driving, but was surprised when something totally unexpected happened. Two men wearing ski masks hopped out the passenger side front and rear doors aiming fully loaded automatic weapons at her.

Plattt! Plaattt! Plaaatttt!

Bullets ripped through April's Jeep like it was made of cardboard. April's mind screamed go, but her body was slow to react. She cringed and ducked low while simultaneously slamming her foot on the gas pedal. She drove about ten yards without being able to see before she crashed into the back of a Cadillac.

Boom!

The airbags released, knocking her unconscious. The two shooters quickly approached April's car to finish the job. Just as they ran alongside April's Jeep, a new burst of gunfire startled both masked men, causing them to scramble and duck beside the

Jeep for protection.

Bok! Bok! Bok! Bok!

Lil Menace's 40 caliber sounded like a cannon going off. Outsiders coming into Park Estates dumping was damn near like a juicy steak being left out on the counter in a house full of roaches. Lil Menace was soon joined by his fellow bangers from the neighborhood.

Bok! Bok! Bok! Pow! Boom!

Before the two shooters had time to adjust, gang members were pouring out of every house on the block. Niggas was on their ass.

"Ahhhh!" One of the masked gunmen cried out, prompting the other to make a dash back to their car where the driver waited with the engine running. He jumped in the car and noticed the driver was dead. "Fuck!"

Boom! Chik! Boom! Chik! Boom!

Slugs hammered into the car, knocking out a window, and paralyzing the last shooter in fear. He prayed for the gunfire to stop long enough for him to push the driver out the car so that he could take the wheel. Just as his prayers were answered, the shooter looked up and found himself staring down the barrel of a sawed-off shotgun.

Boom!

"Grinders, Cuz!" Crazy Cuz barked, glaring down at the dead intruders inside the Impala. "Make sure that bitch isn't alive, Cuz. One-time gonna be here any minute now."

***

April lay in her hospital bed staring up at the ceiling, trying to figure out what the hell had happened. She had spent the last week laying low from the feds, trying to stay out of sight and out of mind. She was baffled by the idea of someone trying to kill her but was even more confused by the fact that she was handcuffed to the bed.

"Hello, my precious," McCracken said with a smile as he

walked into April's room. "Glad to see you made it through that bloody shootout that left three more people dead on my streets."

April glanced up at McCracken like he was crazy. "I don't know anything about three people getting killed. But I do know someone was following me in a black Impala and tried to kill me. I was thinking since you're the police, you might be able to fill me in on what was going on? You are the F.B.I, right? Doesn't that have something to do with intelligence?"

McCracken chuckled softly. "*Intelligence*," he repeated through laughter. "I'd say by the time you get through studying law work on how to win a case on appeal, you're going to be pretty intelligent yourself miss lady."

"Win what case on appeal?" she asked, slightly confused.

"The case that you're being arrested on. I would have thought somebody as intelligent as you would have known that."

April gasped. "So, you're arresting me?"

"Who me? Oh no, no, no." McCracken exclaimed, being dramatic. "I'm with the F.B.I. We do have something to do with intelligence, remember? Besides, looks like the state is charging you with accessory to commit murder. It looks like you and your crew got into it with another crew and well, things got a little ugly, didn't they?"

"My crew? I ain't got no damn crew! I don't know what the hell you're talking about. All I know is some car was following me, then the next thing I know I'm in the hospital with this on my arm." She lifted her arm displaying handcuffs.

"Those are some really nice cuffs," McCracken stated. "They really look good on you, too. Maybe your boyfriend Slim should think about investing in a set for himself. The way I see it, you two will be wearing matching bracelets for a long time." He smiled and spun to leave.

"Wait! Are you just going to up and leave? Isn't there anything I can do to make this right? I haven't done anything to be going to jail for."

McCracken stopped by the door and rubbed his chin like he was in deep thought. "Get a lawyer. I'll work on getting that indictment I was telling you about," he said. "After we lay everything out in front of the judge, maybe he'll let you cop to twenty. That's the only way I can see you making things right."

***

"Man, this shit is crazy," Derrick exclaimed as he walked down the hospital hallway with Stevens, Martina and his son resting peacefully in his arms. "Why should I have to give up my freedom and go into hiding while whoever tried to kill me gets to run the streets?"

Stevens shrugged. "Look at it this way, it'll only be for a little while. Besides, you'll get a lot of one-on-one time with that newborn baby of yours."

Derrick nodded, reluctantly accepting his fate. He did have a lot to be thankful for, but his conscious was starting to weigh heavy on him. Every time Derrick looked down at his son's innocent face, he saw Erica. He was forced to think about the day he would have to explain to his son about what had happened to his mother.

Stevens led Derrick downstairs to an all-black Chevy Suburban that sat parked out front. After everyone was safely inside, he then drove them to a safe house located on the outskirts of Shawnee. The entire ride, Martina sat in the back of the SUV watching Derrick's interaction with Jr. Her heart told her that the baby was not his, but what could she do? It was obvious Derrick cared a great deal for the newborn baby. She wondered how she would ever find the words to explain the way she felt without making Derrick angry with her.

Stevens pulled into the driveway of a gorgeous 4-bedroom house, announcing that they had finally arrived.

"All of this is for us?" Martina squealed, excited to look inside their temporary home, seemingly uninterested with her thoughts from just moments ago.

"It sure is," Stevens stated. "Just wait until you see everything this place is loaded with. You are not going to believe what I'm about to show you." Stevens walked them inside, and just as he suspected, both Derrick and Martina were very much pleased. Every room was fully furnished from top to bottom. New appliances for the kitchen, leather furniture for the living room. Even Jr.'s bedroom was set up like a little nursery.

"This is utterly amazing," Derrick said, standing in the middle of the living room, taking in the beautiful home. "And you all call this a safe house?"

Stevens softly laughed, trying not to wake Jr., who continued to sleep peacefully in Derrick's arms. "We sure do. When the feds seize property, we get it all. We decide what we keep or sell. And in this case, we just decided to keep everything just the way it was." Stevens allowed the couple a moment to take in the beauty of the home they would be living in. After a small tour, he showed them how to work the camera system, gave them a set of keys for their car, and prepared to leave. "If you need anything, and I do mean anything, please don't hesitate to give us a call." He gave Derrick a firm handshake and opened the front door to leave. "Under no circumstance are you ever to try and leave this community. Do I make myself clear?"

Derrick nodded and Stevens left.

"Derrick, there is something I've been meaning to talk to you about, but I wasn't quite sure how to say it."

Derrick sighed, and then put Jr. in his carrier. "What is it, Martina? Say whatever it is you have been meaning to say, just as long as this doesn't turn into an argument."

A look of worry flashed across Martina's face. Derrick could tell she was very reluctant to say whatever it was that was troubling her. "Spit it out!"

"Promise me that you won't get mad."

"Just say it Martina, you're going through all of these changes for nothing."

Martina took a deep breath, took a nervous glance at the sleeping baby, and set her eyes back on Derrick. "Okay, I don't think you're the father of that baby."

Derrick looked at Martina like he couldn't believe what she

had said to him. "There ain't no question as to whether or not I'm that child's father," he exclaimed. "The only thing that's in question is are you going to be around to be my son's mother or not."

Martina's head snapped back as if Derrick's words were a slap in her face. "What the hell is that supposed to mean, are you trying to insinuate that if I don't except that baby as your child, that you're going to leave me?"

"I'm not trying to say anything," Derrick replied sarcastically. "I said it! My son's mother is dead because of me. Because of my bullshit, because I wasn't happy with my marriage. Am I supposed to up and walk away from this baby, leaving him without a mother or a father?"

"So, you don't think he's yours either?"

"I know this is my son!" Derrick yelled. "I'm having this bogus ass argument with you about my own flesh and blood just to entertain your bullshit."

Martina held her tongue because she knew she wasn't getting anywhere in the conversation without having some sort of proof. "Fine, maybe you're right, and I'm the one that's wrong. I'm not trying to be in a full-blown argument with you about this child. I just wanted to talk to you about what's been on my mind."

"Well, what about what's been on my mind?" Derrick countered. "Either you're riding with us, or you're not riding at all."

Martina peered over at Jr. sleeping in his carrier and then slowly sat on the arm of the sofa. She thought about Jonathan, she thought about Erica, and all the crazy things that had been happening as of lately.

Am I really willing to give up the love of my life over something like this? she thought. "I'm with you Derrick, and I always have been. I won't allow anything to come between us again, but I just wanted to make sure this was right."

He walked over to her, "it's right baby." He replied, pulling her up into his embrace. "That's my seed over there, and I don't ever want it to come down to me having to make a choice between you and him."

CHAPTER THIRTEEN

I BEEN LOYAL

"Hurry up and drag that muthafucka over here so we can throw his ass in the back," Slim ordered his goons that struggled to get Devil in the back of a van. "This fool is already tied up, and you, niggas is still having a hard time! We gots to go, hurry up!"

Devil looked up at Slim, hoping beyond hope that his boss would show some compassion for him. "Slim, you know I'll finish the job dawg. Don't do a nigga like this fam!"

Slim opened the back doors of the van while his goons fought to get Devil inside. "It's too late for all that. You should have thought about finishing the job before they blasted your face on the 6 o'clock news!" Slim watched until his young goons finally had Devil in the back of the van and then slammed the doors shut. "Make sure one of you, niggas duct tape that fools mouth shut. That nigga will fuck around and be screaming the whole ride out to the country."

Slim had Devil taken to one of his stash houses deep off in the country. The house was old with no neighbors, and it was located in a heavily wooded area. It had a barn he used for storing various shipments that came in. There was a minimum of four heavily armed men on site at all times, along with three man-eating Rottweilers. If there was ever any chance of someone accidentally stumbling across the stash house, it was almost certain they wouldn't be leaving there with their life.

After arriving at the stash house, the goons wrestled with Devil to get him into the middle of the barn. The horror in Devil's eyes was enough to make the hardest nigga feel some type of sympathy for him. He knew what Slim was about to do to him. At the sight of Slim's attack dogs tugging at their chains to get at him, muffled cries of terror fought to escape the duct tape that covered his mouth.

"Do you have any final words?" Slim asked, snatching the duct tape off Devil's mouth.

"I've been loyal," Devil cried out. "Is this how you gon' play me after all the work I don' put in for you?"

Slim glared down at Devil, seemingly second guessing his decision to kill him. Devil had been one of his most trusted killers since day one, but when Devil fucked up by letting a victim live after seeing his face, everything good he had done in the past was out the window.

"What if the feds find you fam? Are you still going to remain loyal and fade all that heat by yourself?"

Devil peered up at Slim as if he couldn't believe Slim was actually second guessing his gangsta.

"Blood, I always fade my own heat," Devil barked. "You ain't never gotta worry about that fam."

Slim looked back over his shoulder, eyeing his young goons that now held the dogs on chains. He wanted to believe Devil would hold true to the code of silence, but the penitentiary was full of niggas that fell for that.

"Ss-ss, get him!" Instantly, Slim's vicious attack dogs swarmed Devil. One dog went straight for Devil's arms, another went for his leg, and the last went straight for his face.

"Ahhh!" Devil's shrill cries of pain echoed throughout the barn as Slim's man-eating Rottweilers literally ripped the flesh from his bones. The vicious dog that went for Devil's face bit into his cheek, ripping off the whole side of his mouth, leaving his teeth exposed.

"Out!" Slim yelled, commanding his dogs to stop attacking.

The dogs reluctantly backed away and stood within a few feet ready for a second round. "I want each of you muthafuckas to look at this nigga. This is what will happen to you if you ever fail me. If I send you on a mission to kill a nigga and you fuck around and let that nigga live, this is what will happen to you." Slim walked over and picked up a gas can, then went back and began pouring it all over Devil.

"Noooo! Nooooo!" Devil cried out as Slim emptied the can of gas all over him.

"This is how you make sure a muthafucka is dead, especially

when I send you to kill them." Slim reached into his pocket, pulled out his zippo, and then lit it.

"Slim wait! Slim wait!" Devil pleaded.

"Naw nigga, you should have been more thorough." Slim dropped his lighter in a puddle of gas, instantly setting Devil a blaze.

Devil squealed in torment as his flesh sizzled.

"I want that bitch ass nigga Derrick Walker found," Slim yelled over Devil's haunting howls of agony. "I don't give a fuck what you have to do to make that shit happen. Find him and kill him." Slim turned his attention back to Devil's sizzling body. "Whenever this nigga is done cooking, bury his bitch ass out back."

***

Big Crip, the leader of the Steady Grinding Boyz had been blowing Slim's cell phone up ever since he and his crew stopped three masked gunmen from killing April. For the life of him, Crip couldn't figure out why Slim had stopped accepting his calls. One-minute business seemed to be going good between the two organizations, and the next it seemed as if all business ties were cut.

"I wonder why this nigga Slim keep ducking a nigga's phone calls?" Big Crip asked Lil' Menace, who was also a member of the Steady Grinding Boyz.

"I don't know, Cuz. You would think that fool would be glad to talk with us seeing as though we saved his bitch!"

Crip thought about Lil' Menace's line of reasoning, and concluded he was right. Crip couldn't understand it. While the rest of the city still had lots of dope flooding its streets, the Eastside was completely dry. Not so much as one crumb was being sold on any of the Steady Grinding Boyz' blocks.

"Fuck this shit, Cuz," Crip snarled. "We about to push up on them niggas and find out what the fuck is going on."

Big Crip and Lil' Menace left the Crips' spot, hopped in his

Suburban, and smashed to *The Lounge*. It was becoming ever so clear that the C.M. wasn't doing business with the Eastside anymore, but to Crip, that was a harsh reality that he wasn't so willing to accept.

"What if them niggas don't wanna front that pack?" Lil' Menace questioned. "Then what we gonna do?"

Big Crip thought about it for a moment but could sense it was nothing more than a test question. "What if they don't?" Big Crip asked, flipping the same question back on Menace. "What would you say we should do?"

"Psst, I say we rob the fuck outta them niggas! Fuck playing with them fools, Cuz. Them niggas got our blocks hot because we saved one of they people. They owe us, Cuz. They can either pay us, or we gonna get on some gangsta shit."

Big Crip chuckled softly at his young protégé. He loved the standup type of confidence Lil' Menace had. Now all he needed to learn was patience, and how to conduct business without using violence.

"Cuz you gots to chill with all that killa shit you over there on," Crip said, still laughing. "We about to fall up in their little establishment. We have to go in here using our heads not our guns to get what we want."

Lil' Menace cut his eyes over at Crip and smirked. Even though Big Crip was the O.G. from the hood, he was still way too diplomatic for Lil' Menace. Menace was taught to bust first and ask questions later. That peace treaty shit Big Crip was on was not a part of Lil' Menace's program.

After a short drive through the Eastside, Big Crip pulled into *The Lounge* parking lot, banging some old school E-40. *The Lounge*'s security ran outside in a vain attempt to get Crip to turn his music down, but only got ignored. Big Crip continued setting off car alarms until he found a place to park.

"Where Slim at?" Lil' Menace questioned two security guards that quickly approached Big Crip's Suburban.

"Don't you think you're a little bit outta your league?" One of the guards said sarcastically, walking up on Menace as he began exiting the suburban. "This ain't the place for little gang banging kids to hang out at."

"Cuz you got tha locsta fucked up," Lil' Menace spat, sizing both guards up. "I'll see either one of you, niggas one-on-one Cuz!"

"Menace!" Big Crip barked, silencing everyone. "Let me handle this." Both guards turned towards the driver's side of the SUV slightly startled by Big Crips commanding voice. Big Crip was one of them big swollen O.G.s that always kept his hair pulled back in a nice long ponytail. He had jet black skin that was almost so dark it concealed the many scars from turf wars. His menacing glare was enough to command both of the security guards into rethinking their approach to the situation. "We came here to see Slim on business, but all this extra shit is unnecessary."

At the mention of Slim's name, the bigger one of the two guards gave a quick glance at his partner. "Does he know you're coming?"

"What the fuck you think?" Lil' Menace quipped, still feeling some type of way about the comment that was made earlier.

Both security guards stood glaring at Lil' Menace, and one pulled out his cell phone to confirm Slim was expecting visitors. After a brief conversation with someone over the phone, the security guard hung up and turned his attention towards Crip.

"He said you can come in, but your little cousin here has to wait outside." Big Crip gave Menace a head nod to get back in the truck. If Slim was ready to speak with him, it would be business as usual, one-on-one.

Slim sat behind his desk watching his security monitors as security brought Big Crip down the hallway that lead to his office. He had been watching Crip ever since he and Lil' Menace pulled into the parking lot, not to mention that he also had a pretty good idea why he was there.

Security gave a soft couple of taps at the door, before entering.

"Come in—come in," Slim said, standing up from his desk with a Devilish look etched on his face. "Crip what it do, fam? Come in and have a seat." Crip cautiously entered, sure to take in his surroundings before rushing in. The Crimson Mafia wasn't a name given to this organization just because they like the color crimson. Slim and his group of goons were some straight up killers, and one would most definitely need to watch his back if he planned on staying alive.

"I guess you already know why I'm here," Crip began as he quickly crossed the room and took his seat in front of Slim's desk. "Especially seeing as though we ain't heard from you since we saved your girl."

"Grrhmmm!" Slim grunted, clearing his throat when he picked up on Crip's sarcasm. "You haven't heard from us lately because I've had a lot of other shit going on. A few things came up that I needed to give some thought to before I could make my final decision."

Crip nodded his head trying to be understanding of whatever the circumstances could be that was slowing down business. "Peep game homie, we been doing good business with the C.M for a couple of years now, and I want to continue to do so. Now I ain't come in here asking for a handout but seeing as though we saved ya ole' lady and all, I am trying to get some type of understanding why you got the Eastside starved out. We held you down, so technically you owe us! Real niggas do real things, and all we want is to get the business back poppin'."

Slim sat silently trying to put together the proper response. That last statement about real niggas doing real things struck a chord. Was he not to be considered real because he didn't front a pack to someone who had got in the way of Mafia business?

"First of all, we don't owe you niggas shit fam! You and your little crew got in the way of business and ended up killing three of my men—" Slim paused, allowing the reality of what was going on to settle in. "Now the way I see it, you lucky I ain't send my little niggas through the Eastside and burn that bitch to the ground. When a muthafucka takes something of mine, it's only right that I take something of his."

"Send them niggaz, Cuz! My Eastside gangstas ain't duckin' nothing!" Crip hopped up from his seat and stood towering over

Slim's desk. "Whatever you trying to do, we wit it Cuz. In fact, we ain't even gotta do no more talking about it."

"Is that right?" Slim calmly stood, raising a big dumb ass Judge pistol to Big Crips face. "Now normally I woulda shot a muthafucka in his big ass mouth for getting loose at the lips but seeing as though my lounge is packed full of potential witnesses, I'ma let you make it.''

Big Crip glared across the desk at Slim, wishing he could literally rip him apart, limb by limb. But the fact that Slim still had his gun pointed at his face caused him to rethink that. "You got this one," Crip said, easing towards the office door. "I'm going to raise up outta here, but remember, you are the one that started this."

Slim gave a quick nod for his security to escort Big Crip out the building. Regardless of Crip acting as if he was ready for an all-out war, Slim would never give him that much credit. He felt invincible in the streets, untouchable. If the Eastside wanted war with the C.M., then it was a war they would get.

Adrian Dulan

CHAPTER FOURTEEN

WORKING WITH THEM PEOPLE

Slim laid low at his side chick Nessee's house, awaiting word back from April's attorney. Slim had been calling April's attorney's office all day, only to be misled into thinking that nobody knew anything yet. All sorts of negative ideas ran wild in his mind. First, he wondered if April would crack under pressure if the feds ever questioned her. Second, he wondered if April suspected him as being behind the men that tried to kill her. Slim definitely had a lot to think about. To him, one tiny thing overlooked could end up being the key piece of evidence in bringing down the Crimson Mafia.

"Hey, baby, what are you in here doing?"

Slim looked up to see Nessee walking into the living room with a look of curiosity in her eyes. He knew he had been depriving her of his attention all day, but he had tons of other things cluttering his mind.

"I'm just in here trying to figure out a few things," he said, leaning back in the recliner he had been sitting in, allowing Nessee room to sit in his lap. "What's good? You getting hungry, you ready to ride out so we can go get something to eat?"

Nessee sat in his lap and wrapped an arm around the back of his neck. "I'm ready for some of this dick!" she exclaimed. "You been sitting up in this living room all day, and not once have you even thought about breaking me off."

Slim chuckled. He loved to hear Nessee talk that tough shit, like she could really take some dick. Nessee was about 5'5, thick, with bedroom eyes that could hypnotize any man into following her wildest command. She had rich dark-chocolate skin with several tattoos covering her perfectly shaped body. Not one blemish could be seen by the naked eye, so she was never hesitant to walk around in nothing more than a t-shirt and some panties.

"You are always acting like you ready for this dick," Slim continued jokingly. "But once a nigga gets up in this pussy, I bet you your little ass will be trying to run somewhere." Slim ran his hand between her legs, right up to her soaking wet pussy.

Nessee's juices instantly soaked through her thong.

"You wasn't bullshittin' was you?" Slim said, gently massaging her pussy. "You really are ready for this dick, ain't you?"

She stood and slid her thong down to her ankles before standing in front of him. She knew all the right tricks that would drive Slim mad, but before she could work her magic, Slim's cell phone rang, instantly drawing his attention.

"They can wait!" Nessee snapped, looking down at Slim who seemed to be locked in on the phone.

"Nah, this is business and I've been waiting on this call all day."

He quickly accepted the call as soon as he realized it was April. Nessee knew her place as the side chick, so Slim never had to worry about anyone getting caught up in their feelings. "What the fuck is going on?" he snarled as soon as the line connected. "I been calling your attorney all day, but muthafuckas acting like they don't know what the fuck is going on. Somebody need to be trying to tell a nigga something, y'all got me sitting over here in the dark."

"It ain't that nobody doesn't know what's going on," April explained. "I told my lawyer not to talk to you because there are a few things that happened that I'm uncertain of."

Slim sat silently listening. He already knew what April was trying to get at. He knew without a doubt that he had to play his role to the tee. If by chance April got the slightest idea that he had anything to do with what happened to her, it was over for him.

"What are you uncertain of?" he asked, bringing his tone down a notch." All of a sudden you're uncertain about everything when you're in jail, but when you're out here with me you looking at a promising future."

Now it was April's turn to fall silent, already knowing what Slim was getting at. True her and Slim had made an agreement, but the feds had April questioning whether that was a legitimate agreement or just a way for Slim to set her up for a trap. "I'm listening," he stated.

"Did you have something to do with those people that tried to kill me?"

Slim almost dropped the phone in his lap when he heard how bluntly April threw everything out there. There was no question whether the phone call was being recorded or not. There was no doubt whether April knew what she was doing by asking that type of question. The only question that stood out in Slim's mind now was whether April was working with the feds.

"What type of dumb ass question is that to ask me?" Slim fired back, trying to sound offended that April would even ask him something like that.

"I've had a lot to think about over the past month," April explained. "I don't have any enemies. So, why would anyone wanna try and kill me?"

Slim had to think fast because he could tell April was starting to suspect him of being behind the hit. "You know me better than that, April. We go way back don't let them snake ass crackers fill your head up with that bullshit."

"It's just I'm getting ready to come home, and I needed to know who is really in my corner."

"You about to come home?" Slim repeated, "You sitting up in there on accessory to commit murder, they ain't giving you no type of bond on that."

"You know like they know I didn't have anything to do with those people that got killed. The judge gave me a bond because the evidence is circumstantial. If the prosecutor doesn't come up with something concrete, they're going to have to drop the charges."

Slim pondered over April's explanation briefly. Everything made sense, but the question April had asked earlier made Slim question her intentions.

"Whenever they give you a bond, I'll send someone over to pick you up."

April didn't even bother acknowledging Slim's statement about him having someone there to pick her up. She hung up and glanced over at McCracken, hoping that he was satisfied with what she had done.

"Outstanding job!" McCracken exclaimed, pulling off his headphones, and stopping the recorder that had been taping their conversation. "Now if Slim was the one that tried to kill you, he won't be so quick to try and do it again. Being that he knows you suspect him of having something to do with trying to kill you, everything should be a cinch. You shouldn't have a problem finding out everything we need you to find out."

April sat across from McCracken shaking her head in disbelief. She knew Slim like the back of her hand. Slim would never again be as open with information like he was before. "I'm telling you it's not going to be that easy to get back in like that," April said, trying to explain. "Slim is the type that's going to sit back and watch everything I do. If he even thinks for a split second that I'm working for you, I might come up missing."

"Well, my suggestion is don't let him think it," McCracken chimed in, cutting April off. "Either he goes to jail, or you do. Find out his source, and where he's keeping his shit!"

CHAPTER FIFTEEN

NEED TO GET OUT

Several weeks had grudgingly gone past since Derrick and his small family were escorted to a safe house on the outskirts of Shawnee.

The small elderly community Derrick had been confined to, was a far cry from the lifestyle he was accustomed to. Everything there seemed much slower, even quieter, almost to the point of making Derrick feel they were all alone.

Just a few short weeks earlier, Derrick was what he thought to be every woman's man. He had a sex life that consisted of all sorts of exciting twists and turns where even he never really knew what to expect. Now, in what one might say happened in the blink of an eye, all of that had changed. He sat confined to that one house, one relationship, and the sudden change was literally about to make him lose his mind.

"For someone that claims to be happy to be back together, you sure do have a funny way of showing it," Martina said, feeling a tinge of jealousy because Derrick wasn't paying her any attention.

"You know how I feel about you, Martina. Let's not start with all the extras today. I'm just tired of being stuck up in this house. We do the same thing, day in and day out. I feel like I'm the one who broke the law and got thrown in a jail cell."

"Well, how do you think I feel?" she asked. "I'm stuck in this same, damn jail cell with you. I didn't do anything wrong, but I am trying to make the best out of an extremely difficult situation."

He grabbed the remote and clicked off the television. Martina was right, she wasn't the reason they were stuck in this house, he was.

"I'm sorry," he said, giving her a kiss on the cheek. "I shouldn't be so selfish thinking about my wants and desires like you're not in the same position I'm in."

Martina smiled and quickly slid closer to Derrick on the sofa. "Why don't we just go somewhere and have some fun? We can call Georgette to babysit and disappear into the night."

Derrick was instantly intrigued by the suggestion. The idea of doing something wrong when they had been doing everything so right brought its own degree of excitement.

"Where would we go? What would we do? Agent Stevens was very clear when he told us we should never leave the community."

A devilish look twinkled in Martina's eyes. "How do you know I wouldn't enjoy some of the same places that you and your other little dates have gone?"

Derrick was no doubt surprised by Martina's suggestion, but the idea was nevertheless still intriguing. "Are you sure you really want to get out and go to a club? I know I been acting kind of strange lately, but—"

Martina stopped Derrick from talking by giving him a long passionate kiss on the lips. "You're not the only one that needs to have a good time," she said smiling. "I'm sure."

***

Club Kavey turned out to be the perfect solution to Derrick and Martina's problem. The couple was able to get out and have the time of their lives. By the time the night began to wind down to a close, Derrick and Martina were like two young teenagers that had just found love for the first time. Each of them seemingly in a rush to get somewhere and devour the other, but neither of them was conscious of their surroundings.

"What do you want me to do now?" J-Rock asked Mob, who sat on the passenger side watching Derrick pull into the *Holiday Inn* after leaving Club Kavey.

"Pull to the back of the parking lot and call Slim," Mob instructed. "Blood gon' tell you exactly the way he wants you to handle this shit."

J-Rock did as he was told, pulling to the back of the parking lot and blending in with the darkness of the night. J-Rock then dialed Slim's number.

Slim anxiously answered on the first ring. "Where y'all at

fam?" "We back out here on the bloody north," J-Rock stated. "Pretty boy
with the green eyes just checked into the *Holiday Inn*, off 63rd. What do you want me to do now?"

"I want you to lay on them, so you can find out where they staying. If you move on them now, the Jakes is gon' be all over you before you can get outta there." J-Rock sat in silence, trying to figure out a better plan. He had no patience for sitting outside the hotel all night when they could just run in and get this over with. "Nigga, is you listening to me?" Slim asked, after several moments of silence.

"Yeah, I hear you, big homie. I'm just trying to run in and get this shit over with. I don't see the point in—"

"Nigga hold the fuck up, fam! You move the way I tell you to move. You ain't running shit around here, my nigga. All this fronting like you the one making decisions, gon' get that ass put on ice. Just do what the fuck I tell you, find out where they stay and hit me back!"

Click!

J-Rock glanced down at his cell phone, then over at Mob. "Why dude always so turnt up? One minute he wants us to do whatever it takes to put this nigga lights out and the next, the nigga on some you better wait shit."

Mob glared at J-Rock for even thinking he could come to him with his issues he was having about Slim's leadership.

"You got a problem with the way things is being done around here?" Mob snarled. "Cause if you do, you can always get the fuck out! I ain't got no problem with doing this shit myself."

J-Rock nodded and turned to focus his attention back on the Holiday Inn. If there was one thing, he'd come to understand about dealing with Mob, it was that you do as you were told, because if not, the nigga would kill you with the quickness.

***

By the time Slim finally closed *The Lounge*, it was in the early morning hours. Slim walked outside with Nessee hugging tightly onto his arm, hoping he could get her home as quickly as possible. He hated having to drive through the Eastside in the early morning hours. Not only was that the time predators preyed on unsuspecting victims, but it was also a time when the police harassed everyone moving about in the late night.

By the time Slim had safely pulled up in front of Nessee's house, she was pouting. She wanted Slim to spend the rest of the night at her house, but it was obvious he'd made other plans.

"I gotta roll, Nessee. It ain't going to do you any good to sit over there acting like a spoiled brat," he snapped.

"Why do you have to go home? Is it because that gold-digging bitch April is out? I'm surprised you would want anything to do with that hoe. She's probably working for the feds."

Slim sighed and laid his head back on the headrest. It was times like these that made it hard to have a side chick.

"This ain't got shit to do with, April! I got some other shit going on that I need to make sure gets handled."

Nessee cut her eyes over at Slim, then turned to look out her window. Playing second place to another woman had put her state of mind in a dark place. She felt like nothing she ever did for Slim was good enough, or better yet, she felt unworthy.

"Well, at least you can walk me in," Nessee conceded. "Make sure everything is alright. You already know I stay in a fucked-up neighborhood. Would it be too much to ask you to make sure I'm safe?"

He never said another word. He simply responded by doing what she asked. He grudgingly got out and walked Nessee up to the front steps of her house and impatiently stood waiting for her to unlock the door. "What's taking so long? You should have already had your keys out."

She glared at Slim for a moment, then snatched the keys from her purse and dangled them in his face. Slim started to continue to antagonize her, but the look of fear and confusion suddenly appeared on her face, causing him to spin around.

Boom! Chik! Chik! Boom! The first blast missed Slim by

inches, catching Nessee on the hip, forcing her to double over. The second blast caught her in the top of the head, literally blowing her brains out.

Slim dove over the railing that surrounded the porch, then slid and crawled until he made it back to his truck. Just as he opened the door to his Escalade, a candy blue bubble Caprice came to a screeching stop in front of him, blocking his exit.

"Fuck!" Slim yelled, slamming the door shut just as the doors on the Caprice came open.

Several masked gunmen got out, all of them aiming weapons, and all there for one purpose—to kill Slim.

Pop! Pop! Pop! Pop!

Bullets whistled past Slim's head as he ran for dear life. He bobbed and weaved in between houses, doing his absolute best to put some distance between himself and his attackers. The sound of a car engine revving to give chase urged him to run harder. Yet, the mixture of fear and a high adrenaline rush had his heart ready to explode. He needed to find somewhere to hide, and fast.

Frantically, he scanned his surroundings, looking for a place to hide. He knew if he didn't get out of sight quickly, he would surely die. Having little to no options left, he found a dumpster, lifted the lid, and dove inside.

CHAPTER SIXTEEN

NEW BOOTY

Crazy Cuz and C-Loc pulled into the carwash on M.L. King, instantly shutting the scene down. Everybody in sight had to give it up to Crazy Cuz's money green M.C. sitting on 26s that outshined everyone else's ride.

"Pull over there with the homies," C-Loc said, pointing towards Rampage and Sin posting up with a few females that he had never seen before.

"What's up, Grinders?" Crazy said, hopping out of the car, leaving the door standing straight up, stuntin'. "Who tha fuck is this y'all over here posted up caking with?" Crazy Cuz eyed one of the females that looked like Lisa Raye, then turned his attention to Sin for an introduction.

"This is Juicy," Sin said, introducing the young woman he had been talking to before introducing the other two. "The chinky eyed one is China Doll, and the dark skin one is CoCo."

Crazy Cuz walked a few steps closer to Juicy, who leaned on the hood of Sin's candy blue bubble Caprice.

"Who you know over here?" he asked as if Juicy was out of line for being on the Eastside without his permission.

"What—I can't be over here unless I know somebody?" Juicy asked.

Crazy Cuz gave her a once over. "Hell, naw you can't! We fresh out of passes around here, baby girl. If I don't know you, and the homie C-Loc don't know you. You'll fuck around and get fucked off."

Juicy giggled, appearing to be shy. "Well, it sounds like you must be the one I need to be trying to get to know then."

Crazy Cuz bobbed his head up and down, then blew in his hands like he was about to roll the dice. "Walk with me over there for a sec."

Sin sat back watching how the whole play unfolded. Even though Sin thought he was the one that had macked up on these females, he was never one to hate. Crazy Cuz was a front liner from the hood. He lived by all the codes required of a street nigga, so saving a bitch was not part of his program.

After an hour of caking with the females Sin had stumbled on, Crazy Cuz decided to move around. His cell phone had been ringing nonstop, and he had to get out in traffic to collect his paper.

"So, where you fixing to be at later on tonight?" Crazy asked Juicy, walking with her over to his car.

"I'm trying to be wherever you at," she insisted, giving Crazy Cuz a look that said she was about that business.

Crazy Cuz smiled, flashing his diamond encrusted gold fronts. "What's up on getting a room so me and the homies can slide through on you and your friends?"

Juicy glanced back over her shoulder at her friends, then stopped to ask Crazy for his phone. "Whenever you're done doing whatever it is that you do, call me. But don't have me waiting for your phone call all night." Juicy programmed her number into his phone, making sure he didn't leave without it.

"Don't even worry about that. I just gotta make a few stops, I'll be hitting you up shortly."

***

A few short hours passed before Crazy Cuz called Juicy to find out if they were still on for the night. Juicy already had a room reserved, and her and her friends were supposedly waiting for them to arrive.

C-Loc, Rampage, and Sin all rode with Crazy Cuz to go meet up with Juicy and her friends. Everyone was so excited to be able to go kick it with such a beautiful group of young women that not even one of them thought to ask where the fine young women came from? Everyone was so blinded by the allure of sex and having a good time that caution was thrown out the window. Little did they know, they were headed right into a trap.

"Let's smoke this stick before we fall up in there," Sin

suggested as he pulled the filter out of a cigarette to loosen the tobacco in it.

"Come on, Cuz. You, niggas trying to be stuck on stupid while we around all them bad ass bitches?" Crazy Cuz asked.

"Hell yeah!" Rampage insisted. "Hurry up and slam that muthafucka, I'm trying to go in here high and fuck the shit outta one of them bitches!"

After everyone had a few puffs of the wet PCP Sin dipped, they pulled into the *Residence Inn Hotel*. Everyone got out of Crazy Cuz's M.C. walking on cloud 9. The wet made them all feel like kings, and everything appeared picture perfect. Rampage was high stepping so hard that Crazy Cuz had to pull him to the side before they got to the door.

"Cuz is you good? Do you need to wait out here so you can get some air and come back down?"

Rampage gazed up at Crazy Cuz with the most sincere look he could muster up. "I'mmmm straight," he said, sounding like he was either drunk or struggling with a speech impediment. "I'm straight, I'm straight, I'm straight!"

Crazy Cuz couldn't do anything but laugh. It was obvious the homie was fucked up, but it was a room full of bad bitches less than ten feet away. Either he could stand there and waste valuable time, or he could fall up in there and see what them hoes was talking about.

"Fuck it!" Crazy Cuz knocked on the front door, expecting Juicy to answer it, but no answer. He knocked again, this time a little longer, and a little harder, and still no answer. "I know this bitch ain't played a nigga like a sucka." As soon as the words left his mouth, he heard someone unlocking the door.

"Hey, I'm sorry I took so long to answer the door." Juicy stepped aside to allow them in, looking strange. She had a much different demeanor than she had earlier that day. Now instead of some tight-fitting jeans and heels, she wore Nikes, shorts and her hair was pulled into a tight ponytail.

"Where's everybody at?" Sin asked, pushing right between Crazy Cuz and Juicy, immediately admiring the two- story hotel room.

"China Doll and CoCo are upstairs in the bathroom, getting ready," Juicy replied. "If you all would just give me a minute, I'll run upstairs and get them."

Crazy Cuz was left standing somewhat alarmed by Juicy's sudden readiness to leave. She seemed like she was in a rush to get back upstairs. He wanted to ask why she seemed so short with her answers, but as Juicy took off upstairs three men wearing masks stepped out of the downstairs bathroom aiming guns with silencers on them.

Fth! Fth! Fth! Fth! Fth!

Sin was caught in the line of fire because he was the closest one to them. His body danced as he absorbed most of the bullets. Crazy Cuz always being the first to start dumping, pulled out his hammer and let it bang.

Bok! Bok! Bok!

His first shot caught one of the shooters in the throat, dropping him. His second and third missed, so he went for cover.

Fth! Fth! Fth! Fth!

Everybody except for Rampage took partial cover behind a huge sectional. His mind told him that he was invincible, and he could feel no pain. Rampage ran full speed towards the gunmen, thinking he could beat them with his bare hands. The PCP that flowed through his system made him believe he could do anything.

The two mask shooters loaded Rampage up as he charged. He stumbled almost falling but reached out and had one of them in his grasp.

"Gotcha!"

Seeing an opportunity to put these mask gunmen on their heels, Crazy Cuz spared a quick glance, aimed and opened fire.

Bok! Bok! Bok! Bok!

One more gunman down and one more left. Rampage tugged at the fully automatic assault rifle, struggling to strip it away from the gunman. But the more he struggled, the more his adrenaline surged, and the more his adrenaline surged, the more his heart pumped blood out of several bullet holes in his body. Rampage finally crumbled to the floor from the loss of blood, failing to strip the gun away.

Crazy Cuz was petrified from the shock that his friend had been killed, so the masked gunman took aim and squeezed—nothing happened, so he squeezed again—still nothing!

Pop! Pop! Pop!

C-Loc rocked him, sending three shots to the center of his chest, dropping him on top of Rampage. Crazy Cuz took off across the room towards Rampage.

"Come on, Page—please don't be dead. Please!" Crazy Cuz rolled Rampage onto his back to look into his eyes. Rampage had that stare that was far beyond him. "Wake up, Cuz, wake up!" Crazy Cuz sat cradling Rampage's lifeless body in his arms. He couldn't believe that such a fate had fallen on a soldier like Rampage. "Where them hoes at?" Crazy yelled with tears now rolling down his face. "Go get all of them punk ass bitches and bring they ass to me!"

C-Loc took off up the stairs, no doubt ready to pistol whip Juicy and her friends. Once he reached the top step, it was nothing but silence. A deathly silence, the type of silence that signaled that something was lurking in the midst or someone was there, but you just didn't know where. C-Loc scanned the shadowy darkness of the room, looking for any of the three girls that may have been hiding. He slowly crept over to the bathroom door and gently pushing it open. Empty!

C-Loc scanned the room once again, *Where could everyone have gone?* he thought.

There were no signs of CoCo, China Doll and most importantly, no Juicy. C-Loc cautiously made his way back over to the steps, and that's when he heard a noise. Muffled cries of pain came from over by the window. C-Loc rushed across the room, lifted the blinds and saw Juicy two stories down trying to crawl away. "Slimy ass bitch!" he growled, then took off straight downstairs and out the front door. When he ran around to the side of the hotel, he saw Juicy still struggling to crawl away. It appeared as though she had broken one of her legs from jumping out of the window and landing on an air conditioner unit.

"Look at you! You thought you were gon' get away with this bullshit?" C-Loc pointed his gun at Juicy as she tried to crawl away. As she dragged one leg behind her, completely covered in blood, he noticed her shin bone was exposed and clearly sticking through her skin. "Who sent you?" C-Loc yelled, but Juicy continued crawling away as if she might somehow make it to safety. "Bitch did you hear me! Who sent you?" This time C-Loc ran up, cocked back and knocked a patch of hair out the back of her head with the butt of his gun.

"Ahhhh!" Juicy's upper body fell to the grass as she cradled her bleeding head. As she turned over to face her executioner, she confessed, "Slim, Slim made me do it."

"Slim from the Crimson Mafia?" C-Loc asked, but Juicy never verbally replied, she just shook her head yes and closed her eyes.

Pop! Pop! Pop! C-Loc dumped three shots into her face, making sure that her funeral would be a closed casket service.

Moments later, Crazy Cuz came running out the building. "Damn Cuz, you killed her. We needed to know who she was working for."

C-Loc cut his eyes over at Crazy Cuz, then back down at Juicy. "She told me. It was them Crimson Mafia niggas. That's who sent her."

***

Agent McCracken walked out of a meeting with his superiors feeling mentally drained. All the violence going on in the city streets had his bosses with their pants up their asses.

"We need to find a way to get someone inside that organization, and fast," McCracken exclaimed as he and Stevens walked down the hallway headed to the elevator.

"But how do you suppose we do that?" Stevens inquired. "The C.M. is a tight-knit crew. They only supply gangs and other smaller organizations. If we're not one of the two, then we're screwed."

Agent McCracken pressed the elevator button several times. He was anxious to get off that floor and away from the building. "Don't know how we're going to pull this off, but it has to happen. We have one month to bring the rest of Slim's crew down, or they're going to pull the plug on us."

Stevens looked at McCracken, giving him a half smile. "Look at things on the bright side. We still have a case against Slim. As long as we take out the head, then the body will fall as well." The elevator doors opened, and several people exited as McCracken and Stevens stepped in.

"You still don't get it, do you?" McCracken solemnly asked. "Just because we have Slim in custody doesn't mean the drugs and the killings stop. Slim will just put someone else in charge like he did before. We have to get his crew and his supplier. That's the only way we can put an end to all of this madness."

Stevens appeared to be giving McCracken's line of reasoning some thought. "I'll get in contact with April Jordan to see if she's found out anything new for us. In the meantime, I have a special team that I've assembled that I think might be of some interest to you."

McCracken peered over at Stevens slightly intrigued. "To do what?" "Exactly what we need," Stevens exclaimed.

***

Just a few short days had gone by since the tragic murder of Rampage and Sin. Several members of the Steady Grinding Boyz sat around mourning the loss of their fallen comrades before making their way to Sin and Rampage's funeral. The whole set showed up to pay their respects.

Lil' Menace sat in Big Crips Suburban in front of Crips spot, banging *Dreams and Nightmares* by Meek Mill on repeat. He was taking the loss of Rampage a lot harder than everyone else because Rampage was his day one road dawg. The two had grown up together, got put on the set at the same time, and they even caught their first body together. Losing Rampage was like losing a brother, and Menace had no idea how he was going to deal with the mental anguish. It was truly unbearable.

Lil' Menace took a long hard pull from a blunt, trying to smoke it all in one hit. No matter how much he smoked, the pain he carried for his fallen comrade was still there. No matter how much he drank, he could still feel that hollow space in the center of his chest. His best friend was gone, and there was nothing he could do to fill that void.

Big Crip stood on the porch of his spot, watching as his young protégé tried to smoke and drink all his pain away. His heart went out to his young soldier, but that was a part of the life they had chosen to live. Another hardship of the game that Lil' Menace would have to learn how to deal with. Sure, the loss of his close friend left him bitter and feeling completely lost, but soon, he would taste sweet revenge in a manner that was like no other.

Crip walked up to his Suburban, got in, and prepared to leave. Big Crip was never the type to come with any pep talk to uplift his grieving homies. It was already known throughout the streets that if you took one of his, he was going to take ten of yours. It was only a matter of time before he made that understanding clear. The C.M. was due for a reality check.

"Pass that blunt, Cuz. I need to get my head right before we get there." Crip fell in line with a small caravan of Grinders that followed closely behind Rampage and Sin's family.

Any other time the streets would be buzzing with all sorts of action, but today, everything stood still. It was the calm before the storm.

When everyone finally made it to the funeral home parking lot, all the Grinders waited outside to allow the immediate family to get their final viewing moments first. Ms. Jackson, Rampage's mother could be seen struggling to get out of her daughter Chanel's car. The mental anguish resulting from the loss of her son proved to be too much for her to bare. She needed help to do almost everything.

As Lil' Menace observed her struggle, he immediately got out and ran to assist her. Ms. Jackson was like a mother to the younger generation in the hood. Everybody affiliated with Rampage, or that was in his age group, loved her with a passion.

"Will you be coming in with me?" she asked Menace when they reached the funeral home's front doors.

"I-I can't," he stammered, dropping his head, trying to hide the tears in his eyes.

Ms. Jackson smiled at Menace, realizing the pain he carried for her son was genuine. She gently ran her hand over his braids to the back of his neck and gave him a squeeze. "I understand, baby, and he would too." She kissed his forehead and went inside.

Lil' Menace held the front door until the last family member had gone inside. After closing the door behind them, he turned and peered out into a sea of Grinders. The whole Eastside had shown up to give their support. Menace looked around wondering which one of them would have the heart to bring the C.M. down. He gazed off imagining the sweet taste of revenge.

Boom! Boom! Boom! Rat! Tat! Tat! Boom!

Menace was jolted out of his slight daydream by the sound of gunfire coming from inside the funeral home. He quickly pulled out his 40 cal. and tried to rush inside, but bullets came bursting through the glass doors, preventing everyone from entering.

Boom! Boom! Boom! Boom! Boom! Boom!

By the time all the shooting died down, Menace was a nervous wreck. He could only imagine how Ms. Jackson felt, or what she might have been going through. Menace bolted inside, along with Big Crip and several other Grinders. At first, he couldn't see anything but bloody bodies, and family members scrambling around looking for cover and loved ones. Rampage's coffin was turned over with his body lying partially outside of it.

"Fuck!" Menace screamed scanning the room frantically looking for Ms. Jackson. There were so many people sprawled out all over the room that it was difficult to find her, but he kept searching, pushing closer and closer to the front of the room until he finally found her.

"Ms. Jackson! Ms. Jackson!" he cried as he rushed over to

find Ms. Jackson's body riddled with bullets. Her daughter Chanel lay right beside her, eyes open, dead. She appeared to stare right into his eyes. It was almost as if she knew he would soon be standing right there. "Nooooooo!"

Big Crip, Crazy Cuz, and several Grinders ran through the whole building in search of the intruders. They ran room to room until finally making it to the back door, and then outside.

"Is that how these bitch ass niggas wanna play it?" Crip yelled at no one in particular after realizing the shooters had long since been gone. "There ain't no boundaries we can't cross from now on. You see them niggas with their mother, daughter, sister, brothas—murder them bitches on sight!"

Twenty Grinders stood in the alley, glaring down at both ends. Each Grinder made a silent vow in that very moment, that they would avenge their fallen comrades' family. "We ride on them fools tonight!"

CHAPTER SEVENTEEN

IN THE LOUNGE

Young Syke had been sent to keep a close eye on April while she opened and ran *The Lounge* for the evening. Since the threat of retaliation loomed around every corner, Slim had the Goon Squad tighten up on security. The Steady Grinding Boyz would surely want revenge for what the C.M.'s had done to them earlier, and when they came, the C.M.'s would be ready.

"Say fam-o, who the fuck is them niggaz over there in the V.I.P?" Young Syke questioned Puncho as the two sat watching three men they suspected to be possible affiliates of the Eastside.

"I don't know who them niggas are fam. But I do know if they keep flashing all that money, I'ma fuck around and rob them fools."

Syke couldn't do anything but bust out laughing. Slim kept his young hitters so starved that they would rob almost anyone just to come up on some paper.

"You wanna go over there and introduce ourselves so we can see what them niggas is talking 'bout?" Puncho asked.

"It's probably best if we did fam-o. Slim gave us a specific set of instructions, be on the lookout for the Steady Grinding Boyz and keep a close eye on April."

Puncho nodded in agreement as the two began to make their way over to V.I.P. The closer they got to the three men sitting in V.I.P, the more, Young Syke began to realize the dudes definitely weren't Eastside cats. One of the men, positioned in the middle of the booth, appeared to be the boss. He had long dreadlocks that hung down to his chest with a gaze that seemed to calculate everything going on around him. He wore a long-sleeve, black, button-down shirt with designer black slacks. His neck and wrist were so iced out, even Puncho had to wonder if they had made the right decision by approaching the guys.

"What it do fam-o?" Young Syke said, greeting the men. As he and Puncho walked up on the V.I.P. booth, neither of the three men said a word. They just sat glaring at Young Syke like he was on foreign turf. "We saw y'all over here shining on that big boy shit, so me and the homie had to come introduce ourselves."

The man seated in the center of the booth released a soft grunt. "Look at these two lil' muthafuckas." he said in a low tone to one of the other men sitting in the booth. "These lil' niggas is crazy as hell."

The man sat momentarily studying Young Syke as if he was deciding if he would introduce himself. "My name is, A.K., this my nigga Fats, and this one here is Bang," he finally stated.

Young Syke nodded and held out his fist for some dap. "I'm Young Syke and this is, Puncho. You niggaz here with somebody, or waiting on someone?"

A.K shook his head. "Nah, we just came out to enjoy ourselves tonight." A.K nodded his head in the direction of the live band, and glanced over at a section of females.

"I can dig that fam-o. But if you really trying to fuck with some bad hoes, you gotta hit a real club, ya feel me? These old heads in here ain't on nothing. These bitches are washed up, pussy got high mileage, and they flat ass broke! I'ma keep it real with you, fam-o, this ain't the place to knock a bitch. But hey, that's on you, big homie."

A smile cut across A.K.'s face and then quickly disappeared. Syke immediately caught sight of the enormous pinky ring he had on his finger. He could only assume that A.K was a big timer, stunting on him, or even probably there to do business with one of the C.M. bosses.

"Well, playaz, I ain't gonna continue to hold you up from enjoying your night. We just seen y'all over here doing it big and decided that we should come speak." Young Syke turned to leave, but suddenly spun back like he had forgotten to say something. "If you all need anything, me and the homie will be posted up over by the bar. Don't be afraid to come holla."

"Nigga did you see that fool's pinky ring?" Puncho asked, looking back over his shoulder as he and Syke made their way through the crowd.

"Yeah, I seen it. Them niggaz is probably fucking with some major weight," Syke explained. "They might even be here to fuck with Mob, or one of the other bosses. We lucky we ain't get cussed the fuck out. You know how Slim is about fucking with his money, blood is a fool with it."

Both Young Syke and Puncho hurried back over to the bar and ordered more drinks. By the time the waitress brought the drinks to Syke, Bang had already made his way over to them.

"A.K wanted to know if you had something he could smoke on?"

Puncho's face twisted up like it was the dumbest question he had ever heard.

"Hell, yeah," Young Syke exclaimed. "Tell fam-o he can get this right here for free." Syke dug into his pocket, removed a small sack of weed, and then dug out the biggest buds he could find before rolling them into a napkin and handing them over to Bang. "This some gas right here fam-o. Tell blood to bark at me whenever, for whatever." Young Syke then quickly scribbled down his number and handed it to Bang.

Bang looked down at the number, then back up at Syke as if he were about to say something, but instead gave Syke some dap and left.

"Oh, so we giving away weed now, nigga?" Puncho asked in total disbelief. "You don't even know them begging ass niggaz and you over here tricking off our weed?"

Young Syke cut his eyes over at Puncho, then turned his attention towards Bang to watch him make his way back across the floor. "That was an investment fam-o. Them niggaz was trying to see what level of the game they could fuck with us on."

Puncho glared at Syke for a moment, at a loss for words. Had it not been for the sudden sound of shots and the rush of several people running and screaming, the conversation could have gone on for the rest of the night. Shots had been fired and people were on the move, bringing the conversation to an abrupt halt.

Pop! Pop! Pop! Pop!

Syke ducked as someone fired several shots inside the club.

He strained to get a better look at the shooters, but the room was dimly lit. Syke pulled out his Glock, chambered a round, and then made a dash behind the bar.

"Where's April?" he yelled over more shots fired, and several more shrill cries of fear.

"I don't know. The last time I saw her, she was headed towards the back." Young Syke looked over just in time to see several goons headed in their direction. Judging by their eagerness to kill any and everything in sight, Syke could only assume it was the Eastside coming for their revenge. He immediately assumed that C.M.'s call for war had just been answered.

"Go get, April!" Syke yelled over the loud gunfire steadily going off in the club. "I'll hold these niggaz off until you get back."

Young Syke stood from his kneeling position and opened fire. *Bok! Bok! Bok! Bok! Bok!*

Bullets ripped through the group of shooters, causing them to splinter off into smaller groups. Just as Syke begins to think he had stopped the assault, the Steady Grinding Boyz released their own flurry of bullets.

Pldddd! Pldddd! Plddddddd!

Bottles of liquor exploded as hot slugs literally demolished the bar. Syke scurried further down the bar, trying to take cover, but bullets were coming from everywhere. There seemed to be no place the young savage could hide.

Boom! Boom! Boom! Boom!

A sudden burst of new gunfire coming from a different part of the club caused the Steady Grinding Boyz to take cover. Young Syke spared a quick glance over the bar to see why the assault on him had stopped. To his surprise, A.K. and his men were firing back.

Pop! Pop! Pop! Pop! Boom! Pow! Ping!

The extra slew of bullets put the Eastside on defense. The mob of goons that ran in shooting, now quickly back pedaled their way to the door.

"Let's go get them niggaz!" Puncho yelled, after running up

with several other C.M. members and finding Syke still behind the bar.

"Fuck that, where's April?" Young Syke fired back. "She's gone!"

"Gone as in dead?"

"Nah, she made it out the back door." Young Syke scanned the room while people literally trampled over one another trying to get out of the building.

"We need to get the hell outta here!" Syke said, headed towards another exit in the club.

"Are we just gon' let them fools come in here and dump on us, and get away?" Puncho asked Syke, stopping to turn back towards the exit that the Steady Grinding Boyz had left out of.

"Fam-o, if you go out that door, you gon' fuck around and get your face caved in. Now follow me!"

***

Slim was awakened in the middle of the night by the annoying sound of his cell phone ringing on the nightstand.

"What is it?" he answered in a raspy voice. Young Sykes voice came screaming through the line, sounding as if he were panicking. "Wait, wait, wait, calm down dawg. You straight, right? Now, tell me everything that happened."

Young Syke went on to explain everything that occurred at *The Lounge*, including his short encounter with A.K. Slim was furious. He knew the Eastside would answer his call for war, but he never expected them to shoot up *The Lounge*.

"How many people did we lose?" Slim asked.

"Man, I can't say, but it looks like a few homies got bodied. And I think we lost both guards. A lot more are hurt, too."

Slim sighed out of frustration. He grabbed the remote and turned on the TV. "*The Lounge* is on every news station in the city. Ain't no way we can ever go back to operating outta that bitch. We gon' have to find a new spot to meet up at." He sat up in his bed and cradled his head in his hands.

Not only did the Steady Grinding Boyz successfully shut down his legitimate cash cow, but they also told the world who was at war with who. The feds would surely be combing through the club with a fine-teeth comb now.

"I want you to lay low until further notice," Slim said. "By the time this thing finally blows over, shit gon' get as hot as a summer's day in Hell. I'll bark at you in the morning and lace you up on what to do next." Slim disconnected the call and immediately pondered how to capitalize on the tragic situation.

There was pure pandemonium going on back at home on his soil. What better time than now to give a green light to put an end to a potential witness? After all, he was over a thousand miles away on business, so his alibi was solid. The feds were surely combing through his club at that very moment. Why not hit them when they least expected it?

CHAPTER EIGHTEEN

STARS

Derrick drove deep inside Martina while holding one of her legs pinned back. During every long, toe curling stroke, Martina clawed
at his sweaty back. The pain Derrick administered through fucking Martina in their current position only made her cry out for more. She was addicted to the pain because it brought her pleasure.

Derrick sat up on his knees and brought both Martina's legs together. Holding her legs up by the ankles, he then slapped his dick up against her ass and slid inside her.

"Uhhhh!" she cried out, loving it.

Martina eagerly pulled Derrick deeper inside of her, longing for him to pound her back out.

Honk! Honk! Honk! Honk!

The sound of the car alarm going off startled them, but Derrick was reluctant to stop doing what he was doing. It was very seldom that Martina let him fuck her the way he wanted too, so he was trying to take full advantage.

"Babe," Martina whined, holding Derrick's waist so that he was forced to stop. "That car is going to wake the whole neighborhood up. Are you really not going to do anything about it?"

Derrick reluctantly slid off the bed and searched for the keys. Spinning around this way and that way, Martina giggled at Derrick as he stumbled around naked in the dark.

"Look in my purse over on the dresser. I think I remember putting the car keys in there last."

Derrick made his way over to the dresser, feeling around in the dark. After a brief search, and some fumbling through her purse, he found them. *Beep! Beep!* "Now was that so hard?" Martina teased Derrick as he quickly made his way back over to the bed.

Honk! *Honk*! *Honk*! *Honk*! "What the fuck?" Derrick rushed over to the window to see if he could see anything or anyone lurking outside. "Nothing," he exclaimed.

"Check the cameras," Martina suggested, sitting up, nervously wrapping the covers around her. Derrick bolted over to the small table where the monitor and controls to the cameras were. Hitting every angle around the house, Derrick couldn't find anything that looked remotely close to danger.

"Either I'm tripping, or that car is tripping. I can't seem to find anything that would make that alarm keep going off."

"It might just be a dog or pesky cat that's up under the car," Martina reasoned.

"Well, that's exactly why I can't wait to get back to the city. All these animals are just roaming around the neighborhood, it almost makes you wonder why anyone hasn't called animal control."

Martina giggled as Derrick turned off the monitors and quickly got back in bed.

Honk! *Honk*! *Honk*! Martina started kicking her feet, throwing a temper tantrum as if she were a young child.

"Derrick do something!"

He stood in the shadowy darkness of the bedroom, looking at Martina like she had lost her mind. Not only had Derrick lost his erection, but strangely enough Martina wanted him to go outside and face some unknown creature in the middle of the night.

"What if it's a bear or something, then what do you suggest I do?" "*A bear*, Derrick?" She hurled a pillow across the room at his head.

"Do something!"

Derrick began scooping up his clothing that lay scattered around the room. Even though he had lost his erection, he still wanted to finish what they had started.

"I swear—if anything jumps out and tries to eat me, you better come to my rescue."

He stormed out the bedroom and headed straight for the front door. Remembering that he had seen a hammer in the hall closet, he stopped there first to grab a little protection. "I bet if it's a wild dog or pesky little cat, it will be in for one hell of a surprise when I hit him with this."

He opened the front door and stood staring out into the darkness. An urgent feeling suddenly tugged at his conscious. He scanned the shadowy darkness, still unable to find anything dangerous. He chalked it up to paranoia and headed outside. He cautiously made his way down the long sidewalk leading to the driveway. He could only curse himself for not putting the car in the garage like Martina had insisted earlier. But what could he say, who would have known tonight would be the night the alarm started tripping?

The wind blew a stiff breeze, releasing a howl. Derrick stopped. He thought he heard something. *Crunch*! It sounded like someone stepping on a leaf or a branch. Derrick spun around to look behind him, *nothing*! He scanned the front yard and for the first time, he noticed there was no lighting. No porch light, no garage light, no nothing. He was almost in complete darkness.

Crunch! Derrick spun around just in time to get a glimpse of a dark figure moving.

Bink! *Bink*! Stars.

Mob brought the heel of his boot crashing down into Derricks' face. The extreme force of the kick sent Derrick's head slamming into the concrete, almost knocking him unconscious.

In a delusional state of delirium, Derrick reached out for his attackers, but only was met by another devastating blow.

"Wait, what are you doing?" Derrick slurred, "Help! Help!" Mob being the heartless goon, he was, instantly snatched up the hammer Derrick had dropped.

"Shut tha fuck up," Mob spat, hitting Derrick with three bone-crushing blows to the jaw. "And you—" he said to J-Rock, "—help me drag this bitch ass nigga in the house so we can finish this."

Mob and J-Rock dragged Derrick down the long sidewalk leading back to his house. Once they pulled Derrick inside, Mob sent J-Rock to kill Martina while he stayed to finish off Derrick.

"Open your eyes muthafucka! Let me see yo' eyes." *Smack*! Mob slapped fire from Derrick, jolting him back into a state of consciousness.

Derrick's eyes fluttered as he struggled to speak. His jaw lay lax and to the side, all the while his tongue moved freely as he tried to speak. Derrick coughed, trying to hack up the broken teeth that lay lodged in his throat, but the broken teeth literally ripped away at the tissue in his throat, threatening to choke him.

"Do you have any final words?" Mob snarled, peering down at Derrick with pure hate beaming from his eyes. Derrick coughed, fumbling at his throat, tears streaming from his eyes. "You ain't got shit to say now? Well, you had your chance." Mob wrapped both hands around the hammer and raised it high above his head. "This is how all bitch ass snitches should die!"

Whoosh—Splack!

Mob swung the hammer with all his might again and brought the hammer crashing down into Derrick's mouth. *Splack*! *Splack*! Mob raised the hammer once again, preparing to finish Derrick off, but the shrill cries of terror that cut through the silence of the home suddenly grabbed his attention.

Moments earlier, J-Rock ran into Derrick's bedroom and hit the lights. Martina lay curled up naked with a pillow, expecting to see Derrick. She screamed as soon as she realized it was not Derrick, but an intruder instead. "Derrick! Derrick!" she screamed.

J-Rock slowly made his way over to the bed, eyeing Martina with lust in his eyes. "You was expecting to see ya man wasn't you? Well, that nigga ain't coming back." J-Rock reached out and grabbed Martina by the ankles, struggling to force her legs apart. "Let me see that pussy, bitch," he insisted. "I bet that nigga ain't even fucking you the way you need to be fucked." J-Rock pulled Martina down to the bottom of the bed where he stood. He crawled on to the bed, then on top of Martina before quickly unbuckling his jeans.

"Please, don't do this! I'll give you every dime I have to my name." J-Rock paid Martina's cries no mind, he pulled out his throbbing penis and begin forcing his way inside her.

Glocks on Satin Sheets

"Ssss—"

"Ahhhhhh! Ahhhh!"

Mob peered down the long hallway, leading to the back bedroom. *What tha fuck is this nigga back there doing?* Mob thought. He looked down at Derrick's bloody disfigured face and lifeless body assuming he was dead. "Let me go back there and make sure this nigga finishes this job," he muttered.

Fth! Fth! Fth! Fth!

J Rock was silenced by several shots hitting him in the back from Mob's gun before falling dead on top of Martina.

"Get him off me! Get him off—"

Fth! Fth!

Head and throat shots silenced Martina forever. Mob did a quick check over both bodies to make sure they were both dead. He then hurried over to the camera system and proceeded to take it apart. After doing a clean sweep of the bedroom, thoughts of Derrick laying in the living room flashed across Mob's mind. Mob took off down the hall, instantly realizing the mistake he might have made. Even though Derrick appeared to be dead, a bullet to the head on the way out would solidify all curiosity.

Mob ran into the living room to say his last goodbye to Derrick's lifeless body still on the living room floor, but to his surprise, Derrick was gone. Mob shot outside in search of Derrick. When he was still unable to find him, he came back inside hoping to find some type of clue. Mob peered down at the bloodstained carpet where Derrick once lay. He was searching for a trail of blood when the soft sounds of a small child crying touched his ears.

Jr. lay in his crib crying out to the figure that stood peering down at him. Jr. wiggled around, reaching out, kicking his tiny feet. Normally, when he did that his mother or father would quickly scoop him up, but this time was different. No matter what he did, nothing happened.

Jr. cried louder and louder. He cried, and cried longer, but still nothing happened. All of a sudden, a bright red beam burst through the darkness of his dimly lit room. He stopped crying because the red light had commanded his attention. His eyes spread wide as he tossed his head from left to right, trying to avoid the steady beam of light that was now in his face. Finally holding his tiny hands in front of his sensitive eyes, Jr. reached out to take hold of the bright red beam.

Fth!

CHAPTER NINETEEN

ON THE GRIND

Young Syke sat at the dining room table in his house, chopping down yet another half-ounce of some hard white. For the past few days, he had been on the grind stacking more money than he had ever made before. Syke would normally flip a zip every two or three days, depending on how much dope was being sold on the streets. But ever since that big shoot out at *The Lounge* business had been booming. Nobody except Syke had any work. If Syke ever hoped to fulfill his dreams of becoming the next C.M. boss, now was the time. He had the streets on lock and Slim had ordered a halt on all drugs being sold.

Young Syke grew up in the drug infested inner city streets, raised by dope fiends and gang bangers. His mother was a crackhead that literally did anything to ensure that she received her next high. As a youngster, Syke had actually witnessed his mother selling herself just to get another hit of dope. A sad but sickening truth for any child to see, but nevertheless a hard reality he had to deal with.

The game hadn't been too sweet for Young Syke growing up. He was born into the struggle and forced to play a game that seldom, if ever had any true winners. He had to constantly remind himself of the promises Slim made him. Slim said if he got his money right, and proved that he could carry his own weight, Slim would put him down with enough dope so that he would never have to look back again. So, regardless of Slim's orders to lay low, he was full time grinding. He could see his chance to move up in the ranks in the near future, and he was determined to make sure it happened.

"Fam-o, if I keep this shit moving just like this for the rest of the week, I'll have a nine piece by next week," Young Syke exclaimed to Bobo, who stood by the kitchen window serving as a lookout.

Bobo was glad to hear that Young Syke was finally coming

into his own. He too had dreams of doing bigger and better things, so he was also willing to do whatever it took to see that Syke came up.

"Yeah, I sure hope everything works out for you, young blood," Bobo said, intently peeping through the blinds to watch out for police, jackers, or anyone that might try to stop their plans. "The game is always changing. Either you change with it, or you get left behind. Look at me." Bobo looked back at Syke displaying himself as an example of what could happen if Syke didn't change into something positive. The game had a crazy twist to it. One minute you might be the biggest baller, and in the next, you're a smoker.

"Fam-o, you are gonna be straight. Just put that damn pipe down, and we gon' get this money blood." Young Sykes cell phone rang, temporarily distracting him. "What up!" Young Syke said, answering the phone.

"Is this, Syke?" the caller asked. He glanced down at his screen trying to recall if he knew the number.

"Yeah, this Syke. Who is this?"

"This A.K. from the club. Do you remember me from the other night?"

"Aww hell yeah dawg, what's good?"

"I was calling to see if we could meet up and talk about a few things,"

A.K said. "I like the way you handled that one situation the other night. I need guys like you on my team." Young Syke sat beaming with pride that people were starting to see the young hog he had become. Even though he was Crimson Mafia until the death of him, it still felt good to be noticed.

"Yeah, I was thinking something like that about you. Maybe we need to find a place to chill so we can lay all our cards on the table," Young Syke explained.

A.K chuckled softly into the phone at Syke's arrogance. "I'll tell you what, if you're really about hooking up and doing some real business, meet me at the Texas Road House off Penn in one hour. I'll see you there."

Glocks on Satin Sheets

The line went dead. Young Syke looked down at his phone, then over at Bobo, who was still intently scoping out what was going on outside the window.

"This nigga just hung up in my face fam-o. Either this nigga must think he really on something, or he got a young nigga fucked up."

Bobo burst into loud laughter, already knowing how Syke was ready to explode. "Just go meet up with the nigga," Bobo said. "You never know what doors he may open up."

A little over an hour later, Young Syke walked through the front doors of the Texas Road House as if he owned the place. Spotting A.K seated at the bar, he quickly headed in his direction, but was immediately stopped. "You must be twenty-one years or older to be in this area," an older white man said, appearing to be the manager.

"Come on fam-o—do I look like a kid to you?" Syke quickly dug into his pocket, pulling out his I.D along with a huge stack of dope boy money. "Here!"

The manager skeptically looked over the I.D, then handed it back. "Barely," he snarled and stormed away.

"Goddamn, look at you," A.K. exclaimed, checking out Young Syke's clothing. "What, are you a blood or something? I see you with the fresh red Nikes, red fitted, and hoodie. If I were a Crip, I would probably be hella salty, right about now."

Young Syke chuckled. "I don't bang, homie. Me and my niggas is about that bread. We ain't got room to be functioning on that gang shit. If a nigga steady running around the city chucking up the set, how I'm gon' make any money?"

A.K. sat across from Young Syke appearing to be very much intrigued by his conversation. "That's part of the reason why I wanted to talk to you," A.K. said while Syke took his seat and flagged over a bartender. "I need young niggas like you on my team that's about that action. Me and my niggas is about that paper, too. We just need some local guys to help us out and show us around."

Young Syke raised his eyebrows at A.K.'s opening pitch as if something sounded strange. "Let me get this straight, fam-o, you want me to be on your team?"

A.K. nodded while taking a quick sip from his drink. "That's right, youngsta. I want you to be on my team."

Young Syke sat looking like he was trying to figure something out. "And just exactly who is your team?" he sarcastically asked.

"Myself, and the other two guys you met at the club the other night."

"Haaaa!" Young Syke burst into laughter in A.K.'s face because he just couldn't help himself. "Woooo!" he howled, holding his stomach. "No disrespect blood, it's just you said team, and I was thinking like a team. Not just count us all on one hand kinda team. See me and my niggas are thick as fuck. We sliding through rock'n shit. We getting a piece of almost everything being sold around here. Chances are, if you in the same lane I'm in, then I can get you plugged in at a cheaper price."

A.K. sat staring at Young Syke like his revelation meant nothing to him. The slick comments were one thing, but the talk about having a cheaper price was another. "I hear you, youngsta, but until somebody can show me that they can get it to me cheaper than twenty-eight a pop, then I'ma just keep doing what I'm doing."

Young Syke sat staring at A.K. It was almost as if he couldn't believe what he had just said. "How does that feel?" Young Syke asked.

A.K. took another drink from his glass and smirked. "How does what feel?"

"Fam-o, them niggas you coping that pack from is fuckin' tha shit outta you. Do you at least make them take you out to dinner before you let them stick it in?"

A.K. glared at Young Syke like he would slam the glass right against his face at any moment.

"Come on fam-o, don't get this shit twisted. I was just fuckin' with you," Young Syke continued. "But on the real, you speaking on them prices like they all that. That shit is high as hell."

A.K. cut his eyes over at Young Syke then rolled his eyes

while mumbling under his breath.

"I'ma let that little bullshit you just said slide youngsta," he said with a hint of attitude.

"Yeah, me too nigga," Young Syke snarled in response. "I told you I was just fuckin' with you fam-o, but you acting like you over there all in your feelings about it. If you trippin' fam-o, you already know what it is on mines blood, it's whatever."

Both Young Syke and A.K. sat momentarily having a stare down, but in the end, neither of the two made a move.

"I think it might be best if I raise up outta here, fam-o. We both in here giving each other these fucked up looks, and the only thing that's gon' fuck around and happen is one of us gon' get rocked tha fuck to sleep!" Young Syke stood to leave and adjusted his belt so that A.K. could see he had that hammer on him.

"I see you little nigga, but don't none of that flashing ya little pistol bullshit mean shit to me. I live to die for this gangsta shit, but I thought me, and you might be cool enough to at least talk business."

Young Syke stood glaring at A.K. contemplating whether he should scatter his brains all over the floor. "Check this out fam-o, fuck all this back and forth, let's get straight down to business. If you wanna hook up and get that fish scale at a cheaper price, then you need to get at me. But all that other bullshit about getting put on with your little click, fuck that, it's Goon Squad ova here." Young Syke turned to leave.

"What's a cheaper price?" A.K. asked, trying to stop Syke from leaving by showing his interest in what Young Syke had offered.

"Twenty-six," Syke replied, stopping to look back at A.K.

"Well, I'm trying to grab a couple of them thangs, right now." Young Syke spun on his heels to leave like he hadn't heard a word A.K. said. "Answer your phone when I call," Syke said over his shoulder. "I have to run this shit by my people and make sure they cool with fuckin' with you."

Adrian Dulan

CHAPTER TWENTY

BACK IN THE CITY

Slim stood outside the airport stretching his legs after a long flight from Florida while Young Syke and Mob loaded his bags into his Escalade that April drove down to pick him up in.

"So, how have things been looking out here?" Slim asked Mob as he got in the front passenger seat and got comfortable.

"Everything has been way too peaceful out here," Mob stated, hopping in the back. "I don't know if it's the calm before the storm, or what the fuck is going on. There ain't been no feds snooping around trying to catch a nigga slipping, and ain't nobody seen or heard from the Steady Grinding Boyz. It's almost like them niggas done fell off the face of the earth. We dried up the streets to flush them niggas out, but them bitches ain't going for the bait. They still somewhere lurking in the cut."

Slim sat appearing to be in deep thought as to what could be going on. "Everything is all good," Slim insisted. "As long as the streets is dry, then sooner or later they gotta come out to try and re-up, and when they do—" Slim paused, turning his attention towards April. He still didn't trust her yet. In fact, the only reason she was still breathing was so he could see how the feds were using her, or if they really were using her. "What's been going on with you, Ms. Thang?"

April glanced over at Slim, flashing a forced smile. "I'm good. I have been chilling at the house, trying to stay out the way until you came back. All that madness that went down at *The Lounge* the other night was way too much drama for little old me."

Slim smirked. "You still alive ain't you? Well, that must mean that I left you in good hands then?" Slim turned back towards Young Syke, who sat directly behind April. "I heard you did ya thang, baby boy! You was dropping them bitch ass niggas like you was a certified sniper or some shit."

"Yeah, well you know a nigga 'bout that action fam-o. I just wish I could have done more to keep them muthafuckas from doing so much damage to the speezy."

"Blood fuck that spot! We'll get another one. In a situation like that, you did all that I'd expected from one soldier. I'm proud of you."

Syke sat in the backseat stuck on cheesy face. He'd finally done something that grabbed the attention of the boss.

"When you go to re-up, I got a little something for you," Slim continued. "This ought to help you get ya bread right where you need it to be."

"What! Oh, hell yeah!" Syke celebrated, slamming his fist into the palm of his hand. "I have been out here on the low making moves so I can try to move up in ranks."

Slim chuckled softly. "What you think you ready to move up in ranks now?"

"I been ready! I even got some new clientele that wanna grab a couple of them thangs. That should lock me in on a new position. I got my own buyers, and I can build my own little squad from there."

Slim's smile slowly faded into a frown. "Some new clientele?" he asked. "Dawg what the fuck is you talking about?"

"Remember I told you about them cats I met at the club? Well, I went and had a drink with one of them niggas today. At first dude was on some, trying to get me to choose up with him and his little click. But when I broke a few things down about how we do things, fool was all in. He wanna get down with us and grab a couple of them thangs."

"Hold up!" Mob insisted, cutting in on Young Syke. "That might be the Steady Grinding Boyz using someone else to connect with us so they can get back on again."

Young Syke sat shaking his head. "No that isn't the case." Even though Mob was considered to be the new under boss, Syke still wasn't willing to allow anyone to come between his chances to become a young boss. "Fam-o, I'ma tell you straight up, them niggas is one hunnid. They was right there beside me knocking them niggas off as they ran up. My right hand to God fam-o, them niggas ain't no Eastsiders."

Slim sat in silence pondering on how he should deal with the situation. It's not like he didn't trust Young Sykes' judgment, it's just no telling what the Steady Grinding Boyz might do to get back on again. "When is ya boy trying to grab that work?" Slim asked.

"Fam-o ready now. I just rode with Mob to pick you up because I needed to make sure I personally ran this by you."

Slim nodded with understanding, then peered back at Syke again. "From now on, run that shit through Mob before it gets to me. I remember what I promised you a long time ago, but this organization has structure. There is a chain of command that you have to follow before you get to the top. Do you understand?"

"I gotcha, big homie. This right here will never happen again. I just needed to make sure you was with me on this."

"'I'm always with you lil' nigga. But if this shit fuck around and blow up in your face, you already know what it's gon' be."

Young Syke nodded and rode the remainder of the ride to Slim's house in silence. In the back of his mind, he had a feeling that he had just made a big mistake. No matter how much he wanted to believe that

A.K. was official, something was telling him that he wasn't.

April drove quietly soaking up the new information about this new group of hustlers trying to connect with the Crimson Mafia. She had hoped Young Syke might say enough so that she could identify who the new group was, but he must have known better. He kept the details to who was who limited. April made a mental note to inform McCracken of Young Sykes' promotion. Hopefully, that new bit of information would be enough to make the feds back off her for a little while.

April's phone rang, prompting her to pick it up and check the number. She had eight missed calls, all from a private number, and several unopened text messages. As much as she wanted to answer her phone, she couldn't. That private number that kept calling back-to-back was none other than the feds. If Slim had the slightest clue that that's who was calling, she was as good as dead.

"Who the fuck is that blowing your shit up like that?" Slim inquired, suspiciously peering over at April. "You got some other nigga on your bumper that I don't know about?"

April spared a quick glance over at Slim, trying to give him a look that would downplay his assumption. "See there you go," she fussed. "It ain't nobody but Juicy calling. She has been trying to get me to come out and kick it ever since you went out of town. But I told her that I was good. I was really just laying low until all the heat died down." In all reality Juicy hadn't been answering any of April's calls.

Slim glared over at April contemplating if he should blow her brains out right then and there. He had personally sent Juicy to her death well over two weeks ago, but here April was saying that was her calling.

Slim played it off, keeping his cool. "Oh, that's Juicy blowing your phone up like that?" Slim inquired, sounding as if he actually believed April's story.

"Yeah, that's her silly ass," April insisted. "I done told her to stop calling my phone like she's fuckin' crazy. I don't know what I'ma have to do to make her get the picture." Slim caught movement out the corner of his eye. Mob had his gun out and pointed at April's head.

"Tell Juicy I said hello when you see her," Mob snarled, wanting to pull the trigger.

Slim slightly shook his head, ordering Mob to stand down. "Oh, I will," April said, clueless that she was mere seconds from death. "But I don't know why you want to speak to her, you ain't been speaking to her."

Slim continued to play it off, showing no indication that he suspected April of anything. If he ever wanted to find out what April was up to, then he had to play his role to the tee, especially in order to get her to reveal her intent.

***

Agent McCracken stood up from his desk and tossed his cell phone down on it. After letting out a loud, frustrating sigh, he walked over to his office window that overlooked the city. "If she doesn't respond in an hour, I'm snatching her ass right back off the streets," he said to Stevens. "What do we need with someone who can't produce any new leads, or respond when we try to contact them?"

Stevens just shrugged. He knew McCracken was stressed out with the case. All he could think to do was say something positive, something that wouldn't further agitate the situation. "If we can get this buy to go through, then we won't need April's cooperation. She might be dragging her feet, right now, but sooner or later, she'll be wishing she hadn't."

McCracken ran both hands through his salt and peppered hair before locking his fingers on the back of his neck. "We can never have enough evidence, Stevens. I'm overreacting, and I know I am. I just know that something had better give, or it's over for us." McCracken's office door suddenly came flying open and crashing into the wall behind it. Director Timothy Liggens stormed inside of the office, startling both Stevens and McCracken.

"Can one of you hard working gentlemen please tell me why, Mr. Walker was found again—almost beaten to death?"

"Say what!" McCracken yelled in disbelief.

"You heard right," Liggens stated firmly. "His wife is dead, someone put two bullet holes in her body and their beautiful newborn baby boy—" Liggens' voice trailed off like he was fighting to maintain his composure.

"How the fuck could this be happening?" McCracken said to no one in particular.

"Oh, no, no, no," Liggens' exclaimed. "You're going to have to do way better than that. The way I see it, if someone doesn't get to explaining what the hell is going on around here, it's about to be two senior agents looking for a new job."

Adrian Dulan

CHAPTER TWENTY-ONE

I NEED THAT

Lil' Menace had been scoping out Young Syke's dope house ever since the night at *The Lounge*. Menace had been dying to get some payback at the young savage that put on like he was invincible. The way Young Syke stood up against the Steady Grinding Boyz while they charged full speed firing rounds had Menace slightly curious as to who Young Syke actually was.

Lil' Menace sat behind the jet-black tint of his rented Charger parked a few houses down from Sykes spot. Menace had watched Syke leave to make a run, come back with a small duffel bag, and leave again to return with a McDonald's sack. "Now either this nigga got the munchies late at night, or that's money in that sack. But either way, I need that!"

Menace hopped out, chambering a bullet into the barrel of his 40 cal. Being that he had been watching Syke's spot for the last few nights, he was certain his presence was undetected. Lil' Menace made a mad dash across the yard and up to Bobo's wooden shack, Young Syke was using as his spot. He quietly crept up the wooden steps of the front porch and cautiously peered through the busted blinds on the window. Young Syke sat at the table rolling a blunt with a bag full of money sitting on the table in front of him. Lil' Menace positioned himself in front of the front door, preparing to kick it in, but as soon as he lifted his foot off the floor, his attention was caught by the sound of the backdoor slamming.

"Damn!" Menace put his back against the wall, allowing the darkness to conceal his presence. He knew Young Syke's lookout was probably just doing his rounds, and moments later his assumption proved to be correct. Bobo came from the backyard to scan up and down the block. He walked right in front of the porch, pulled out a cigarette, and lit it. He never heard a thing as Menace crept up behind him and slept him with one solid blow to the jaw. *Bam*! "Night, night nigga!" Menace growled.

Lil' Menace quickly made his way around to the back of the house, deciding that the front door might create too much of a scene. He slowly crept up the back steps and listened closely. Syke was inside coughing off the smoke he had inhaled from a blunt, Menace assumed. Knowing it was time to make his move, Menace reached out for the knob gently turning it.

"Goddamn!" Young Syke said, coughing and fanning at a thick layer of crack smoke that hovered in the air. "A nigga gotta let some air up in this bitch. That nigga Bobo got it smoky as fuck in here." Syke walked to the back door and opened it. "What the—" Young Syke was caught off guard by a dark figure standing at the back door. He was just on the verge of asking what this person was doing when he spotted a gun. Syke instantly went off on him, swinging like crazy.

Bink! Bink! Bink!

Lil' Menace got rocked and stumbled backward down the stairs before accidently dropping his gun in the grass. Young Syke came off the porch, putting them thangs on Menace. Even though Menace wasn't anywhere near ready for Sykes sudden attack, he still managed to find his bearings. Lil' Menace dropped his head and rushed in with fists flying. The two were locked up like vicious pitbulls, fighting to the death.

Young Syke seemed to be overwhelming Lil' Menace with his strength and a barrage of connecting blows. After every swing Menace threw, four more came flying back at him. Spotting a weakness in Menaces defense, Syke threw a hook that caught Menace right smack on the chin. That was all it took. Syke grabbed a fist full of braids and pulled Menace into a headlock.

"I got your bitch ass now!" Syke put his weight on Menace, forcing him to the ground.

Lil' Menace knew he was in trouble. He knew if he didn't figure out a way to get out of his current position, it was a wrap! Menace dug his feet into the ground, wrapping Syke up by the legs and pushed. The sudden burst of force caught Syke off guard as he fell onto his back, but he still somehow managed to keep a firm grip on Menace's head.

Glocks on Satin Sheets

Lil' Menace laid on top of Syke while his head remained under Sykes arm pit. He fought with all his might to break free but couldn't. Lil' Menace's last option was a vicious over the head swing, hoping that he landed something. *Bink!* Menace hit Syke in the nose so hard that Syke temporarily loosened his grip. Menace snatched his head free and fought for dear life.

Syke tried his best to protect himself against the steady reign of blows pouring down on him, but it was nearly impossible in his position. Menace caught Syke with several monstrous blows, leaving Syke punch drunk and fighting to regain his bearings.

"What now?" Menace spat, crawling off Young Syke, struggling to catch his breath. "I said what now mothafucka?" Lil' Menace stumbled over to the back steps in search of his gun. "You thought you had me, didn't you?" Lil' Menace picked up his gun and spun around just in time to see Syke on his knees trying to stand. "Ain't no need to waste your energy playboy, you might as well gon' and get comfortable."

Bok! Bok! Bok! Bok!

Menace fired several rounds at Syke, dropping him back into the grass. Menace realized firing his gun had raised the risk of someone hearing the shots and calling the police, so he ran inside Syke's spot to collect the money. Once Menace had the bag of money in his possession, he ran out the front door and straight into Bobo.

"Please don't kill me," Bobo begged. "I don't know shit, and I ain't seen shit."

Bok! Bok! Bok! Menace lit him up with several rounds. "East up, bitch ass nigga!"

Adrian Dulan

CHAPTER TWENTY-TWO

WHAT'S IN HER PHONE

Slim woke up a little earlier than normal the next morning. His goal was to get inside that phone April protected so religiously. He slowly slid the covers off himself and eased out of bed, trying not to wake April. He quietly tiptoed around the bed and over to the nightstand where April's phone sat. He disconnected her phone from the charger and began to go through it.

April had six messages marked urgent and several missed calls. Slim opened one of the messages that only displayed the phone number and read it. : I need you to come in as soon as you get this message. If you're not able to come in, then give us a call ASAP! Slim read the message again, trying to get a better feel for what was going on.

"Come in where?" Slim repeated softly, then quickly moved on to April's voicemail.

"Ms. Jordan whenever you hear this message you need to give us a call immediately. It's imperative that we speak with you. Thanks!"

Slim suddenly felt dizzy. He knew the sound of the police when he heard them, but it was hard to believe April was actually working with the feds. Slim glared down at April who still slept peacefully under the covers. He contemplated killing her, but if he did what would the feds do? Slim was certain that the feds were somewhere watching his every move, so he had to figure out a better way to handle this situation.

"Wake up, baby girl," Slim said, reaching down and palming April's ass, gently shaking it. "It's time to wake up. We have some very important shit we need to handle today."

April slowly turned over, peering up at Slim, squinting her eyes. "What time is it?"

He smiled and turned to head downstairs. "It's time to get up. I have something very special for you. I can promise, you'll love it."

***

A couple of hours flew past, and April and Slim were finally dressed and headed outside to his truck. Slim hit the locks, and the two quickly climbed inside. When he turned on his truck, the sounds of 'TGT' I Need came rumbling through his subs. At first, April thought he might have been allowing only a small portion of the song to play. But as he continued to drive deeper into the city, she noticed that's all he wanted to listen too. She pulled off her shades and curiously peered over at him. Slim wasn't the type to listen to R&B, let alone listen to it while he was with her.

"What's on your mind?" she asked.

Slim hit April with the biggest puppy dog eyes he had ever laid on a woman. "Us," he replied. "I wanna get back to that special place in life when I was the number one nigga in your heart, and you was the number one woman in mines."

April gave him a warm smile, hearing the sincerity in his words. Hearing him talk the way he was talking now reminded her of the old Slim, a kind-hearted, loving man that catered to her every need.

"I don't know how to respond to that," April said. "You kind of caught me off guard with that one. I would have never expected you to say something like that, considering everything that's happened on both of our behaves." Slim nodded in agreement, and April thoughtfully asked, "Do you really believe we can ever get back to that special place where it can be just you and me?"

Slim acted as if he was giving April's question some serious thought. "I think if we continue to hold on to yesterday's baggage then we can't properly prepare for today's challenges." He left no room for rebuttals. He immediately hit the button on his remote and let the subs bang.

April couldn't do anything but look at Slim with newfound admiration. This new person he was showing himself to be was somebody she could very well get used to.

Slim made his way through the early morning traffic, and out to the country where April had been countless times before. The sight of the stash house Slim only used for dogfights instantly made her uneasy.

"You woke me up, to bring me to a dog fight?" April questioned in disbelief.

"Come on now. You know me better than that. If I express to you that I'm feeling you, then you should already know I got something real nice for you, so just chill."

April took a deep breath to try to calm her anxiety. She could remember years ago when Slim showered her with nothing but the best. All she could hope for now was that this was about to be one of those times.

"Okay, okay, I'll sit back and let you do your thing."

Slim leaned over and gave her a passionate kiss before hopping out and going around to open her door.

"Here put this on," he said, standing with the passenger door open, holding a crimson colored rag in his hand. "I'm going to walk you inside. I don't want you to see your surprise before it's time."

April reluctantly allowed Slim to blindfold her and walk her inside. She was never the type that really liked surprises. She always liked to know what she was getting, or where she was going. However, she let him do it.

"We're going to play a little game called Ask and Tell," Slim whispered in April's ear after bringing her to stand in the middle of the barn. "I'm going to ask you a question, and you have to give me the correct answer. But—" Slim paused to create suspense and excitement.

April was literally on the verge of having an anxiety attack because she was so thirsty to receive some type of expensive gift.

"If I ask you a question and you give me the wrong answer—"

April stood anticipating his every word. She had both hands locked together like she was praying.

"I lose?" she asked, trying to finish his sentence. "What— you're not going to give me my surprise?"

Ping! Poom! Pow!

Slim's goons swung aluminum bats, hitting April in the knees, thighs and lower back.

"Slim!" April cried out, crumbling to the ground. "Help me!"

Slim reached down and snatched the blindfold off April's eyes. The look of fear, confusion, and shock sent him into an overly dramatic laughter.

"I'm here, bitch! I would never leave you around these crazy muthafuckas. It ain't no telling what these niggas plan to do to your ass." Slim knelt beside April, forcing her to look at him by holding her chin. "You're going to tell me everything I want to know, and everything I need to know. How you respond to my questions will determine how much more time you have on this earth."

April peered up at Slim, not really knowing what to think. She had all kinds of questions dancing around in her mind. But none of them really made sense to consider. She was certain he knew nothing.

"Slim why are you doing this to me? You just told me we were going to be together."

Slim chuckled softly, "I got cho' dumb ass, didn't I? I didn't wanna be with no snake ass bitch! I'm trying to find out how long you been working for them people."

Her heart felt like it dropped down into the pit of her stomach. She could no longer stand to hold eye contact with a man that seemed to have the ability to read her darkest secrets.

"I would never do anything like that against you," she cried. "I held you down while I was locked up."

Slim shoved April's face away from him in disgust. Standing to his feet, dusting his hands, he immediately sent his young hitters into action. "Show this rat ass bitch I ain't fucking around!"

Ping! Poom! Pow! Bing! Ping! Poom! Poom! Pow!

Slim's young goons literally beat the shit out of April. April screamed so loud and for so long, her voice grew hoarse.

"You still think this shit is a game?" Slim snarled, towering above April. "I got all day to sit here and beat yo' muthafuckin' ass until you tell me everything I wanna know."

April lay rocking back and forth on her side in severe pain.

She looked up at Slim barely able to recognize the person she was looking at. Slim looked like a mad man that enjoyed every second of her pain. April knew right then and there she would not walk out of there alive. Whatever she needed to say or do to get it over with, she was ready.

"Fuck you, Slim!" April yelled. "I told the feds everything I could think of about you. I told them about Derrick, the drugs, Flocko."

Slim winced. "Bitch you gave up the plug?" he asked in disbelief. "Nigga I gave up everything," April fired back. "You don't give a fuck about me! All you care about is yourself and these broke ass niggas you keep around you."

Slim paced back and forth while his men awaited his orders. The only thing he could think about was the real war that could possibly be brewing once Flocko found out April gave him up.

"So, the truth is out. You a ratty ass bitch that's working for the feds?"

April cried harder, regretting that she ever told that lie. The truth be told, she would never snitch on Flocko. He was like a God in the streets who giveth life, and taketh life away.

"Slim, I'm sorry. They made me—" she started, but Slim held up one hand silencing her.

"I don't wanna hear shit else you got to say," Slim growled. "You've already said enough!" Slim peered back over his shoulders at another group of young goons that held his vicious Rottweilers on chains. "Let the chains go," he demanded.

April's eyes went buck. "But Slim I only said that because—"

"Bitch when I said I ain't trying to hear nothing you got to say, that means nothing." he looked back over to his dogs. "Kill that bitch! Ss— ss!"

Adrian Dulan

CHAPTER TWENTY-THREE

NEW WAY IN

Puncho crept as quietly as possible from his grandmother's home, trying his best not to awaken her. Every morning around 8, Puncho met up with Syke at Bobo's house. They started each day in the dope house, trying to make money, or plotting and planning a major move.

Birds sang their morning song as they hopped across the lawns in search of food. Puncho couldn't help but feel like he was like them, up early trying to get his money right.

"The early bird gets the worm," Puncho said, spotting a bird that had just plucked a worm from the soil before taking flight to the safety of the heavens. "That's why I'm up early just like you. I gotta get mines, too!"

As Puncho continued to draw closer to Bobo's house, he noticed someone was stretched out on the front lawn. His first thought was that Bobo was drunk and had passed out from having too much to drink. But the closer he drew near to Bobo's house, the more he realized that was not the case. Bobo lay dead with dark red spots covering his oily white t-shirt. His once fluffy white beard was now speckled with dried up blood. Puncho peered up at Bobo's house, then back down at his lifeless body. He could only hope that his best friend hadn't fallen to the same fate.

Puncho cautiously walked up the front steps and went inside. He carefully went from room-to-room, finding nothing. He pulled out his cell phone quickly dialing Syke's number. Moments later the sound of a cell phone ringing somewhere in the house startled Puncho. He followed the sound.

Puncho followed the sound of the cell phone ringing until he stumbled upon it laying by the back door. How did this get here? He whispered to himself. Did Syke drop his shit while in a rush to get out the back door?

Puncho opened the back door and instantly saw his best friend lying face down in the grass. "Syke! Syke!"

Puncho was off the back porch and over to Young Syke's side in a flash. "Wake up blood! You can't be dead dawg, wake up!" Puncho carefully rolled him over, lifting his head onto his lap. It was the closest he had ever been to a dead man, let alone a dead man that he had love for. "Please wake up, fam," he begged. "You the only nigga I fucks wit' out the whole set."

Puncho's eyes filled with tears as his emotions overcame him. He pulled Syke into a tight embrace, wishing he had the power to reverse the painful tragedy.

"Who did this to you?" Puncho asked, slightly shaking Syke. "When I find them niggas, I'ma kill every last one of them." Young Syke's eyelids fluttered as he released a soft groan.

"Syke?"

Syke's eyelids fluttered again and he groaned much louder.

"Oh, shit—I got you fam. Just hold the fuck on, I'ma run and get help!"

***

Mob sat at the bar inside his luxury condo while Puncho told him everything that happened that morning. Mob was mentally beating himself down for not being on point and being the one to see this coming. Mob was convinced that he had allowed the unknown buyers the opportunity to double back and take back the money they had just spent. He also allowed Derrick to slip through his fingertips, too.

His head hung low from disappointment. He knew Slim would be furious about him slipping up and not completing the mission he was sent on. Since Young Syke was laid up in the hospital, and Derrick was still alive, things stood the chance of getting real ill out in the field. He thought back to Devil's sizzling body on the barn floor and it instantly sent a chill up his spine. Even though Mob was far from having any fear whatsoever of Slim, it was the thought of going against what he lived to die for, and that was crushing him. The Crimson Mafia was all he knew, and his loyalty was with that family until the death of him.

Mob poured himself another double shot of Vodka and took it straight to the head. Being the underboss came with many mentally strenuous responsibilities, the kind that even he had failed to uphold. "They'll never get away with what they've done," Mob swore to Puncho, who sat in the living room with his head held down.

"Blood, I ain't trying to hear that shit! When is all this extra bullshit gon' end dawg?"

Mob spun around in his chair, slightly moved by the aggressiveness in Puncho's tone. "Every day it's something. We got beef with niggas that y'all been breaking bread with for years. No soon as the big homie forces us to start fucking with that rat ass bitch, shit gets fucked up. Now we got funk with muthafuckas that ain't done nothing but make us money."

"Hold tha fuck up, lil' nigga," Mob snarled. "Don't push your hand too far on this fam. I totally understand how you feel about this shit, because I feel the same way, too. But my loyalty is with Slim and this organization we've built. Respect and honor is everything. You can either respect the game for what it is, or you can move tha fuck around!"

Puncho knew he had gone too far with expressing how he felt. If no one else had the heart to speak on the bullshit that was going on, then he would. "Look dawg, you told me to count on you as you would also count on me. You said that's how we gon' be able to maintain out here in the streets getting this money. We move as a unit—no weak links. Ain't that what you said? Think about it— why we at war in the first place? Why Syke even fucking with some new niggas that he don't even know? Fam out here trying to eat damu, plain and simple. If that punk ass bitch hadn't ever came around, then none of this shit woulda happened dawg."

Mob rubbed his temples, feeling a major migraine quickly coming on. There was nothing he could say to what was being said, because all of it was the truth. Even his own pockets were starting to feel the effects of all the drama going on in the streets.

"You're right," Mob reluctantly stated, turning back to the bar and pouring another drink. "I'll put everything on the table when I speak with Slim. Even though I'm never one to question his judgment concerning certain things, I can honestly say I feel you on this one."

"What about this new situation?" Puncho pressed on. "When are we gonna handle this shit? We have been sitting here all day waiting on Slim to answer the phone, but for some reason he ain't got back at us. Ain't no telling where them fools A.K. and his crew are. We need to try to get on them fools line as soon as possible."

Mob peered back at Puncho once again at a loss for words. Even though Puncho was barely twenty-one years old, he was wise well beyond his years. Mob now understood why Young Syke insisted on Puncho being allowed the chance to become a part of the Goon Squad.

"Give me Syke's phone," Mob ordered. "I'm going to try and call that nigga A.K. from a different number to see if he picks up. If he does, we'll have to set something up so we can lock in with them fools."

***

Agent McCracken stood alongside Young Syke's bed, while he lay in a coma. To him it seemed as if every time he gained some type of hold on operation Slim Pickings, death came crashing its mighty fist down on it, practically destroying everything. Finally, growing tired of all the ups and downs that Slim's case had presented him with, McCracken felt it was time to make a decision. Either he was going to close the case and arrest Slim on the charges that he had against him, or he would turn the case over to someone else. The wrong decision could cost him dearly, especially considering he was nearing retirement.

"I want April Jordan picked up off the streets immediately," McCracken told Stevens, who sat on the other side of Sykes bed going over police reports. "We can't risk losing our only witness in a case that's splitting apart at the seams."

"Would you like for me to send a few units to her address to see if she's there?" Stevens asked.

"No, I think we should go about picking her up a better way," McCracken stated. "Have your team GPS her location using her cellphone. We can go pick her up after they've found her, that way we can get a free search of Slim if she's around him."

Stevens quickly put away his reports so he could attend to the task at hand. There were too many bodies popping up around a city that wasn't accustomed to that much violence going on around it.

A soft knock at Young Syke's hospital room door captured both agents' attention.

"Good afternoon—do you mind if I have a word with you?" Agent Avery Jefferson said, peeking his head in from the hallway.

"Sure, come right on in," McCracken said, giving Jefferson a warm smile while extending his hand for a handshake.

"How's he coming along?" Jefferson asked as he came alongside Young Syke's bed and gazed down at him with pity in his eyes.

"Well, Doctors say it's up to him now. They've done all they can do, considering all the damage that's been done," McCracken stated plainly. "If he's going to pull through this thing, then he's gon' have to do it alone. It's no longer in our hands."

Jefferson appeared to be slightly moved by McCracken's statement. "I can't help but wonder why so many young men are literally running to get involved with this deadly game? I mean it really makes me wonder why they can't tell the difference between a war and a game. These young guys come into this thing thinking they're going to get rich over night, but they have no clue. It's much harder than that, my friend. Much, much harder than that."

"This was a pretty sharp kid, I bet," McCracken said. "I hate to see that he chose this path to go down in life. Now if, and when he wakes up, he's looking at spending quite a few years in the penitentiary, or he's going to just lay here and die!" McCracken shook his head in disappointment, then peered over at Jefferson. "I've decided to close the case. I understand how—"

"You've got to be kidding me," Jefferson interrupted in disbelief. "After what I just did for this case, now you're telling me you want to shut everything down?"

"I understand what you've done for the case," McCracken continued. "But you've got to understand what's on the line. Too many people are coming up dead behind these guys and the drugs they're selling. Even though you were able to buy two kilos, our way inside is laying right here in front of us."

Jefferson walked over to Young Syke's window, thinking of several different scenarios that could possibly keep the case open. He thought about trying to go above McCracken's head, but the only thing that could come of that was him getting fired. In the midst of Jefferson trying to figure out a plan, his cell phone rang a special ring tone that he had programmed for the investigation. "We've got a caller," Jefferson excitedly stated.

Stevens glanced over at McCracken who appeared to be deciding on what to do.

"Well, answer the damn thing for crying out loud," Stevens exclaimed. "Just because he said we're shutting down the case, doesn't mean it's closed down yet!"

"What up, who is this?" Jefferson asked, answering his phone, instantly transforming his role into a street thug. "Buggzy?" Jefferson repeated as McCracken and Stevens looked on. "How you get this number, homie?" Jefferson stood listening while the caller explained how he got the number and why he was calling. "I ain't seen or heard from Young Syke since last night," Jefferson continued. "But if and when I do, is this the number that I can reach you at?" The caller continued to talk for a little while longer, and Jefferson's face lit up at what he was hearing. "So, I can call you if I need anything? That's cool—I should be ready for y'all real soon. A'ight bet!" Jefferson disconnected the call.

"We have another way in," Jefferson announced. "But it won't do any good to have a way in if you're still closing the case."

McCracken took a nervous glance over at Stevens, then down at Syke. Too many people were dying behind this young man and the drugs him and his crew sold. His own words seemed to echo in his head as he pondered his next move. If he decided to close the case, who would really be winning, the killers who would still be on the streets, or the federal government?

"The case stays open for now," McCracken stated reluctantly. "But I want April Jordan picked up off the streets immediately." He peered over at Jefferson with seriousness in his eyes. "Don't let me down son. We've got too much riding on this. We have to make this work."

***

Lil' Menace posted up with Big Crip in his hotel room preparing to slam yet another cigarette inside a vial. For the past several days, the Steady Grinding Boyz had been laying low, allowing the Crimson Mafia to comb the streets in search of them. Lil' Menace on the other hand, being the live wire he was, took it upon himself to scope out a lick and came up on fifty-two racks, never telling a soul how much he hit for. Lil' Menace stashed the money and kicked back with Crip telling the tale of how he pulled it off.

"Man, Cuz—you shoulda seen how that nigga was begging me not to beat his ass. I mean this nigga was like—please Menace! Please don't hit me again." Menace mocked, cowering away as if he were ducking a vicious blow. "I started to slap the shit out his ass for acting like a straight up bitch. That nigga went from a hardcore dope boy, to a gay ass nigga like that," he said snapping his fingers. Afterwards, he pulled the filter from the cigarette and loosened the tobacco.

"You didn't make him tell you where none of their major stash houses were?" Big Crip asked.

"The way that nigga was crying and getting loud with that shit, I thought Cuz was gon' wake up the neighbors. I just went on and rocked his ass to sleep, ran in to get the money, and did what I had to do."

Big Crip smirked, already knowing it was more to the story than Lil' Menace was saying it was. Lil' Menace was the type that put ten on ten. Meaning by the time you heard whatever new information that was floating around, it was a good chance it was watered down, and cut with his own twist.

Big Crip flipped through the channels on the television while Menace lit the stick. Still unable to fully except Menace's explanation of what happened, Crip continued to press on, "So, if you beat that nigga's ass the way you say you did, why you got all them knots all around yo' shit?"

Lil' Menace ran his fingertips over his forehead, feeling the knots Young Syke put on him. "You tryna be funny, Cuz? I told you them niggas had bats when I ran up in there. I had to take that shit from them niggas before I could get back on top!"

Big Crip fell out laughing. "You know that nigga beat yo' muthafuckin' ass, Cuz," he howled. Every time he looked up, there was Lil' Menace with knots around his head and a busted lip. He couldn't help but see the situation for what it was. Lil' Menace looked like somebody had gotten dead off in his ass.

Lil' Menace waved Big Crip off and took a long hard pull from the wet cigarette. He was sitting on fifty-two bands of dope boy money. Couldn't nobody talk down on him, especially somebody that was still waiting to get fronted a pack?

The sound of somebody's bass came rumbling through the hotel room, prompting Big Crip to look through the peephole. "Is that, Crazy Cuz?" he questioned, not really able to see exactly who it was.

"Let me see." Lil' Menace hopped up to peek through the curtains, grabbing his 40 cal. "Yeah, that's him."

Crip opened the door and stepped out to greet Crazy Cuz.

"Got damn! What tha fuck happened to you?" Crazy asked Menace as he walked up to shake it up with Crip and Menace.

"Oh, you got jokes too?" Menace quipped, looking around to make sure no one else was within earshot of what was being said.

"Naw, I'm just saying my nigga, it looks like somebody done straight blinded yo' muthafuckin' ass."

Crip busted into loud laughter, unable to control himself any longer. Now there was no denying it, someone else was seeing the same thing he was.

"Come on, Cuz, leave that nigga alone," Crip said. "I been going hard on his ass all day." Crip lead Crazy into the hotel room and the three of them sat down to chill.

"You, niggas ain't heard about what's been going on with them C.M. cats?" Crazy asked, taking a few puffs from the cigarette Menace had just passed him.

"Heard what?" Big Crip inquired. He was all ears to hear any new information. Especially seeing as though Menace claimed to have robbed one of them.

"The Fed's ran up in one of Slims spots today. They caught him and a few other niggas trying to dispose of a body. The streets is saying them niggas got caught with hella dope and money. It's a wrap for them niggas, Cuz."

"Put that on something!" Lil' Menace demanded.

"I put that on tha set, Cuz! Even though it's about to be drought season around this bitch, we can come out of hiding and let our nuts hang."

That was music to Lil' Menace's ears. He hopped out of his chair and towered over Crip and Crazy Cuz as he celebrated. "I'm trying to throw a block party and pull up stuntin' with some bad bitches," he exclaimed. "Now that them mark ass niggas is out the way, the city is ours!"

Big Crip sat quietly listening, trying to decide how they would deal with the new information. If the feds were involved, there was always the chance that the feds had something on them as well.

"Did you hear how many of them niggas got popped up in Slim's stash house?" Crip inquired.

"It was only a handful of them niggas Cuz, it's still a lot of them fools out here running around," Crazy Cuz replied. "But without that dope and they big homie behind them with all that bread, it's a wrap for them niggas, Cuz. Them mark ass niggas can't afford to go to war."

Crip knew how the Crimson Mafia was known to lay low whenever drama presented itself. But as soon as the smoke cleared, they would be right back in the mix, but stronger than ever. "Let's just dip back to the hood to see how this situation plays out," Crip finally said. "We need to sit back and watch how the rest of them niggas move, that way we can make the proper adjustments."

"So, what we ain't throwing no block parties?" Menace quipped. "Once we see what we're really up against, I'll let you know what's next."

CHAPTER TWENTY-FOUR

BACK ON THE BLOCK

Using the help of Puncho and an old head named Dooney, Mob moved the whole operation over to a new spot off Lake Hefner. Mob had been brainstorming all day, trying to figure out how he could keep the Crimson Mafia afloat. In the midst of all the new turmoil that had suddenly surrounded them, he had assigned Dooney to watch over the C.M.'s last existing stash house. The three of them sat trying to come up with every reason in the book why they should all walk away, but the conversation kept leading to the same conclusion, The Crimson Mafia was for life. There would be no letting go.

"Who brought you into this organization?" Mob questioned Dooney, who seemed to be showing little regard to his authority.

"Slim brought me in," he exclaimed. "I came up with Slim's father, and after he died, I looked out for him until he was the man he is today."

"But why would you choose to get down with us if it wasn't all or nothing? It looks like you trying to jump ship just because shit's looking hectic out here in the streets. The last time I checked, it was because of the C.M. that you got food on your plate. You got what you got from the work we put in!"

Dooney shook his head in disappointment. If they didn't walk away from this thing, right now, everyone associated with Slim would soon fall. "I've been out here in these streets for over thirty years young blood. And I ain't never, and I mean never, seen the inside of a jail cell. You gotta learn how to read the signs of the times. There's always thunder and lightning before the storm."

Mob wasn't getting the point he was trying to make. "Man, if you don't miss me with that ancient Hebrew bullshit you talking about," Mob remarked. "I'm going to do what I know Slim would want me to do, and that is hold this shit down. Now being that you and Slim's relationship is what it is, I'ma give you a chance to step."

Dooney was in between a rock and a hard place. If he left, he figured he wouldn't be able to survive. He had no retirement plan, no social security, no family, nothing! Dooney had been hustling on the streets for so long the C.M. was now all he had.

"I ain't got nowhere to go, Man," he said reluctantly. "I'm too old, and you know that."

"Well, what makes you think I'm ready to up and just walk away from what I got going on?" Mob replied. "The C.M. is a big part of my life as well. That's why I'm so willing to guard this thing with my life." Mob saw that his point had been made and wasted no time moving on to the next order of business that needed to be discussed. "I hear them Eastside niggas are back on the block, looking mighty comfortable since we been laying low. They must think shit is sweet, or that we done fell off?" Mob sparked up a blunt and took a long hard pull from it. "I say we pull up on them niggas and give them an ultimatum. These streets is still ours, either they can start back doing business with us, or we gon' dead them niggas right there on the spot."

"That's what tha fuck I'm talking about," Puncho finally chimed in. "All that other shit about this my life, and I ain't got nowhere to go, had a nigga ready to cry up in this bitch. I'm trying to get to this money and murder them niggas that shot the homie, Syke!"

Both Mob and Dooney had a good laugh at Puncho. He was young and didn't fully understand the commitment the streets demanded. But as long as Mob was the new boss of the Crimson Mafia, he vowed to teach Puncho everything no one ever took the time to teach him.

Mob stood up, picked up his 45 off the table, and placed it in the small of his back. "You know what youngsta, I ain't had the chance to see what your murder game is like," he said, passing Puncho the blunt. "All this talk like you ready to ride. Well, it's time to put up or shut up lil' nigga!"

***

Crazy Cuz and Big Crip hopped out in traffic, shining like new money. It felt good to be back out on the block with the homies again. There was no threat of war, no police combing the streets trying to arrest them, and the hood was almost right back to where it needed to be.

As Crazy pulled into the car wash off MLK, smokers that scrambled around trying to do anything for a hit came running up as soon as they saw Big Crip riding with Crazy Cuz.

"Hey, Crip," Boochi Boo excitedly greeted. "I hope you working, cause I got something real special for you."

Boochi Boo licked her chapped lips as she ran alongside Crazy Cuz's M.C. Boochi Boo boasted to have the best head on the Eastside. Young hustlers were known to drop her a few rocks just to see if the gossip was true.

Crazy parked his M.C. under one of the stalls, and they both got out. "Back tha fuck up," Crip snapped, towering over Boochi Boo and several others that formed a small circle around him. "You muthafuckas know not to be running up on me like that." Crip turned his attention to Boochi Boo and flinched. "Bitch if you don't get yo' crusty lip, anorexic built, no teeth having ass tha fuck out my face—I'ma cave yo' fuckin' face in." Crip pushed through the semicircle around him and made his way over to C-Loc who sat on a crate pocket checking some smoker about his money.

"Oh, shit, look who's back on the block," C-Loc exclaimed, standing. "I see you back bending corners with Crazy Cuz again? That must mean you back on again."

"Pssttt, I wish," Crip replied. "I'm just trying to see what it looks like out here. The homie Crazy Cuz got a little something if you trying to get on. It ain't nothing major, but he still on, though."

C-Loc took a brief look around, making sure Crazy Cuz wasn't within hearing distance. "If it's that same shit Cuz been pushing, then I'm cool on that. That shit takes too long to lock up. You gotta keep fucking with it and fucking with it. That's too much work homie— not to mention the clockers keep saying that it leaves a funny taste in their mouth."

Adrian Dulan

Crip just soaked up the little info and kept it pushing. "Trust and believe, we working on getting something better, but the hood gon' have to learn how to work with what's on the table." Crip scanned the parking lot, trying to see who else was on the scene. He wasn't about to spend the whole day listening to homies complain about something that he had no control over.

"Hey homie, I'ma be right back. I'm about to push over there to the store and get something to drink," Crip said and quickly made his way across the street to the store.

Once inside, he bought a blue cream soda and a pack of Newport shorts. As Crip stepped back outside, he couldn't help but take notice of a black four-door GMC truck on 28s parked in front of the store. "Damn, that muthafucka is clean as a bitch," he exclaimed.

"You like that?" someone asked, standing to Crip's right, next to an out of order pay phone.

"It's cool, that's you?" Crip asked, gesturing towards the truck, but watching the man suspiciously.

"Yeah, that's me," the man replied.

"No offense, but do you know where you're at? Niggas get they shit pushed back for pulling up in the hood stuntin' especially when niggas don't know who they is."

The man chuckled softly as if that was the damnedest thing he had ever heard. "Yeah, I know where I'm at, but I don't think you fully understand just who tha fuck I am." Crip instantly picked up on the irony in the way the man was talking and went for his gun.

"I wouldn't do that, big homie. I would hate to have to fuck up that pretty little ponytail you got." Puncho pulled the hammer back on his pistol, letting Crip hear that snap, crackle, and pop in his ear to ensure that he knew it was not a game.

"You, niggas might as well go on and do what you came to do. I ain't getting in the truck, and I damn sho ain't kissing no ass."

Mob smiled, inwardly respecting Crip's gangsta. "We ain't come here for no funk, fam. We came to talk in peace, so we can get this money back poppin'."

Crip seemed surprised. "You, niggas wanna talk peace after

you done murked my lil' niggas and disrespected they families! What type of shit do y'all think this is?"

Mob walked up pulling his nickel plated 45 from the small of his back, aiming it at Big Crip. "We can either talk peace, or you can rest in peace. I really don't give a fuck what you decide to do. But understand this, you'll either live or die based on your next response."

"Like that?" Crip asked, staring down the barrel of the big dumb ass 45 Mob held in his face. "You, niggas making muthafuckas fuck with the C.M. now?"

"Naw homie you got us fucked up with them Italian muthafuckas. You got options." Puncho nudged the barrel of his own gun into the back of Crips head.

"We can both cut our losses and get back to the business or you most definitely will be the first one that will take another loss."

Crip peered over at the car wash, then back at Mob. There were no wins in this situation, and he would surely be killed if he resisted. "It's over," he grudgingly said. "But at the same time, we ain't trying to get caught up in that fed heat you, niggas is caught up in either."

"This is straight up business," Mob stated firmly, putting his gun away so that Crip could relax. "We wouldn't bring any heat to our own money supply. What type of sense would that make?"

Puncho dug in his pocket and pulled out a contact number for Crip. "Take this," he said, tapping Crips arm as he walked from behind him. "Hit that number when you get at ya people and let them know how this shit is about to go down."

Crip snatched the number and stood watching as Puncho and Mob got in the truck to leave. Part of him wanted to pull his gun out and light they ass up for coming in his hood, but his better judgment kept him from doing it. For Crip to swallow his pride meant his hood would eat without the threat of war, and more importantly, without anyone else being killed.

***

"Gabriel Lewis, your attorney is here to see you," Slim was awakened by two hillbilly C.O.s at his cell door, who were there to escort him to an attorney visit. "Turn around and cuff up!" the guard stated as Slim came closer to the cell door.

"Is all that barking necessary?" Slim inquired. "You make it seem like I don't already know the drill. Or is it you just like being able to tell a grown ass man what to do?"

"Yeah, whatever! Just do what I tell you and we won't have any problems today."

Slim turned, allowing the C.O. to place the handcuffs on him. "Damn, them muthafuckas is way too tight fam. Loosen them thangs up!"

"I see you ain't so hard after all?" the C.O. chimed. "I was hoping for that kind of response." The two C.O.s snatched Slim out of his cell and led him down the hall to a small conference room where his attorney awaited him.

"What the hell are all these people doing here?" Slim questioned, staring into the small room where several agents and his attorney sat staring back up at him.

"Calm down, Slim," his attorney stated. "These gentlemen approached me down the hall and made an offer I didn't think you could refuse."

Slim appeared to give his attorney's statement some thought. "They ain't the judge or the D.A., what type of offer can these muthafuckas offer me?"

McCracken stood from his chair and approached Slim. "I can offer you a shorter sentence. Maybe short enough that you still have a few years to enjoy life."

Slim smirked, peering over at his attorney, then back at McCracken. "If this is one of them conversations that's going to end with you asking me to work for you, miss me with that bullshit!"

McCracken chuckled and eased a few steps closer, standing so close to Slim that the two could literally smell each other's breath. "It's up to me whether you live or die in a federal penitentiary.

Either you can come work for me, or you just earned yourself a life sentence for keeping it gangsta."

Slim glared at McCracken so hard both C.O.s came to stand next to him. "So, it's up to you if I live or die in the penitentiary?"

McCracken slowly shook his head with a smile forming on his face.

"So, I assume all you want from me, is for me to give up somebody else. So, I guess you want me to put them in the same situation I'm in?"

McCracken grunted and smiled. "In so many words, yes! That's exactly what I want."

Bink!

Slim headbutted McCracken so hard, he went stumbling back into the table. "Now that's in my power muthafucka," Slim snarled as the guards instantly slammed him against the wall, restraining him. "I hope all you snake ass peckerwoods die! Fuck you muthafuckas! Fuck You!" Slim yelled as he was being restrained.

***

Hours later, McCracken sat in his office holding an ice pack to his nose. McCracken swore he would make Slim's life a living hell for what he had done to him. Not only had Slim embarrassed him, but he had made a mockery of the government as well.

"Good afternoon, how you hanging in there?" Agent Jefferson asked, entering the room carrying a file. "Ewwww, looks like you have a little swelling going on around your eyes."

McCracken looked up at Jefferson like he was crazy. "Yeah, why don't you tell me more about it? Better yet, what are you doing in here in the first place?

"I have a few papers I need you to sign off on so I can get the okay on the buy money. We're all ready to go on my end. I've already spoken to Agent Brown who was with me the night I met Young Syke at The Lounge. He's going with me to make this buy, so as it stands, we're ready to roll!"

McCracken opened the file and thumbed through several

papers. "Have you already made contact to make sure this is the real deal?"

"Yes, Sir, we're meeting Buggzy at the 36th Street apartments tonight at 7 p.m. I'm taking Agent Brown for precautionary measures, just to make sure everything runs smoothly."

"The 36th Street apartments off Kelly?" McCracken repeated. "Pssttt, you guys had best be on full alert in that area around evening time. That's a very hostile area, so you'll need additional units on standby just in case. What's your gut telling you about the guy that you're dealing with?"

"I feel like he's in a rush to make some cash," Jefferson insisted. "Slim and his little crew have been taking hit after hit. First Slim, and one of their main stash houses, then Young Syke. I believe they're chasing the wind but have no clue that they're only digging themselves a deeper hole."

McCracken sighed, taking a moment to dissect everything Jefferson had just told him. No matter how good Jefferson made it sound, something wasn't sitting right with him. Why would a crew that was so closely knit be so willing to do business with a newcomer? The C.M. is a very discreet organization with very loyal and steady clientele. There was no need to deal with someone new, especially when they didn't know if they could use them.

"I want you to be extra careful on this one," McCracken said seriously. "There is so much going on in this city that involves this crew. I wouldn't want them to try to get one over on us, trying to make up for some of their losses by using us."

Jefferson stood with a puzzled expression etched on his face. Where is all of this coming from? he thought. In the back of his mind, he knew he had covered all corners, making sure the case was airtight. "I'll be on the lookout for anything that looks out of the ordinary," Jefferson stated. "But once again, I think this thing should go over rather smoothly tonight.

McCracken could sense the doubt Jefferson held in regards to his advice. "You seem to have gotten this all figured out, don't you?" he asked, picking up the file and quickly adding his signature. "Here take these," he said, handing over the file. "We'll see you when you get back in tonight."

Adrian Dulan

CHAPTER TWENTY-FIVE

THE TAKE BEGINS

Derrick laid in his hospital bed fighting to hold back the warm tears that streamed down his butchered face. Thoughts of his once peaceful and normal everyday life flashed before his mind, sending his heart plummeting into a neverending abyss of misery. Everything that made up Derrick's life had suddenly been violently stripped away from him. Derrick was left to rot mentally, becoming nothing more than an empty shell that could be used to harvest evil.

Derrick thought back to the night when he stood in hiding and witnessed his only child being murdered. He remembered rolling over to his stomach and coughing up the teeth that had been painfully wedged deep in his throat. A few brief moments after that, he had struggled to his feet and stumbled down the long hallway to Jr.'s room. His only focus was on saving his son, because he believed his wife was already dead.

He had entered his son's room and quickly scooped him from the crib, but Jr. cried, sensing the evil going on in his very own home. Derrick being afraid for his life, as well as his son's, quickly laid Jr. back in his crib and concealed himself in the darkness of the closet. As Derrick stood as still as he could, he silently prayed, hoping beyond everything that there was a God that would answer his prayers. He had never truly been a religious man, but in that very moment, a prayer was all he had.

A tall, dark figure slid into the room and came to stand over Jr.'s crib. Derrick stood deathly still watching as his son reached out to the man holding a gun just inches from his son's face.

"Father give me the strength, he's just a child," Derrick prayed. "If you're really up there, then please do something!"

Derrick closed his eyes, willing himself to burst from the closet and attack the dark figure, but a calm, soothing voice seemed to come from all around him, literally paralyzing him. "Be still," the voice commanded, and in the next moment—

Fth! It was over.

Derrick had spent the last week being forced to relive that horrific moment a million times. Why fate would bestow such a heavy burden for him to carry alone completely baffled him.

"Mr. Walker," Stevens said, entering Derrick's room to stand over his bed. "I'm glad to see that you are finally awake. Normally, when I come in, you're asleep because they keep you so heavily medicated. I just wanted to tell you face-to-face, man-to-man that I'm going to do everything in my power to bring those killers to justice. Even though you can't talk, right now, I'm going to need you to focus on your memory. Within the next couple of weeks, I plan to have you try to write down everything you can remember from the night you and your family were attacked. As soon as possible, we have to figure out a way we can get started on this."

Derrick stared up at Stevens, seeing nothing more than a dead man talking. It was because of him that he ever decided to trust the government in the first place. Everyone that had anything to do with the demise of his family would soon feel his wrath. It was only a matter of time.

***

Lil' Menace slowly ran his hand through Teresa's hair while gently tapping his dick against her soft pink lips. "Say, ahhhhh," he jokingly teased, demanding that she open her mouth and let him inside.

"I can't stand your crazy ass." She giggled, opening wide and taking the helmet in like it was a juicy strawberry. "Uhmmmm you taste so good, though," she moaned, flicking her tongue on the slit at the tip of his dick. "Is this my dick?" she asked, becoming aroused by Menace's moaning and groaning.

"You know it is," he stated. "So, why are you trying to play that little game with me now?"

Teresa smiled, knowing she had Lil' Menace right where she wanted him. She lifted his dick and ran her tongue between his

238

balls, then back up to the tip of his dick again.

"If this is my dick," she said, gently jacking him off. "then why you been giving my shit away to all them nothing ass hoes?"

Menace was in a whole other world. He could see Teresa's lips moving but hadn't heard one single word she said. He slowly eased his hands around her head, locked both hands together and tried to force feed her.

"No—umm, umm. Stop Menace! I want you to answer my question before I do it!"

Menace peered down at Teresa having no idea what she was talking about. He assumed she was tripping because she wanted something. "I'm going to move you out of the hood, get your car fixed, and take you shopping. So, stop acting like that!"

Teresa giggled softly to herself, but still managed to maintain her composure. If Lil' Menace was about to do all he said he was about to do, then she had no problem doing what he wanted her to do.

"Ahhhhhh!"

***

"Man, it's slow as fuck out here," C-Loc complained to Menace who sat on the passenger side of C-Loc's parked car, exhausted from his sexual experience with Teresa. "I thought Big Crip was supposed to link us back up with the Crimson Mafia again. Why are we still out here pushing this bullshit instead of that A-1 them niggas be having?"

"Cuz, I don't know what the fuck Crip got going on," Menace stated. "When he came talking about that peace treaty shit, Cuz lost me. Ain't no way I'ma let that shit ride with what they did to Rampage and Sin.

On the set, it's on, upon sight! Any nigga get caught slipping with them, or get in the way gon' get some, too. I ain't sparing none of them niggas." Menace sat up and glared at C-Loc, trying to get a read on where he stood.

"I know it's fucked up," C-Loc started. "But sometimes you

gotta let shit go in order to grow. Everybody ain't sitting on paper that they just came up off from a fresh lick. If I had a few stacks saved up, then maybe I would feel the same way you do. But being as though I don't, then to eat, I gotta do what I gotta do."

Menace looked away disappointed that the hood had come to this. "That's a damn shame. What's next Cuz, you about to get out here and start selling some ass to make some paper?"

"Cuz you got the locsta fucked up! I'm about to raise tha fuck up outta here, cause, I can see you over there in one of your little moods." C-Loc started his car and sat waiting for Menace to get out.

"You better watch yourself, Cuz," Menace said, grabbing the door handle to get out. "Every nigga that ain't with me, they against me. I don't give a fuck who it is. Cuz or blood, Crimson Mafia or Grinder. Any muthafucka can get it!"

C-Loc sat acting like he could care less. Even though he was a young rider himself, today wouldn't be the day he took it there with Lil' Menace. Once he got back to the Estates, he would fill the big homies in on everything Lil' Menace planned to do.

Menace slammed C-Loc's door and turned to watch as it drove off and made its way towards the exit. Part of Menace wondered if he had gone too hard on the homie, but his better half knew he had said the right thing. Just as Menace turned back around to go back inside Teresa's apartment, he spotted someone wearing a Crimson colored ball cap. Menace squinted, inching closer to get a better view. "Is that?" Menace moved a little closer, ducking down, and straining harder to see. "Say it ain't so. Say it ain't fucking so! That's that mark ass nigga from the club. I can't believe that nigga is out here slipping like that!"

***

Puncho stepped out from the breezeway, pulling his fitted ball cap down on his head. He tried his best to make sure his identity was concealed. He was about to catch his first body. There would be no second chances if he slipped up. Puncho pulled out his 9 mm and checked to make sure it was ready to go. His nerves were so far gone, he trembled a bit like it were cold outside. "Come on dawg, get a grip Baby," he told himself, trying to pump himself up. "I gotta do this. I'm here now and ain't no turning back." As if right on cue, his phone rang a special ringtone, letting him know it was time to get ready.

A.K. pulled into the 36th Street Apartments driving a silver Malibu. Puncho watched nervously as A.K. pulled into the parking spot by the dumpster. "What up, youngsta?" A.K. said as he hopped out the car. "This my boy Bang, I know you remember him from The Lounge, right?"

Puncho was momentarily at a loss for words. There was only supposed to be one person that he was going to have to shoot. Now there were two, and he was starting to doubt whether he could actually pull it off. "Damn, fam, I thought you were coming by yourself," Puncho said trying to buy himself some time, and a better situation.

"With all this hard-earned cash I'm bringing to the table, I'm sure your people will understand why I felt like I needed to bring somebody to watch my back." A.K. opened the back door and pulled out a red book bag. "I got the cash, so let's do this!" he said, slinging it over his shoulder.

For a moment, Puncho stood nervously staring at both men. It was about to be his first lick ever. No one was there to tell him he should wait and try to follow them to a better place. It was a decision he had to make on his own.

"Damn, youngsta, you alright?" A.K. asked. "You just standing there looking lost like I don't have a hunnid racks in this bag."

Puncho instantly snapped out of his little trance. "My bad fam, what tha fuck was I thinking?"

A.K. and Bang chuckled and smirked at the bewildered expression on Puncho's face. But just as quickly as their smirks had appeared, they disappeared as Puncho pulled out his hammer and let that bitch bang.

At sight of the gun, A.K. and Bang attempted to dodge as if

Puncho was about to throw hot water at them, but it was too late.

Bok! Bok! Bok! Bok!

The shots tore through A.K.'s body, causing him to dance all over the sidewalk until he finally went crumbling to the ground. Puncho quickly tried to take aim at Bang, but he had somehow managed to find safety between the cars. Puncho bent over and snatched the money bag off A.K.'s lifeless body.

"This is for, Young Syke, you bitch ass nigga!"

Bok! Bok! Bok! Bok! Bok! Bok! Bok! Bok!

Puncho emptied his clip into A.K.'s body.

"Freeze!" Bang yelled coming out from between the cars. "Drop your weapon and—"

Pop! Pop! Pop! Pop!

Mob's chrome 45 rang out loud and clear, making it seem as if the whole world had gone deathly quiet.

Pop! Pop! Pop!

"Run nigga!" Mob yelled as he ran towards Bang, sending hot slugs flying towards his head.

Puncho took off like a bat out of hell. He ran as hard as he could until he finally reached the back side of the apartments. "Shit!" He heaved as he neared the gap in the fence they were to climb through. "A nigga way too outta shape for this shit." He took a moment to catch his breath, putting his hands on his knees as he stared down at the ground. The soft patter of feet hitting the ground, caused Puncho to relax, relieved that Mob was finally there. "Thank God you made it dawg," he said without looking back, sounding winded.

"You muthafuckin' right—thank God I made it!" Menace spat, panting from all the running he had to do just to keep up. "Let me get that bag up off you playboy."

Puncho raised up and spun around, startled by Menace's unexpected presence. "Nigga what tha fuck is you doing here? This ain't got shit to do with you!"

Menace racked a slug in the barrel of his sawed-off pump. "That's just what the fuck I was going to say to yo' mark ass. Now don't make me have to tell you again nigga."

Puncho ice grilled Menace. There was no way he was going to hand over that bag full of money. He needed to stall Menace a little while longer to give Mob enough time to get there and even the score.

"Why is you tripping, fam? We already squashed the beef with you, niggas. I don't understand what all this extra bullshit is about."

Boom! Chik! Chik! Boom! Chik! Chik!

Menace blew his whole face off, leaving him mutilated and disfigured. "That's what tha fuck it's about nigga!" Menace walked over and pulled the bag from Puncho's grasp. "If I would have known getting money off you, niggas was going to be this easy, I would have been knocking you bitch ass niggas off a long time ago."

Menace knelt to check the contents of the bag. "Jackpot!" Stacks on top of stacks of dead presidents stared back up at him. "Gotdamn, you, niggas is really out here eating."

All kinds of ideas ran rampant in Menace's mind. He smirked devilishly as two of the ideas stood above the others. One, it was time for him to take over the Eastside. Two, it was time to get all the way in with the Crimson Mafia. Once he found out where their main stash house was, he planned to rob them of everything they had.

He zipped the bag and slung it over his shoulder. As soon as the opportunity presented itself, he would begin The Take Over.

To Be Continued…
Glocks on Satin Sheets 2
Coming Soon

Submission Guideline

Submit the first three chapters of your completed manuscript to ldpsubmissions@gmail.com, subject line: Your book's title. The manuscript must be in a .doc file and sent as an attachment. Document should be in Times New Roman, double spaced and in size 12 font. Also, provide your synopsis and full contact information. If sending multiple submissions, they must each be in a separate email.

Have a story but no way to send it electronically? You can still submit to LDP/Ca$h Presents. Send in the first three chapters, written or typed, of your completed manuscript to:

LDP: Submissions Dept
Po Box 870494
Mesquite, Tx 75187

DO NOT send original manuscript. Must be a duplicate.

Provide your synopsis and a cover letter containing your full contact information.

Thanks for considering LDP and Ca$h Presents.

Glocks on Satin Sheets

Coming Soon from Lock Down Publications/Ca$h Presents

BOW DOWN TO MY GANGSTA

By **Ca$h**

TORN BETWEEN TWO

By **Coffee**

THE STREETS STAINED MY SOUL **II**

By **Marcellus Allen**

BLOOD OF A BOSS **VI**

SHADOWS OF THE GAME II

By **Askari**

LOYAL TO THE GAME **IV**

By **T.J. & Jelissa**

A DOPEBOY'S PRAYER **II**

By **Eddie "Wolf" Lee**

IF LOVING YOU IS WRONG… **III**

By **Jelissa**

TRUE SAVAGE **VII**

MIDNIGHT CARTEL III

DOPE BOY MAGIC III

By **Chris Green**

BLAST FOR ME **III**

A SAVAGE DOPEBOY III

CUTTHROAT MAFIA II

By **Ghost**

A HUSTLER'S DECEIT III

KILL ZONE **II**

BAE BELONGS TO ME III

By **Aryanna**

THE COST OF LOYALTY **III**

Adrian Dulan

By **Kweli**
CHAINED TO THE STREETS III
By **J-Blunt**
KING OF NEW YORK V
COKE KINGS IV
BORN HEARTLESS IV
By **T.J. Edwards**
GORILLAZ IN THE BAY V
TEARS OF A GANGSTA II
De'Kari
THE STREETS ARE CALLING II
Duquie Wilson
KINGPIN KILLAZ IV
STREET KINGS III
PAID IN BLOOD III
CARTEL KILLAZ IV
DOPE GODS II
Hood Rich
SINS OF A HUSTLA II
ASAD
TRIGGADALE III
Elijah R. Freeman
KINGZ OF THE GAME V
Playa Ray
SLAUGHTER GANG IV
RUTHLESS HEART III
By **Willie Slaughter**
THE HEART OF A SAVAGE III
By **Jibril Williams**
FUK SHYT II

Glocks on Satin Sheets

PAID IN KARMA III
By **Meesha**
I'M NOTHING WITHOUT HIS LOVE II
By Monet Dragun
CAUGHT UP IN THE LIFE II
By Robert Baptiste
NEW TO THE GAME II
By **Malik D. Rice**
Life of a Savage II
By **Romell Tukes**
Quiet Money II
By **Trai'Quan**

<u>Available Now</u>

RESTRAINING ORDER **I & II**
By **CA$H & Coffee**
LOVE KNOWS NO BOUNDARIES **I II & III**
By **Coffee**
RAISED AS A GOON I, II, III & IV
BRED BY THE SLUMS I, II, III
BLAST FOR ME I & II
ROTTEN TO THE CORE I II III
A BRONX TALE I, II, III
DUFFEL BAG CARTEL I II III IV
HEARTLESS GOON I II III IV
A SAVAGE DOPEBOY I II
HEARTLESS GOON I II III
DRUG LORDS I II III

Glocks on Satin Sheets

Adrian Dulan

CHAINED TO THE STREETS I II
By J-Blunt
PUSH IT TO THE LIMIT
By **Bre' Hayes**
BLOOD OF A BOSS **I, II, III, IV, V**
SHADOWS OF THE GAME
By **Askari**
THE STREETS BLEED MURDER **I, II & III**
THE HEART OF A GANGSTA I II& III
By **Jerry Jackson**
CUM FOR ME I II III IV V
An **LDP Erotica Collaboration**
BRIDE OF A HUSTLA **I II & II**
THE FETTI GIRLS **I, II& III**
CORRUPTED BY A GANGSTA I, II III, IV
BLINDED BY HIS LOVE
THE PRICE YOU PAY FOR LOVE
DOPE GIRL MAGIC
By **Destiny Skai**
WHEN A GOOD GIRL GOES BAD
By **Adrienne**
THE COST OF LOYALTY I II
By **Kweli**
A GANGSTER'S REVENGE **I II III & IV**
THE BOSS MAN'S DAUGHTERS I II III IV V
A SAVAGE LOVE **I & II**
BAE BELONGS TO ME I II
A HUSTLER'S DECEIT I, II, III
WHAT BAD BITCHES DO I, II, III
SOUL OF A MONSTER I II III

Glocks on Satin Sheets

KILL ZONE

By **Aryanna**

A KINGPIN'S AMBITON

A KINGPIN'S AMBITION **II**

I MURDER FOR THE DOUGH

By **Ambitious**

TRUE SAVAGE I II III IV V VI

DOPE BOY MAGIC I, II

MIDNIGHT CARTEL I II

By **Chris Green**

A DOPEBOY'S PRAYER

By **Eddie "Wolf" Lee**

THE KING CARTEL **I, II & III**

By **Frank Gresham**

THESE NIGGAS AIN'T LOYAL **I, II & III**

By **Nikki Tee**

GANGSTA SHYT **I II &III**

By **CATO**

THE ULTIMATE BETRAYAL

By **Phoenix**

BOSS'N UP **I , II & III**

By **Royal Nicole**

I LOVE YOU TO DEATH

By Destiny J

I RIDE FOR MY HITTA

I STILL RIDE FOR MY HITTA

By **Misty Holt**

LOVE & CHASIN' PAPER

By **Qay Crockett**

TO DIE IN VAIN

Adrian Dulan

SINS OF A HUSTLA
By **ASAD**
BROOKLYN HUSTLAZ
By **Boogsy Morina**
BROOKLYN ON LOCK I & II
By **Sonovia**
GANGSTA CITY
By **Teddy Duke**
A DRUG KING AND HIS DIAMOND I & II III
A DOPEMAN'S RICHES
HER MAN, MINE'S TOO I, II
CASH MONEY HO'S
By Nicole Goosby
TRAPHOUSE KING **I II & III**
KINGPIN KILLAZ I II III
STREET KINGS I II
PAID IN BLOOD **I II**
CARTEL KILLAZ I II III
DOPE GODS
By **Hood Rich**
LIPSTICK KILLAH **I, II, III**
CRIME OF PASSION I II & III
By **Mimi**
STEADY MOBBN' **I, II, III**
THE STREETS STAINED MY SOUL
By **Marcellus Allen**
WHO SHOT YA **I, II, III**
SON OF A DOPE FIEND
Renta
GORILLAZ IN THE BAY **I II III IV**

252

Glocks on Satin Sheets

TEARS OF A GANGSTA

DE'KARI

TRIGGADALE I II

Elijah R. Freeman

GOD BLESS THE TRAPPERS I, II, III

THESE SCANDALOUS STREETS I, II, III

FEAR MY GANGSTA I, II, III

THESE STREETS DON'T LOVE NOBODY I, II

BURY ME A G I, II, III, IV, V

A GANGSTA'S EMPIRE I, II, III, IV

THE DOPEMAN'S BODYGAURD

Tranay Adams

THE STREETS ARE CALLING

Duquie Wilson

MARRIED TO A BOSS... I II III

By Destiny Skai & Chris Green

KINGZ OF THE GAME I II III IV

Playa Ray

SLAUGHTER GANG I II III

RUTHLESS HEART I II

By Willie Slaughter

FUK SHYT

By Blakk Diamond

DON'T F#CK WITH MY HEART I II

By Linnea

ADDICTED TO THE DRAMA I II III

By Jamila

YAYO I II

A SHOOTER'S AMBITION

By S. Allen

253

Adrian Dulan

TRAP GOD

By Troublesome

FOREVER GANGSTA

GLOCKS ON SATIN SHEETS

By Adrian Dulan

TOE TAGZ I II

By Ah'Million

KINGPIN DREAMS

By Paper Boi Rari

CONFESSIONS OF A GANGSTA

By Nicholas Lock

I'M NOTHING WITHOUT HIS LOVE

By Monet Dragun

CAUGHT UP IN THE LIFE

By Robert Baptiste

NEW TO THE GAME

By **Malik D. Rice**

Life of a Savage

By **Romell Tukes**

LOYALTY AIN'T PROMISED

By Keith Williams

Quiet Money

By **Trai'Quan**

Glocks on Satin Sheets

<u>BOOKS BY LDP'S CEO, CA$H</u>

<u>TRUST IN NO MAN</u>

<u>TRUST IN NO MAN 2</u>

<u>TRUST IN NO MAN 3</u>

<u>BONDED BY BLOOD</u>

<u>SHORTY GOT A THUG</u>

<u>THUGS CRY</u>

<u>THUGS CRY 2</u>

<u>THUGS CRY 3</u>

<u>TRUST NO BITCH</u>

<u>TRUST NO BITCH 2</u>

<u>TRUST NO BITCH 3</u>

<u>TIL MY CASKET DROPS</u>

<u>RESTRAINING ORDER</u>

<u>RESTRAINING ORDER 2</u>

<u>IN LOVE WITH A CONVICT</u>

<u>Coming Soon</u>

BONDED BY BLOOD 2

BOW DOWN TO MY GANGSTA

Glocks on Satin Sheets

www.ingramcontent.com/pod-product-compliance
Lightning Source LLC
Chambersburg PA
CBHW070837280626
47161CB00015B/1017